TH[E]
FOURTH
SPECIES

BY A. E. WARREN

Tomorrow's Ancestors

Subject Twenty-One
The Hidden Base
The Fourth Species

PRAISE FOR THE TOMORROW'S ANCESTORS SERIES

'A stonking good sci-fi & coming-of-age story all wrapped into one ... a book that tackles humanity, hardship, and classism at the deepest level.' *Magic Radio Book Club*

'An unputdownable exploration into the ethics of science.' *Buzz Magazine*

'Unbelievably compelling and readable.' *Ink and Plasma*

'Incredible ... without a doubt one of the best YA sci-fi books I've ever read.' *Out and About Books*

'Unique and engaging with full *Jurassic* vibes to boot.' *Fictional Maiden*

THE
FOURTH
SPECIES

A. E. WARREN

1 3 5 7 9 10 8 6 4 2

Del Rey
20 Vauxhall Bridge Road
London SW1V 2SA

Del Rey is part of the Penguin Random House group
of companies whose addresses can be found at
global.penguinrandomhouse.com.

Penguin
Random House
UK

First published by Del Rey in 2022

www.penguin.co.uk

A CIP catalogue record for this book is available
from the British Library.

ISBN 9781529101362

Typeset in 10/14.5 pt ITC Galliard Std
by Integra Software Services Pvt. Ltd, Pondicherry

Printed and bound in Great Britain by Clays Ltd, Elcograf S.p.A.

The authorised representative in the EEA is Penguin Random House
Ireland, Morrison Chambers, 32 Nassau Street, Dublin D02 YH68.

Penguin Random House is committed to a sustainable future for
our business, our readers and our planet. This book is made from
Forest Stewardship Council® certified paper.

MIX
Paper from
responsible sources
FSC
www.fsc.org   FSC® C018179

For Ella, with all my love

'Nothing is so painful to the human mind as a great and sudden change.'

Mary Wollstonecraft Shelley

CHAPTER 1

* *

Elise

Not many people would choose to enter the crematorium in Cytosine at two in the morning, but it was the living Elise feared, not the dead. After three hours of waiting, the canyon base was finally free from prying eyes, so she clipped herself to the electronic winch line normally reserved for the last journey of Cytosine's recently deceased, and pressed the button at the base of the cliff to send herself sailing up its side. Once at the top, she slipped out one of the short push knives strapped to her thighs and thrust it into the ground. Holding on to the handle, she ignored the two-hundred-foot drop below and unclipped herself from the line before pulling herself over the edge of the precipice. She secured the knife back into its leather holder and silently rolled away from the brink of the cliff, her heartbeat barely raised. There, lying flat against the grass, she took a moment to assess her surroundings.

Behind her another set of knives were thrust into the ground, only the hands holding them visible. After a few seconds, a well-built man dressed entirely in black pulled himself over the cliff with ease. Crawling through the grass, he stopped when he was next to Elise.

'Have we missed him, Ma'am?'

'No one has entered or exited the building, so he's still inside,' Elise responded sharply, not looking at him. 'But only one way to find out.'

Without waiting for Milo, she stood and walked to the hatch that comprised the entranceway to the crematorium. She stamped on it twice and waited. A few moments later the wooden hatchway creaked open a few inches from the inside. Signalling for Milo to follow, she pulled it up the rest of the way before swinging onto the ladder that ran deep into the ground. The heat from below was already unbearable. She savoured the last few seconds of cool air before descending, electric bulbs providing a clear view of the compacted earth and stone the ladder was bolted to.

Reaching the bottom, she jumped the last two rungs and landed firmly before turning to face the man waiting for her. The hatch-opener wiped his face with the back of his hand, leaving a streak of soot behind, and a sheen of sweat covered the skin beneath his open shirt. He frowned as he watched Milo climb down behind her.

Elise waited until Milo had landed beside her before speaking. 'You're burning them late tonight, Eli.'

'We've had a spike in numbers here the last month ... I suppose that's what you're here about.'

Elise glanced over Eli's shoulder to the wide tunnel stretching to the incinerators. The golden light of the fires behind cast him in shadow, and Elise tried not to think of the chimney openings a mile away pumping out the heavy smoke of the dead.

'How many?' Elise asked.

'Fourteen deaths last week; fifteen the week before,' Eli responded, leaning against the compacted earth of the entrance-way.

Elise frowned; that was an increase of over a third since the last time she'd visited. 'How many of them were from the containment centre?'

'Nine this week. I think ...' Eli responded. 'I heard talk of a sickness in there.'

Elise straightened. 'Can you find out more for the next time I come? I want to know if it's actually a sickness or if their standards of "care" are dropping.'

Eli nodded. 'So, you'll be making this a regular visit then?'

'At least until the numbers have fallen.'

'That's better for me,' Eli said. 'I don't like it when you just pop up. Puts me on edge.' He glanced over to Milo again. 'Why's that one all dressed in black? Don't he know what it means?'

Elise glanced behind her. She hadn't noticed the colour of Milo's clothes before. She should have.

'It's his first mission out. He doesn't know that his clothing shouldn't be black. We'll get him changed for next time.'

'What does it mean?' Milo asked, pulling the front of his jacket out and staring at it, his square jaw pressing down on his chest.

Elise looked up at him. A whole foot taller than her, and probably four years older, but he knew so little of the other bases. That was what came from being born and raised in Uracil.

'It means you're dressed like the Protection Department,' Elise said. 'In the bases, only the Protection Department can wear all black clothes. So, on your first mission, you managed to come out dressed as our enemy.'

Milo grimaced at the implication. 'I didn't know, Ma'am. I'll change for next time.'

Elise looked him up and down; it was the only mistake he'd made the entire mission. 'I've got a grey jumper in my bag that might fit you. But you can't keep it. It's not mine and the owner might want it again when he returns.'

Turning to leave, she tried to avoid thinking about the jumper's owner.

'One more thing, before you go,' Eli said, looking between them. 'Maybe you could pass a message to the Tri-Council for me? I'm only a year off my seven years of service and I was wondering if Uracil would consider finding someone to replace me and take me back early.'

Elise rounded on him, her eyes narrowed. 'And who exactly would replace you?' Eli had no response for her, so she answered for him. 'No one, that's who! We're stretched thin as we are and we need all the eyes we can get. If we don't monitor the deaths here no one else will.'

Both men stared at her in silence, looking surprised at her vehemence – she'd gone too far. Elise adjusted her tone and tried to smile. She could feel the mechanical pull of her lips upwards but the light didn't reach her eyes. It never did these days.

'Anyway, Eli, it's only another year. It'll be over in a snap. And then you can be back in Uracil foraging, working the fields, or building tree houses; whatever takes your fancy. You'll never have to see the inside of this burned-out hole again.'

Eli snorted. 'You try being told you've got to do another year down here and see how long that feels.'

Elise reached for the ladder and placed her foot on the first rung. 'We've all got our burdens, Eli.' She pulled herself up. 'I'll see you in a month.'

Two weeks later, with Milo on his way back to Uracil to continue his training, Elise waited by an ancient oak tree, thirty miles due east of Guanine. She was the first to arrive in the dense forest, chosen as it was the most central point of Zone 3. It was late in the evening and the rest of the Collective would be with her by dawn.

With nothing to do but wait, she settled on the ground and lit a fire to signal her position. She leant away from the fire's warmth, the day having taken her by surprise with one last burst of heat before autumn set in. Once the twigs had caught, she moved farther away so she could keep wearing Samuel's grey jumper. The broth she had made with the hare caught earlier that day was soon bubbling away. She sat quietly as she waited for the cooler midnight hours.

She didn't hear the soft footsteps until they were close behind her. Leaping to her feet, she reached for her sling, ready to defend herself against the member of the Protection Department who had found their meeting point. But as the footsteps drew closer, and Elise finally made out the features of the approaching figure, she relaxed.

'You nearly got me that time,' she said, as Maya crossed to the other side of the fire.

'Maybe these bones are getting a little old,' Maya responded. 'Still, I enjoy testing myself.' She gave a broad smile that showed the large gap between her front teeth. 'So, what did you decide to do for Milo's first mission in the end?'

Elise rubbed her forehead; she was tired but rest would have to wait. 'I took him to Cytosine to check on Eli at the crematorium.' She glanced up. 'The numbers are rising again, Maya.'

The older woman frowned. 'I thought you had stopped doing that? I was breaking a number of rules by telling you about Eli, and every time you check in on him is a risk to Uracil's security. What's more, it won't help. You can't monitor all deaths in the bases – we don't have any undercover agents at the other crematoriums.'

Elise began rummaging through her bag for the screen where she kept her records. 'If you don't have anyone in the crematoriums, then maybe you have an agent you could put me in contact with in the records off—'

'We can talk about this later, but you know I can't divulge any more of our undercover agents' locations to you. It's not safe for Uracil, and it's definitely not safe for the agents,' Maya said, placing her hand on Elise's bag. 'Tell me, how did Milo do?'

Elise looked up. 'He's certainly fit enough, took instructions, didn't go beyond his remit.' She paused. 'He kept on calling me Ma'am, though.'

Maya chuckled. 'You'll get used to it as you get older. To a sixteen-year-old fresh out of Uracil's academy, you must seem very worldly.'

'Sixteen? Worldly? I'm not worldly! And how is he sixteen? I thought he was in his mid-twenties!'

'You should know by now that in our time, you shouldn't judge a person's age just by what is presented to you, little miss.' Maya's eyes flashed with amusement. 'And don't worry; you'll always be younger than me.'

Elise frowned. Milo was younger than she had been when she had first started working with Kit. She felt bad now that she'd been so curt with him on their first mission together. On reflection, she had been trying to assert her authority with someone she'd believed to be older than her.

Maya broke into Elise's thoughts. 'How did the mission go otherwise?'

'Cytosine was quiet,' Elise responded as she spooned the broth into two bowls. 'But Eli asked to come back to Uracil a year early.'

Maya frowned. 'And what was your response?'

'I told him that Uracil needed him out in the bases. That a year would pass quickly enough.'

There was silence as Maya processed her response. Elise grew uncomfortable as the minutes ticked by.

'Do you think I made the wrong decision?' she eventually asked.

In the last eighteen months of completing missions for the Infiltration Department she had come to trust her own judgement, but she would always view Maya as her trainer.

Maya leant back. 'Why did you say no, instead of passing on his request to the Tri-Council?'

'We're at war,' Elise responded, 'whether the undercover operatives can see it or not. A silent war at the moment, but we might soon need every operative we've got. The Tri-Council know that.'

'I can see your reasoning and I think it was the right decision. The operative is safe for the moment anyway. It's not as if he believed that his cover was compromised.' Maya leant forwards. 'Just don't lose sight of the reason we do this. We work to provide the best lives possible for as many as we can. I've noticed how fixated you are with monitoring the Potiors and I worry that you act out of revenge.' Elise tried to interrupt but was cut off. 'I know what they did to you in the containment centre in Cytosine was unforgivable—'

'I'm fine. It's been two years now, and I've healed better than they expected.'

'But the doctor said—' Maya fell silent. 'Someone's coming.'

Elise hardly breathed as she scanned the area. And then she heard it: in the distance there was a rustle as someone, or something, brushed up against foliage. She turned in the direction of the noise and moved to silently crouch behind the cover of a sprawling holly bush.

Maya was by her side in two steps. Both believed that it was better to be prepared than assume they knew who was approaching.

A woman's voice called out. 'Something about birds that fly away and summer ... or maybe winter. There was definitely a bird and a season.' She stopped. 'Why are the passwords never about pigeons? Always about the fancy birds that bugger off for half the year.'

Maya stood up with a sigh and waited for the woman of middling years to come closer to the light of the fire before speaking in a low voice. 'It's "Where do the swallows go in autumn?", Raynor. And it's not that hard to remember if you ever actually listened during the meetings.'

'Consider me suitably chastised,' Raynor said, as she began shrugging her backpack off. She nodded to them both. 'Put some water over the fire, please. It was hotter than the surface of a star today and it's been a long trek. How on earth are you still wearing that jumper, Elise?'

Elise ignored the question, walking over to help with her backpack instead. 'It's good to see you.'

'And you too, sugarling.'

Maya held back. 'I'm glad you made it safely.'

'So am I. Now how about some water?'

The three women sat and discussed their recent missions from the Tri-Council. In the last few years, unless something was considered top-secret – and many things were – an air of openness between Infiltration operatives had been encouraged by the leaders of Uracil. They had learnt from the disastrous policy of total secrecy that had been in place until the end of Faye's reign.

'So, I shuffled through the marketplace,' Raynor said, a look of glee passing across her features. 'Not one person glanced my way and I was able to pass on the message while pretending to purchase a new saucepan.'

She gave a wide grin that showed a few of her back teeth were missing.

Elise shook her head and smiled. When she had first met Raynor, they had been sent on a mission in Adenine together. Having never been to the capital, known for 'Guidance and Governance', she had prepared for weeks. She had scoped the surrounding area for three days, selected some innocuous-looking weapons that she could carry without raising suspicions and then dutifully set up their base camp.

When Elise had returned that evening with fresh spring water, Raynor had wandered into the small glade. Without introducing herself, she had plonked herself down, taken her shoes off and pulled out the camera they had been sent to collect, before starting to massage her feet.

At first, Elise had been annoyed by this operative who clearly preferred to work by herself and was so dismissive of the protocols that had been drilled into Elise during training. But it hadn't taken long for her to realise that she had much to learn from someone so skilled at looking unremarkable that she could pass through most situations unnoticed. Raynor's prime strength was her apparent insignificance; she could blend with a group of Sapiens as if she had known them for three generations.

Just as Raynor was about to recount another tale, Maya stood up and began to prowl the circumference of the clearing. Elise tensed. Raynor carried on eating.

A rush of air blew into the circle; the flames of the fire flickered and nearly went out. 'Sorry if I'm late,' said the young man who'd arrived.

He'd run in so fast and silently that Maya and Elise barely had time to react to his approach.

'No need to apologise, Maxmilian, you're not late,' Maya responded. 'We aren't all due until tomorrow morning, but a few of us arrived early.'

Elise tried to relax as Maxmilian sat down. At first, she had struggled with his inclusion in the Collective. Tall and lean, he moved with a languorous strength that reminded her of Fintorian. He had done his best to conceal as much of his Potior beauty as he could by letting his black hair curl scraggily around his ears. But the effect was a mere token when faced with unblemished skin that glowed with health, broad features that perfectly complemented each other, and deep grey eyes flecked with sea-green. In a way, his scruffy countenance added to his charm.

Even though he didn't foster the air of mystery and almost tangible self-confidence that the other Potiors had, it had still taken Elise a while to dispel her initial belief that 'once a Potior, always a Potior'. Eventually, Maya had managed to persuade her that he was no threat; he had passed all of the rigorous checks and was just as disillusioned with their world as Samuel's father had been when he had co-founded Uracil. On the few missions she had completed with him, Elise had found Max to be more puppy than wolf.

'Hello, Madam Ray,' Maxmilian said, as he sat down next to Raynor.

'Good to see you, Max. How was the journey to Zone 2?'

Max was limited in the work he could do in Zone 3 as he was over seven feet tall and clearly a Potior. People like him didn't go unnoticed.

'Took bloody months. I'd wake up every morning, hang my head over the side of my sailboat and stare at the sea. Next morning: sea. Day after: sea. I started to fantasise about soil, sand, even *clay*. I would lie there with my eyes closed, drifting along, creating these elaborate chimeras of finally landing the boat, dropping to my knees on the beach and rubbing my cheek against the sand.' His eyes widened. 'I think I went a bit mad.'

Raynor snorted in amusement and Max grinned back at her.

'I can laugh now, Madam Ray,' he carried on with enthusiasm. 'But at the time I think you nearly lost this colleague of yours. I was so close to forgetting my reason for going there that by the time I landed, I had to take two weeks to recover. Next time, I'm taking some company.'

He accepted a bowl of broth and set to it with a large spoon that he pulled out of his backpack.

As the hours ticked by, more members of the Collective assembled. Elise hadn't slept in close to two days, but she forced herself to stay awake so she could greet each of the arrivals before they moved to the safer location where the meeting would be held. As each one entered the glade she looked up expectantly. None of them were Samuel.

As she waited, she twirled the bracelet that she had not taken off for almost two years; it contained the latest pill that would erase all her memories of Uracil, last updated three months ago during her most recent visit to the hidden base. She hoped she would never have to use it again; last time she had only lost three months of memories and that had been enough to change the course of her life. Over two years would be much worse.

One by one, the elite members of the roaming section of Uracil's Infiltration Department assembled. The agents who were undercover and planted in Zone 3's four bases, as Samuel had been, were naturally unable to leave their posts and so did not attend these bi-annual meetings on the autumnal and spring equinoxes, the halfway points between the winter and summer solstices.

Once they had all arrived, Maya stood and silently led them out of the forest to the cave to the east. Elise kept her head down the entire way, not wanting to make small talk with the other operatives. Her left eye was twitching due to her lack of sleep and she didn't want anyone to comment on it. When they arrived, she took position at the front of the cave so she could look out at the river that surrounded it. It had been chosen for these meetings as the river acted as a natural deterrent for any wandering or lost people, and the interior of the cave meant that they could hear a winged camera if one had been sent in to spy on them.

Before Maya could call for the customary five minutes of silence to check for cameras before the meeting was held, Elise asked quietly, 'Is Samuel not back yet?'

'No, he's still in Zone 5 looking for his father; he may have a lead,' Maya responded before giving a loud whistle.

Elise tried not to dwell on the news. Samuel had good reason to be away. He'd needed to know whether his father was still alive and so had decided to trace his last known movements. Before he had left, he'd asked Elise to join him, but she'd refused. She hadn't felt right leaving when so much was still to be done here. How could she come and go when so many others couldn't even begin to imagine the freedom she had? Her reasoning had frustrated him, and they'd barely been on speaking terms when he had left over a year ago. She had made her decision and tried not to regret it, but with her refusal she worried she'd snuffed out any chance of their friendship developing into what they'd once had. She smiled to herself. She couldn't even remember what they'd once had, so it wasn't as if she could miss it, but that didn't seem to help the small ball of grief that flared whenever she thought of him.

Maya took her place in front of the operatives. 'Thank you all for coming. We shall begin with the customary five minutes of silence.'

Everyone dropped their heads and Elise strained to hear for the minute winged cameras. No one so much as coughed.

After what felt like an hour, Maya raised her head to begin. 'As we all know, Fiona stepped down as Head of the Infiltration Department last month and I've agreed to take her place.'

There was some whooping, which Maya shut down with a glance. 'We have a lot to thank Fiona for. She worked tirelessly for years to make Uracil safe and I have a lot to live up to.'

The semi-circle of twenty-three operatives quietened down.

'As the new Head of the Infiltration Department I want to keep you regularly updated on any changes that may be happening. To that end, I must inform you that our focus is shifting. I've spoken to the Tri-Council at length these past months,' Maya continued, 'and both they and I believe that we've worked in the shadows for too long. With this in mind, we are changing our core aim. In short, we are going on the offensive.'

Elise stilled her features. She had spent eighteen months trying to persuade Maya of the benefit of this change of tactic. To hear this announcement made her hands tingle. They were finally going to take some action.

'When Uracil was formed fifty years ago we knew that in order to survive, we had to protect ourselves. This strategy was a success, but whilst Uracil has thrived, the Potiors' grasp over the other bases has also strengthened. Their scientific advances have only increased that control and we fear it won't be long until they will be unstoppable. We therefore have a five-year plan.'

Elise's stomach sank. Five years? That was too long. How many would die in that time at the hands of the Potiors? How many more would go through what she had in the containment centres?

'Our long-term aim for Zone 3 is to have a mix of what were once termed "Sapien", "Medius" and "Potior" leaders. Many of the Potiors will not go quietly, but Maxmilian and the other

Potiors who are part of Uracil assure me that there are others like them, who believe in equality and can be convinced of our vision. Therefore, our first step is to collect information on each of the Potiors and categorise them, whilst also gathering as much information on the base's current scientific research and breakthroughs as possible. While we have turned our attention outwards, it is also important for us to proceed with caution, and work steadily towards our end goal.'

Raynor cleared her throat with a frown. 'I thought "For Uracil" was what guided us. Not "For All The Other Bases First".'

Maya looked as though she had been expecting the question. 'We'll always protect Uracil. "For Uracil" will always stand. But from now on, we also want to help the bases form a new leadership. We must work to protect all, including those who have never even heard of Uracil.'

There were mumblings in the circle; to Elise's ear, it didn't sound as if everyone was in agreement. A woman sitting at the front raised her hand.

'You have a question, Septa?' Maya said.

The woman with the spiky bleached-blonde hair sat up straight. 'I just wanted to say that I'm sure that the Tri-Council would have given such a huge turnaround in policy a lot of thought, so it must be the right thing to do.'

Raynor rolled her eyes and began picking the dirt out from underneath her nails.

Elise tried not to react to the presence of the operative who had broken her out of the containment centre in Cytosine and then tried to throttle her that same evening. She only saw Septa at these meetings and always avoided speaking to her. Elise still couldn't believe that Septa had gone unpunished for what she had done to her.

Maya nodded. 'And it's not just the Tri-Council; all the leaders of the different departments in Uracil have been involved. A decision like this needs the agreement of everyone and also a careful gathering of information that is assessed at each turn. Therefore, each of you will be working in small teams. You will be sent on individual missions assigned specifically for your group's specialism.'

Everyone looked around at each other as this news sank in.

'Melanie, Justin, Tia and Thomas, you'll be on the team reviewing the Potiors in Thymine.'

The four operatives whose names had been called glanced at each other and nodded. Elise looked over at them enviously before reminding herself that there were three other bases with Potiors. She shot a silent request up to the stars that she would be placed in the Adenine group where most of the Potiors resided. She wanted to find out everything there was to know about the Premier.

'Raynor, Maxmilian, Septa and Elise. You'll be in the scientific research wing ...'

The scientific wing ... with Septa. Elise stared up at Maya. It was one thing for Septa to go unpunished, but why would Maya put them together, knowing their history? Elise barely listened as the rest of the operatives were divided into teams.

Before she found an opportunity to object, Maya drew the meeting to a close. 'Report to me tomorrow morning to get full details of your first missions. In the meantime, try and get some sleep. I need you all fresh-faced for this one. And before you all swarm me, I'll not be answering any individual's queries or complaints about your groupings. We don't have time for petty grievances.'

Maya stared around at them all until her eyes came to rest on Elise. There was nothing she could do but wait.

Elise woke with a start to find someone leaning over her. Trying to focus in the early-morning light, she stared at Septa, who was squatting next to her.

'Thought we'd better make amends,' Septa said, crouching so low that she almost grazed the forest floor.

Septa was as petite as Maya, but Elise remembered that she used her fragile appearance to her advantage; she had always been one of Uracil's best fighters.

'How do you make amends for nearly killing someone?' Elise asked. 'I don't think a badly timed, insincere apology is the best start.'

She sat up, pulled on her jumper and tried to flatten her hair.

Septa stared over Elise's shoulder. 'I told Maya you wouldn't want to hear it.'

'So, Maya asked you to do this?'

'Yes, she wants us to work alongside each other. And apparently the air might need clearing, although I don't see that I've done anything wrong.'

Elise pushed back her hair. 'You tried to kill me.'

'I was acting on the Tri-Council's orders. Once I came out of hiding and they realised that Faye had given me the order, all was forgiven. And I got you out of Cytosine's containment centre. We had fun on the way, didn't we? Saved your midget friend too. You should be thanking me for that.'

'I'm not thanking you for anything. Do you just follow any orders you're given?'

Septa stared at her, unblinking. 'Of course I do, I'm loyal to Uracil.'

'So, you just go around killing anyone they tell you to? Why didn't you question those orders, raise it with the other members of the Tri-Council? You knew I worked for Uracil as well.'

Septa raised an eyebrow. 'I wasn't trained to question the orders of a superior. I'd be failing Uracil if I did. Anyway, I've apologised so I've got a clear conscience. Any awkwardness between us is now your fault.' With that, Septa sprang to her feet. 'Meeting's in ten minutes so you better get up.'

Elise watched in disbelief as Septa walked away.

Fifteen minutes later, Maya led Elise and Septa's newly formed team back to the edge of the forest in silence. They carried on walking until all they could see were wild sheep and deer grazing; the grass was low.

'Before we start,' Maya said, 'I want you to know that we're keeping mission details confined to the groups you're assigned to. We know from experience that openness is important, but for a mission of this size, we can't have one capture leading to the exposure of all our plans.'

Elise now understood why Maya had brought them here – no one could hide themselves and listen in on their discussions. She looked around at her three new associates. They each nodded in response to Maya's announcement; the protection of Uracil never had to be explained or justified.

'You've each been assigned to one of the research wings. In brief, that means that we want to know what the Potiors are currently researching and where their scientific discoveries are taking them. We're hearing rumours of a new project in Adenine but our spies in the museum can't get close enough. A whole wing has been shut off for the last year since they received a delivery from Guanine. If we can keep tabs on that, we can pre-empt any changes they make in the four bases.

'So, we need you to go to Guanine and find out what they sent. We believe the delivery came from either their museum or the university there. Any questions?'

Elise raised her hand. 'Should we collect information on any of the Potiors we might come across? We could look at the Director of the museum for a start.'

'No. There are other teams tasked with that, and too much activity could make them suspicious, as well as possibly contaminating the legitimacy of our research.'

Elise was about to respond but then thought better of it. The last thing Maya needed was Elise testing her authority after the tepid reception from the rest of the department to the news that they weren't focusing entirely on Uracil any more. But she didn't understand how she'd ended up being put on the research team when she'd run more infiltration missions in the past eighteen months than most of the other operatives. Instead of tracking down Potiors, she would be doing something Milo could have been tasked with.

'As she's worked in one of the museums, Elise will be leading this mission,' Maya said.

Elise kept her face still. All three of her colleagues had been in the Infiltration Department much longer than she had. Plus, last time she'd infiltrated a museum it hadn't exactly gone to plan.

Septa's face reddened before she mumbled, 'Great. We'll probably all be captured by the end of the week.'

Maya didn't break eye contact with Septa. 'She's leading. And if you carry on like that, I'll arrange that she leads the next mission too.'

CHAPTER 2

. . . .

Twenty-Two

Twenty-Two enjoyed the warm evening breeze as she stood in the open doorway of the cabin.

Eighteen months.

Eighteen months of the same four walls, the same visitors at the same times, food that rarely changed and conversations that skirted around the edges of what needed to be said.

In that time, she had grown to dislike the number eighteen. She had pondered it for a long time, and decided that the number eighteen had no special qualities to it. Her time in the cabin had not been wasted: she had made full use of the screen she had been given and had read two hundred and sixty-three Pre-Pandemic works of fiction during her solitary imprisonment. And not once had she come across the number eighteen being a central character or theme in any work of literature. An insignificant, pointless number.

She decided she would not think of it again. Today was different. She had finished her term of punishment for the death of Faye and was free to leave the cabin, though as part of the condition of her release she couldn't leave Uracil. They couldn't have her scampering off into the distance – not with her know-ledge of its location.

She stretched her arms above her head and turned to face the crescent moon. She was at the edge of the island that was home to Uracil and could hear the water lapping at the pebbled shore beyond the next set of trees. That was one of the things she had missed most whilst in her little cabin – the sound of nature con-ducting its daily business. Taking a deep breath, she scrunched her eyes as she recognised the scent of jasmine; one of her favourites.

The guard coughed. He was still standing to one side, hold-ing the door open for her. Twenty-Two glanced over at him. He pulled the door even wider and raised his eyebrows, clearly wanting her to move forwards.

Why doesn't he just ask me to move?

These Sapiens and their odd ways.

The guard coughed again, more loudly this time. Twenty-Two stretched her arms even higher to give herself another moment to think. She then tentatively took a step towards Ezra, who was waiting patiently for her past the threshold.

'That's a very tickly cough,' Ezra signed to Twenty-Two, while nodding at the guard.

Twenty-Two scrunched her eyes at her best friend and stared down at her feet, willing the right one to follow the left and take a further step.

'Why don't you let me help you?' Ezra signed.

He moved towards her and took Twenty-Two's hand, break-ing the spell. She took the next few steps by herself.

'Thank you,' she signed, after letting go of his hand.

She looked around; there was no one else waiting to meet her.

Perhaps today is not special to them?

She kept her features still to try and hide her disappointment. 'Where is Kit? I thought he would be here to meet me.'

Ezra bounced on the balls of his feet before responding. 'We thought it best if it was just me that came to meet you. Kit wanted to be here, but he's in a meeting with the Tri-Council. He wants to request that another Neanderthal is freed from a museum.'

'The next one? Already?' Twenty-Two responded.

Ezra lowered his head. 'Well, it's been two years now since you left Cytosine. Come on, let's get you back home.'

Twenty-Two nodded and followed Ezra towards Uracil.

The word 'home' was jarring to her. To take her mind off it, she considered the implications of more Neanderthals being freed. On one hand, she would no longer be one of only a few – no longer special. But then, on the other hand … the more Neanderthals that joined her here, the less the Sapiens would stare. That was what she wanted.

She scrunched her eyes to reassure Ezra. 'I'm glad that another might be joining us. Who is it?'

'Twenty-Four. A female. Around eleven years old, I think.'

'What happened to Twenty-Three?'

Ezra looked away for a moment. He quickly recovered when Twenty-Two continued to stare at him. 'Twenty-Three isn't with us any more.'

Twenty-Two nodded. She had expected as much. The lives of her brothers and sisters who had been brought back from extinction were tenuous at best while in the care of the museums. She mourned them in her own way but rarely dwelt on their demise. In a way, that was their trade for a second chance at living. There was nothing she could do to change what had already happened and they were with the stars now, along with all her other ancestors.

'Is there something else you want to tell me?' Twenty-Two signed, aware that Ezra had still not relaxed into his usual jovial self.

'Ahh ... yes. The Tri-Council want to see you. Michael's asked that you meet him at the first appointment tomorrow morning.'

Twenty-Two stopped walking. Ezra had kept her up to date with all the shifts in the structure of Uracil over the past eighteen months and she knew that Michael had replaced Faye as the third member of the Tri-Council. With all the changes that had been made, she had often worried about what would happen to her after she was released. She had served her sentence but wasn't so naive as to imagine she would go unnoticed now that she had been freed.

'You don't think he's going to wipe my memory and expel me, do you?' she asked, fearful of the power that Michael, along with the other two members of Uracil's Tri-Council, wielded. 'I wouldn't be able to survive out there only knowing what I did back at Cytosine's museum.'

Ezra looked flustered. 'No, of course not. Not a chance. You're too unique and important to Uracil. There's no one else like you ... Well, apart from Kit. And Twenty-Seven ... And Bay. But they don't have your ... your *authenticity*.'

Twenty-Two studied Ezra's countenance. 'So, you do think he will try to expel me?'

Ezra frowned. 'No, that's not what I *think* will happen. Only what I'm scared of happening. Kit feels the same.'

Ezra continued walking and Twenty-Two followed as she pondered this development. In a way, it was reassuring to know that she wasn't the only one afraid of what might happen. She stared up at the night sky as she considered the potential out-comes of her meeting with Michael. Like the sky, her thoughts were ever turning. Kit had once told her that when their ances-tors had been alive 40,000 years ago the stars had been in a different position in the sky. The night sky, or her view of it, had slowly revolved over thousands of years.

Ezra took a deep breath before speaking again. 'We can always appeal. I've spoken to Tilla about it and we can ask to speak to all three members of the Tri-Council if we need to.' Ezra took another gulp of air as his words tumbled out. 'And if the worst comes to the worst, I'll leave with you. Then I can help you learn how to live outside of the museum again.' He frowned. 'Hopefully they won't erase so far back that I'll be gone from your memories too. Either way, I've always wanted to explore outside of the bases, maybe even visit another Zone. Even better to do it with you.'

Twenty-Two tried to scrunch her eyes. It wasn't often that she mimicked appearing happier than she was, but she didn't want Ezra to worry about her. She tried to remember the stars' blessings for granting her Ezra. He was all that she really needed. She had survived her first fourteen years with only Dara, so she could survive the next with only Ezra. At the thought of her old friend and Companion, she glanced up at the night sky again and sent her a silent greeting.

Ezra began to walk more quickly. 'Come on, we'd better get you back to your cabin.'

'Can we go around the edge of the lake?' Twenty-Two asked. 'I don't think I'm ready to walk through the centre yet.'

'I thought you might not be; it's why I asked for them to release you in the evening.'

In unspoken agreement, they walked more quickly, both lost in their thoughts.

When they arrived at her old cabin, Twenty-Two surprised herself by being pleased to see it. She had never been particularly attached to this square wooden box with its low ceiling and excessive amount of furniture, but knowing that she could enter and leave the tree house at will produced a lightness in her chest. As was often the case, it was the removal of the pressure that made her realise that it had been present all along.

Ezra hung back and she stepped in front of him to slide open the cabin's door, hoping that he'd be able to spend the rest of the evening with her.

'Surprise!' Georgina exclaimed, as she pulled back the cabin door from the other side.

Twenty-Two stared at Georgina as she tried to process what was happening. The nurse's smile began to fade when Twenty-Two did not respond.

'Come in, come in,' Georgina signed and Twenty-Two stepped inside. 'We wanted to give you a little party and thought it best to do it in your cabin.'

Twenty-Two glanced around. Tilla was standing on the opposite side of the cabin door holding a slightly wonky iced cake covered in minute fairy lights shining in the darkness of the shuttered cabin.

Kit was standing behind Georgina, scrunching his eyes at Twenty-Two. She couldn't pull her gaze away from the brightly coloured paper hat he was wearing. She realised everyone had them, aside from her and Ezra. She wondered if the inclusion of these hats escalated a gathering of people into a party.

Behind Tilla, Bay was trotting in a continuous circle in the middle of the cabin, clearly overcome with the excitement of being allowed to stay up late and attend the evening event. Her long hair was scraped up into a ponytail at the top of her head; it bobbed and danced with her movements as it had always done. Unable to sit upon her head, Bay's orange paper hat hung halfway down her back and was kept in place by a string around her neck. Twenty-Two was pleased to see that Bay had grown into a solid, strong little girl. Her thick legs were encased in slightly sagging tights that were handsomely offset by a multi-coloured gauze tutu, which she twirled around her as she circled the room.

'You've taken all of the furniture out,' Twenty-Two signed to Georgina. There was only a sleeping roll placed underneath the window and a shelf with a few items left in the cabin.

'Yes ... we can bring it back if you want,' Georgina signed.

Tilla stepped forwards. 'Kit thought you might prefer it this way.'

Twenty-Two scrunched her eyes. 'Yes, yes I do. It is much better. And Bay can run more freely, like she should be able to.'

Georgina visibly relaxed.

Twenty-Two stepped into the cabin and glanced at the three other Sapiens standing awkwardly in the corner. She did not know who they were, so she decided to ignore them until a further explanation was given. She would have to ask Georgina about all of the new residents of Uracil in the coming days. Her memorised records clearly needed to be revised and updated.

Instead of openly staring at the Sapiens, Twenty-Two knelt down in the centre of the cabin and smoothed her tunic over her legs. She felt the slight pressure of a hat being placed on her head and she pulled the string under her chin. Bay stopped her circling and stared at Twenty-Two. Twenty-Two had only been allowed visits from adults – children had not been permitted – so they had not seen each other for eighteen months and Twenty-Two understood that Bay would not recognise her.

Twenty-Two gestured for Twenty-Seven, who had been unsuccessfully hiding behind Tilla's legs. He had grown so much in the time that had passed. He was still shorter than her, as he was only a child, but she could see the beginnings of his transformation into an adult. His previously missing teeth had been replaced by his adult ones, and sturdy legs supported his barrel chest. She was pleased that he could no longer be confused with a Sapien boy, as he had when she'd first met him back in Cytosine. His long brown hair still flopped over his eyes, so she had difficulty reading his expression. She was relieved when he came without hesitation – he hadn't forgotten her. The three of them sat together in a small circle and scrunched their eyes at one another in turn.

There was a small sniff from the unknown Sapien woman standing in the corner. Twenty-Two glanced up at her.

'I'm so sorry,' the woman signed. 'I didn't mean to disturb you; it's just seeing you all together ...'

Georgina gestured at the three Sapiens. 'This is Elise's mother, Sofi. Her father, Aiden, and brother, Nathan. We thought they could come to your party because Elise is away at the moment ... She's away a lot at the moment.'

The tall man stepped forwards. 'She wants you to know that she's very happy you've been released.'

Twenty-Two looked over at Elise's family and took them in. The man was big for a Sapien but did not seem to have confidence in his strength; instead, his nerves seemed to guide him. The woman was calmer, more at peace with her surroundings, but she watched everything and everyone carefully. The boy reached his mother's shoulders and looked to be shy. Twenty-Two warmed to his alert eyes and interest in his surroundings; he clearly took after his mother. Twenty-Two decided that she wanted to know more about him.

'I am pleased that you have made it to Uracil,' Twenty-Two signed in response. 'It is different to Thymine as there is no Museum of Evolution. I understand that Uracil is the only base without a Museum of Evolution. Kit thinks that is a good thing, but I liked being able to see all the animals.'

Everyone was silent. Twenty-Two realised she had said the wrong thing. Ignoring the awkwardness, she gestured for Elise's brother to join the circle. He looked up at his mother for her agreement before sitting cross-legged next to Twenty-Two.

'I've never had a party before,' Twenty-Two continued. 'I've read about them and thought that I would like one.' She adjusted her hat, so it was centred on her head. 'It turns out I was correct.'

'Well, let's liven this up a tad then,' Tilla exclaimed. 'Who wants cake?'

'Me. Definitely me,' Georgina signed, smiling over at her partner. 'Let's put that ridiculous, strengthened tooth enamel I've got to good use.'

Bay clapped her hands in delight, and everyone visibly relaxed, united in the pleasure of watching a small child enjoy herself.

*

Twenty-Two had met Michael a few times while working as Faye's assistant. As one of the heads of the Agricultural Department, he had spoken to the Tri-Council on a regular basis regarding the amount of food he and his team were able to supply to the residents of Uracil. He was strong and tall for a Sapien, but even with these advantages he had always been clearly uncomfortable in Faye's presence.

While Twenty-Two waited to meet with him the next morning, she wondered why he had campaigned for a place on the Tri-Council when he'd once told her he preferred being outside of Uracil, in the fields he tended to. Tugging her acorn-brown tunic farther down her legs, she took a seat on one of the same carved ledges in the oak tree that Faye used to preside over.

Twenty-Two heard Michael's approach before she saw him. From behind her, his heavy boots banged against the wooden walkway. His pace was steady and as the noise of his footsteps began to increase, Twenty-Two felt her anxiety about her future match their volume.

Should she apologise for what she had done to Faye? No. She did not believe that she had acted incorrectly. She could not apologise as that would be deceitful. No matter how many times Kit had tried to persuade her that she should not have acted so hastily, she had stayed firm that her actions had been necessary – she had done what no one else had the strength to do. She had saved lives; she was sure of it. Faye had ordered Septa to kill Elise. Who else had Faye disposed of in this secretive manner? And if Twenty-Two hadn't stopped Faye when she had, who else would have suffered at her hands? Perhaps she should try to explain this to Michael, hope to make him understand her reasoning. He was a sensible man; perhaps she could persuade him of the logic of her actions.

As Michael neared the rear of the tree trunk where Twenty-Two was seated she stilled her nerves and turned to face him.

He did not greet Twenty-Two until he had sat heavily on the chair facing her. He positioned his legs so they stretched out in front of him with only the heels touching the wooden platform and the toes pointing upwards. His wide frame looked too large for the chair even though Faye, who had been much taller than him, had always managed to perch upon it.

'Hello. How have you been?' he signed slowly.

Surprised by his knowledge of sign language, Twenty-Two warmed ever so slightly to him.

'I am well. Much better than my last months in Cytosine's Museum of Evolution. I was cared for here. Thank you.'

Michael nodded and glanced towards the waiting area, which was already beginning to fill with visitors for the day.

'You must be wondering why I asked you to come so early.'

Twenty-Two nodded.

'I have spoken with Raul and Flynn and we are all in agreement—'

'What I did was not wrong,' she signed quickly. 'Faye was corrupt, and she used her power only to serve her own interests. If I had not done what I did then more people would have died because of her actions. I did it for Uracil and I would do it—'

Twenty-Two dropped her hands. She would not lie to Michael, but that did not mean that she had to tell him all her thoughts. She had gone too far; they would definitely expel her now ... She could not lose her memories, they were part of her, as much as her fingers and toes.

Michael leant forwards. 'That is not why I asked you here. As far as I am concerned, you have served your term of punishment and deserve a second chance. In fact, I asked you here because I need an administrative assistant. And I think that you're a wise choice for the job.'

Twenty-Two's eyes widened. 'But—'

'Do you want the position?'

Twenty-Two thought for a moment before responding. 'Yes, I do.'

'Can you start tomorrow?'

'Yes.'

'Then there's no more to discuss,' Michael smiled. 'I will see you then.'

Twenty-Two left the platform and made her way straight to Ezra to tell him her news. Things were looking up.

CHAPTER 3

. . . .

Genevieve

Genevieve opened one eye and then the other. It was two in the morning and fully dark outside. She had slept for only three hours, but, thanks to one of the gifts of genetic engineering she had inherited from her father, she was refreshed enough to turn her mind to the rest of the day. With a brightness she tried always to display, she swung her legs out of her vast bed and placed both feet firmly on the carefully polished floorboards. Reaching her arms above her head, she went through her morning stretches – equilibrium and routine were key to her wellbeing and she tried to enter the day in the calmest manner possible.

When she had finished, she crossed the bedroom, taking the time to run her hand along the shot-silk cover of the tête-à-tête chair looking out to the south-facing gardens. The light clicked on automatically as she entered her dressing room, and the soft hum of cooled air being pumped into the room accompanied it. Outside, the early autumn heat in Adenine would be stifling, but inside her carefully controlled home a constant temperature was maintained.

Flicking through her dresses, she selected an elaborate affair made of russet chiffon she'd forgotten she owned. Slipping it over her head, she stepped into the small mirrored side room so she could inspect herself from every angle.

Frowning at her reflection, she decided that she didn't like the way the dress sat on her hips and pulled it back over her long, lean figure. Instead of returning it to the hanger, she placed the dress in the recycling basket. The russet dress would soon sit in the closet of another Medius who had more slender hips than her own. She pondered the next selection.

After finalising her attire, she sat in front of her dressing table and pulled the stopper out of a bottle of Dermadew. Dabbing the glistening golden syrup across her high cheekbones, she hummed to herself as she decided on the other areas of her skin that required attention. Left to soak for a few hours, all traces of the previous day's strain would be removed and she would maintain the flawless complexion that was so admired in the Potiors. Its cost of fifty Medi-stamps was high, but it left her skin looking plump and dewy; the resulting light sheen made her glow with health and vitality.

Adding the final touches to her appearance, she smiled at her reflection – she would do for the day. She closed the bedroom door behind her and crossed to her study where she would work until dawn without once raising her head.

'A vision! A vision, in teal!' Mortimer exclaimed as he looked up from his breakfast plate three hours later. 'It is quite your colour, my dear.'

Genevieve closed the dining room door behind her and bent to kiss the top of his head. 'You say that about every colour, Father.'

'Well, that's because it's true!'

Genevieve smiled at him before taking a seat to his right. She looked down the long dining table; all of the other eighteen chairs were empty. They would remain so until Thursday evening when they would be hosting a small dinner party for their neighbours, colleagues and associates. As she pondered the menu for two nights' time, she tapped her finger against her glass.

'Thank you, Dina,' she said when her usual breakfast of smoked salmon and the tiniest smattering of dill was brought to her.

She did not look up at the owner of the hand that placed the small plate in front of her; several Sapien servants helped run their home and she knew each just by the way they presented her breakfast. Instead, she started to flick through her screen, scanning the dinner options that were available from the Emporium – if you had the tickets.

'Another busy day?' Mortimer enquired.

Genevieve looked up. 'As busy as the rest, but I've been asked to report to the Museum of Evolution today. I don't know why; nothing generally happens there that requires my input.'

'Maybe they have a new display? I wonder what they have brought back this time,' Mortimer said, while carefully slicing the duck egg on his plate into quarters.

He liberally sprinkled salt over each piece before popping them one by one into his mouth.

Genevieve leant back. As the recently promoted Assistant Director of the Disclosure Department, she was required to work for each Potior in Adenine and had to be ready to visit a different building every week if necessary. Preparing releases and updates for the population's screens required an adaptability that she had always possessed, even as a child. It was unusual, though, for anything to occur at the museum that required someone of her rank to assist; it was usually kept for the more junior members of the team. There was only so much one could say about a chameleon being brought back from extinction. But she would never directly query why her attendance was required today – she would marvel at the unveiling of a new chair leg design if a Potior requested her to. You didn't get to her rank by openly questioning the Potiors' decisions.

'Perhaps they finally want to put the Neanderthals back on display and require a screen release about it,' Genevieve said. 'After what happened in Thymine, they may need to move more quickly this time.'

Dina entered the room again to clear their plates.

'Anyway,' Genevieve continued hurriedly, 'I've been considering Thursday's dinner and I think we should start with roasted mushrooms and shallots.'

Mortimer leant back in his chair and smiled at her. 'You always have the best ideas, my dear. You delight me yet again.'

An hour later, Genevieve left their home. It looked like rain, so she had slipped on a light coat that reached her ankles. As she walked, she enjoyed the feeling of the material swirling around her feet. She found protection in her layers of clothing and make-up, gaining strength from even a dab of blusher and an artfully draped scarf. Layer upon layer of attire to bring the confidence she needed to set foot outside of her home.

Genevieve took the most direct route to Adenine's Museum of Evolution, even though it was the busiest. She weaved her way through the crowds of Sapiens and Medius making their way to their daily workstations. Her home, along with those of all of the other high-end Medius families, was a short walk to the centre along the recycled rubber pathways.

Crossing yet another small wooden bridge, she stared at the water trickling beneath her feet. The original Potior leaders had chosen a vast island of meadows, criss-crossed with streams and brooks, as the centre of Zone 3. It meant that for the majority of its residents going about their daily business, the fear of the untreated water kept them alert and mildly on edge. Consequently, thousands of its residents only ever felt at peace when they were securely inside one of Adenine's many buildings. Having crossed the bridge, she lifted her head and kept her gaze forwards, scanning the route, deciding whether to hang to the left of the busy footpath or to the right.

Up ahead were the twelve offices in the centre of Adenine. They were designed to resemble segments of an orange. Each one was identical and pointed inwards to the Premier's residence – the political hub of Zone 3 – and affectionately referred to as 'Father's Kitchen Table' by most of the Medius. Circled around the outside of the offices were a few Medius schools, the courthouse, the Emporium and the Museum of Evolution. Beyond their walls were the residential properties, distinguished by the importance of their occupants, fading away in grandeur until they reached the lowly Sapien homes fashioned from handmade clay bricks and reused materials. The only buildings beyond the Sapien dwellings were the crematorium and recycling centre.

To reach the museum, Genevieve had to cross to the other side of the wheel of offices. As she entered the broad lane that split the Office of Communications from the Office of Justice, she smiled at the few Medius acquaintances she passed and stopped to talk to one of Mortimer's colleagues who had recently been promoted to Assistant Director of Shipping. She invited him to their little party on Thursday even though they didn't have a spare seat for him. To resolve the matter, she decided that she would not mention the invitation again to another of the guests to make room for this unexpected acquisition. Constant adjustments were required to keep abreast of her ever-shifting circle of peers.

As she crossed over the stone boulevard in front of the Premier's home, she looked up at the large building. It could easily accommodate every Medius and Potior in the city. The Premier only employed Medius servants and had a whole retinue of Potiors by his side. It was the centre of Adenine and every other building seemed to have sprouted from its unchanging presence. A small river circled its walls and the entranceway could only be accessed via a single arched bridge, and every visitor was required to have their credentials checked by one of the ten Medius guards. A small, orderly line was already beginning to form. She knew enough about Pre-Pandemic history to be aware that the river that circled it was called a 'moat' and based on the designs of castles from the medieval era. Its presence was essential – no one would ever dare to swim across the moat to avoid the bridge.

Crossing to the other side of the boulevard, Genevieve took the lane that ran between the Office of Provisions and the Office of Production, two departments that worked closely together to provide for the needs of the Potiors and Medius. What the Sapiens required was rarely a priority.

Approaching the museum, she briefly checked her screen – she had made it in good time. Genevieve's height – six and a half feet – her swirling coat and her fixed eyes meant that the lower-end Medius and all of the Sapiens had parted for her. Quickly making her way to the museum's front entrance, she merely nodded at the two Medius guards positioned at the bottom of the stairway. She never willingly engaged these types in conversation. What would be the point?

Taking the stairs leading to the main atrium two at a time, she did not glance around as she entered the vast glass structure. The museum had never held much of her attention. Her interests lay elsewhere.

She tried not to grimace when she saw Anthony, one of the Collections Assistants, leaning against the reception desk.

'I thought I would come and wait for you, Genevieve,' Anthony said, before he looked at her appraisingly. 'New coat? Or have you shrunk?'

'It looked like rain,' she responded. 'Is Constalian in this morning? She asked to meet.'

'Yes, she's in one of the rear laboratories. I'll take you over,' he responded. He began to amble towards the double doors that led to the inner workings of the museum. 'I'm sure she'll want me in on this one.'

'Don't bother yourself; she asked only for my attendance.' Genevieve smiled before continuing. 'Strict instructions that no one below clearance grade seventeen attends.' She met his gaze. 'Remind me, you're still sixteen, aren't you?'

She waited patiently for his response.

Anthony pursed his lips. 'Fifteen, actually. But bound to be sixteen by the end of the year.'

'Still two short, though. Aren't you?' Genevieve said.

With a smile that didn't reach her eyes, she swept towards the side door, not waiting for any further reply. She had already known Anthony was grade fifteen rather than sixteen, but she wanted to hear the admission from his own lips.

After several tries, she found Constalian in one of the laboratories. Genevieve had to pass through three sets of identification scanners before she could push open its door. Rolling down her sleeve, she glanced at the tattoo on her wrist before covering it.

She was surprised at the size of the room, no larger than her bedroom at home. Plain concrete lined the walls, and there were no windows and only one doorway. 'Functional' was the word she would use for it.

'Ah, just who I wanted to see,' Constalian said, beckoning Genevieve over to her.

Genevieve looked up at the towering woman and smiled warmly. Constalian's midnight-blue eyes, her perfectly waved white hair, the sheen to her skin; all of it was designed to overwhelm Genevieve and she had to concentrate to appear as was expected.

To give herself a moment of composure, Genevieve bowed ever so slightly before squeezing Constalian's hand in return. 'It is always a pleasure to assist you. What can I do to help? Is it to do with the Neanderthals?'

Constalian waved her hand at Genevieve as if to dismiss the idea. 'Oh no, we have far more important matters to attend to.' She leant forwards. 'Between you and me, the Neanderthal Project is growing a little stale. Years of resources and energy and what do we have to show for it? A dozen or so misfits who seem unable to appreciate the gift of life that they have been granted.

It will be phased out soon. But don't worry; there are other, more exciting projects afoot.'

Genevieve tried not to look shocked. People had devoted their lives to the Neanderthal Project and it would seem that it was being stuffed under the bed like an outdated toy, no longer of use or interest. She smoothed her features after reminding herself that it was not her place to question the Potiors' decisions. It was better not to indulge those thoughts.

'So, what can I help you with?' Genevieve asked, brightening her voice.

Constalian beamed at her. 'This is one of the most pivotal moments in our society's development. A project that we have been working on for a while has come to fruition and we need to release it to the masses.' She let go of Genevieve's hand and began gesturing with both of her own, plucking intangible points from the air. 'It requires a degree of dexterity. It could be perceived in a somewhat ... negative manner and it is up to you to make sure that the Sapiens understand that they will benefit.'

Genevieve dropped her head slightly as she thought about what was required of her. 'Of course. I will do everything in my power to assist you, Constalian. Can you provide an outline before I receive the full brief?'

'Yes, I can. I want you to start on this immediately.'

Constalian pulled out a chair and took a seat. Genevieve hadn't had much contact with her previously but knew that she was known for her straightforward manner. She was believed to be one of the original founders of Adenine, along with the Premier, which placed her as one of the oldest of her kind. Despite having lived for over a hundred years, she did not look a day over forty-five.

'As I said, we've been working on this for nearly two decades, and in fact, it was originally proposed over fifty years ago,' Constalian told her. 'It's so key to our development that it has been worked on in Adenine, Guanine and Cytosine.'

Genevieve took a seat next to Constalian. She had wanted to ask why it hadn't been developed solely in Cytosine, the scientific base of Zone 3 which heralded itself as 'Ingenuity and Innovation', but she knew that Constalian had a habit of anticipating most people's questions. She would decide whether Genevieve needed to know the Potiors' reasoning.

Constalian leant back in her chair and stared at Genevieve. 'Yes, a project of this size has required all of our finest minds. In short, we have decided that a new species is required to assist with the workings of Zone 3.' Genevieve opened her mouth but shut it once Constalian continued. 'And not just any new species. A new species of human.'

Genevieve nodded and kept her features still as she tried to process this.

'They will assist the Sapiens in Zone 3 with the ever so essential, but perhaps somewhat repetitive, work that we require of them. This, in turn, will relieve more of the Sapiens to take jobs in the production centres and other neglected areas, such as the docks. We have to redouble our efforts in this regard.'

'You plan to ... create ... this new species, then?' Genevieve said.

Constalian smiled and crossed her legs. 'We do. Just as we did with the Medius and Potiors.'

There was a pause while Genevieve tried frantically to guess the possibilities.

'Oh, don't worry,' Constalian said. 'I don't expect you to come up with any of the logistics for this development; it's taken us years to perfect this one! There will be a new lottery. Half of the future Sapien pregnancies will be genetically engineered to create this fourth species of human.'

Genevieve blinked but did not speak. She thought she had guessed the rest but didn't want Constalian to suspect that she had.

Constalian smiled, excitement radiating from her. It was almost infectious. 'Half of the Sapiens' future progeny will be gifted these genetic enhancements, but there will be no selection process. The decision will have already been made for them. They will be granted gifts that will ease the tediousness of their working day, suppress any resistance that could upset their mental equilibrium and reduce their stress levels and general anxieties.'

'They will become compliant,' Genevieve said.

'Well, yes,' Constalian said. 'But I don't think we'll lead with that in the screen releases, will we?'

'No, of course not,' Genevieve responded. 'I'll come up with something much more suitable.'

'We also need a name for them,' Constalian said, frowning for the first time. 'We have a few potential ones, but see if you can come up with anything and we'll consider it alongside the others.'

Genevieve tried not to look flustered – she could be responsible for naming the Potiors' new creations.

Constalian raised an eyebrow. 'So, what do you think of it all?'

Genevieve smiled and leant forwards in her chair. 'I think it is ... sublime.'

CHAPTER 4

. . . .

Elise

On her first day as team leader, Elise had decided that they should try and cover as much of the distance to Guanine as possible. She had pushed the group to walk over halfway and had only stopped when the evening light drew so dim that they couldn't see where they were placing their feet. When they couldn't walk any farther, they had set up camp in an open stretch of meadow. The grass was high enough to cover them from view when lying down, but the open ground meant they couldn't risk lighting a fire that evening and signalling their position.

'If we'd stopped four miles ago we could've camped at the edge of the forest and lit a fire,' Septa said. 'Then we could be eating properly and not using our reserves.'

'I've already explained my reasons to you,' Elise said, her voice rising ever so slightly before she corrected it. 'I chose to cover more ground, so we'd get to Guanine in the early afternoon tomorrow. We need to scout the area for a few days before deciding when to enter the museum. Our reserves can always be replenished tomorrow, when it's light.'

'It's not the decision I would've made,' Septa continued, unrolling her sleeping mat a little more vigorously than necessary.

Elise shot her a look. 'What? I'm just being honest. And honesty is a quality that should be encouraged, not dismissed.'

'I don't really need your input on simple things like where we're camping,' Elise said, as calmly as she could. 'I'll take suggestions for the main section of the mission, but right now, we're camping here.'

Septa pulled some dried meat out of her bag. 'I'm only offering an opinion. We're allowed an opinion, aren't we? Or do you prefer us to blindly follow your orders?' she smirked.

Elise opened her mouth to respond, but Max spoke before she could continue. 'What am I going to do on these missions? I can't really stroll around Guanine making subtle enquiries.'

'You're our safety net,' Elise responded, unrolling her own sleeping mat. She glanced up at him. 'Maya said every group should have one person who remains in base camp and reports back immediately if the other three operatives don't return on time. That way there are no delays in knowing the status of a failed mission.'

Max raised an eyebrow. 'Call it what you want, but I can smell the sweaty feet of a messenger boy when I'm near one.'

'It's a shame,' Septa said, sitting down on her own mat. 'All your skills, Max, and you're put to the back.'

'I can also recognise a soup stirrer when they're next to me,' Max said, glancing at Septa.

She shrugged. 'Better than a messenger boy.' She threw an imaginary ball at him. 'Fetch!'

Elise sighed; this was not going as planned. She decided to retreat and take advantage of the full moon to walk around the circumference of where they were camping.

After a few minutes, Raynor caught up with her.

'Don't tell me,' Elise said. 'You don't like where we're camping either?'

'I don't give a monkey's where we camp,' Raynor replied. 'As long as it's dry and safe.'

Elise smiled, relieved that at least one of the team wasn't disgruntled with every decision she made.

They walked in silence for a moment before Raynor spoke. 'What I came to say was, don't be scared of ruling with an iron fist sometimes. You can't always wriggle your way into everyone's hearts.' She pulled out an imaginary screen and started tapping at it. 'Day One: Elise is so great. She's such a great team leader and makes all the right decisions. I wish I had her athletic figure and quiet control. She's the bestest!'

Elise raised her eyebrows. 'I was trying to be diplomatic. She's only sulking because I was made team leader. And I thought it was better than fighting with her ... There's just something about her that gets under my skin and makes me want to floor her.'

'Well, you're not going to win her over with the nicey-nice stuff. You could give Septa a place on the Tri-Council, change the name of Uracil to Septaville, have a national holiday in her name and it still wouldn't be enough. She'd still think she'd been cheated.' Raynor cleared her throat noisily and spat the resulting deposit on the ground. 'The only thing she understands is strength, and you're not showing any.'

Elise thought about it for a moment. Raynor was right.

The next morning, they set off at first light. Elise set the pace without looking for the rest of the group's agreement.

After a few miles, Septa spoke. 'Do we really have to go this fast? We'll be exhausted by the time we get there.'

'Is it too much for you?' Elise asked. 'Not as fit as I remember you were?'

Septa bristled. 'I was just thinking of Raynor.'

Elise stopped and faced Septa. 'No, you weren't. You never think of anyone but yourself. If you don't like it, then leave. I'm sure Maya will find something for you to do back in Uracil.'

'I told you, I was just thinking of the oth—'

'You told me the reason you followed the order to kill me was because you never question a superior when it comes to the protection of Uracil,' Elise said, not breaking eye contact with Septa. 'But all you've done since I was made team leader is question everything I've said. So, which is it? You should have questioned the order to kill me or you shouldn't be questioning me right now? You can't have it both ways.'

'I follow the orders of my superiors,' Septa responded, cocking her chin upwards. 'But I don't include you in that category. You think you're so special because you go on so many missions, but you're not special. You have volume but you don't have quality. And you'll be dead in a few years because of it.'

Elise squared up to Septa, ready to snap at any moment. 'Well, it's a few years longer than I would have got if you'd had your way. And if you don't follow my orders then you're also not following Maya's as she's the one who put me in charge. Shall we report that to Maya next time we see her? Or shall I send you packing now?'

Septa shrugged and mimed zipping her mouth closed. Elise realised that, in that moment, Septa hated her.

They set off again.

I can't please everyone, and do I really want to get on Septa's good side anyway? Does she even have a good side?

Elise pushed the thoughts away. She had more important things to worry about, such as whether Septa could be trusted to follow orders in the middle of a mission.

An hour later, Max, who could have run the distance they had covered without breaking a sweat, nudged Raynor.

Since he towered above the older woman, this meant prodding her in the neck with his elbow. 'Guanine's your old two-step shuffling ground, isn't it? Have you always been "Education and Enlightenment"?'

Raynor raised her head. 'I was born and raised there, yes.' She stared down at her feet again.

Elise studied her; she looked tired. 'Let's stop for a break and eat something,' she said, making sure not to look directly at Raynor. 'We'll be at the outskirts of Guanine in about two hours.' She gave Septa a quick glance. 'Septa, keep watch.'

Septa reddened and Elise mimed closing a zip over her mouth.

Max chuckled.

When they were settled and he was stretched out on his side, he addressed Raynor again. 'When did you leave Guanine, then?'

'In my early twenties, when I was young and still vaguely beautiful,' she said wryly.

Max snorted but quickly recovered.

Raynor shot him a look. 'Beauty is overrated – we all age eventually. Well, perhaps not you, but I don't envy you one bit.'

'You don't?' Max said. 'I thought everyone would want to live in a young body for at least a hundred years.'

'The Potiors don't really live, though, do they? They don't mix, they don't relax, they don't enjoy the small things that this world has to offer. That's not living in my view.'

'But don't you miss looking young, feeling strong?' Max asked.

'The arrogance of youth,' Raynor said staring across at him, almost pityingly. 'It was a relief, actually, when my beauty began to fade. Everyone else was so focused on replenishing what was so clearly slipping away, but I thought, bugger it! Let it slip; let my features alter and age. I've got other qualities that can be improved. There is still hope for the inner beauty, if you only provide a place for it to blossom.'

Max tipped an imaginary hat at her. 'Wisdom indeed, Madam Ray.'

'Where did you grow up, Max?' Elise asked as casually as she could.

She didn't know much about him, or any of the Potiors really.

'Adenine,' Max said, biting into an apple. He chewed for a moment. 'That's where all the Potiors are born and raised. We only leave for the other bases when we are fully grown.'

He took another bite and Elise stared at him, willing him to continue.

Max saw her watching him. 'Wouldn't be very impressive if we were caught wetting ourselves at age three because we couldn't get to a toilet in time, would it?'

'They're clever bastards, the Potiors,' Raynor said to Elise. 'They do everything to keep themselves as distanced from the rest of us as possible. Fresh pish down the trousers narrows the gap.'

'They're also very possessive of their gifts,' Max continued. 'They have a strict one-in-one-out policy.'

Septa had stopped patrolling and drawn closer; she too was clearly interested in learning more about the Potiors.

'There's only a thousand of us, you see,' Max continued. 'A Potior can make a request to reproduce, but they have to wait for another Potior to pass on. Trevilian was the name of the Potior that I replaced. In a way, he was a parent to me as well, as I wouldn't be here without his input.' Max smiled. 'Or maybe I wouldn't be here without his output is a better way of phrasing it.'

'What do Potiors die of?' Elise asked.

She had been brought up to believe they were practically invincible. Since then, she had learnt that they could bleed. She'd seen Fintorian go out that way.

Max snorted again. 'They're capable of dying of the same ailments as the Sapiens and Medius, but they have access to better medical facilities. They have a monthly health check, which catches most cancers and diseases before they spread. Their enhancements mean that they rarely suffer from any cardio issues and their ageing process has been slowed down too. Old age hasn't had the chance to catch up with any one of them yet. So that only really leaves unattended trauma.'

Max smiled around at his colleagues. 'In conclusion: they break, just like you do.'

Elise thought about what Max had said. 'Why do you refer to the Potiors as "they" and "them"? You're a Potior yourself.'

'Physically, yes,' he replied, carefully wrapping up the apple core and stowing it in his bag. They were all careful not to leave any trace of human activity outside of the bases. 'But I don't have access to the medical attention that they do, I don't align myself with them and I don't believe in what they do, so I don't think I am one any more.'

'What do you call yourself, then?' Septa asked.

She had edged closer to the group.

'Does it matter?' Max responded. He stood before Septa could reply. 'I'll continue the patrol for the rest of the break.'

Elise loaded a small stone into her sling and took aim. Crouching behind a granite ledge, she waited patiently until the guard stopped for a moment to take his cap off and pat down his hair. She looped her arm above her head in three accelerating swings, her confidence growing with the familiar circles. At the beginning of the fourth, she released the stone.

The whipping noise echoed across the deserted streets. The guard jumped at the sound. Whirling through the air, the stone's journey ended with a satisfying clunk on the window ledge at the front of the museum, fifty metres to the right of the entranceway. Her aim was perfect, even in the depths of night.

The guard shone his torch in the direction of the noise, but the beam didn't reach the window. Glancing over his shoulder, he checked the entranceway. All was quiet. Torch still facing the window, he set off to investigate, his thumb hovering over the portable button that Elise knew would bring ten more guards if pressed. Instead of facing the enemy head on, creating distractions using the sling was her preferred method in situations like this, as it left no unconscious body to be stumbled upon.

Slipping around the edge of her hiding place, she took another brief moment to check there were no other guards nearby. The stone steps stretched up in front of her, leading to the heavy oak doors of the museum.

Elise had decided to take point, much to Septa's obvious, but thankfully unexpressed, annoyance. Eighteen months of training with Maya had made Elise's tread as light as the first snow of winter. She could blend into crowds without drawing anyone's gaze and had perfected the ability to merge into a setting – one moment visible, the next gone. But none of this impressed Septa.

Elise looked around again. Something was bothering her; she had expected the rear entranceway to Guanine's Museum of Evolution to be heavily patrolled.

Over a hundred years ago, Guanine had been chiselled into the mountainside in the western region of Zone 3. To prove their worth, Medius students wishing to study at its university had to climb the thousands of steps that led up to the settlement's entranceway, past all the residential Sapien homes that were burrowed into the rock face. Guanine's museum, located near the peak of the mountain, was the first of its kind, built for the student population, and, therefore, one of the jewels in the Potiors' self-appointed crown.

It had taken three days of circling Guanine's borders for them to find a way they could slip into the museum unnoticed. But their patience had paid off, and an opportunity for them to enter the museum had presented itself yesterday when Raynor had wandered through Guanine's Emporium by herself.

Reporting back, Raynor had told them that she'd been casually inspecting a table of palm-size models of double helixes when the store owner had informed her that he was doing a roaring trade at the moment. They were considered good-luck charms by the student population, and their final examinations were the next day. With the students feverishly trying to cram the last bits of knowledge into their already overloaded minds before their final day of tests – and the rest of Guanine support- ing this by having a quiet night in preparation for the following all-night celebrations – not a soul would be out on the streets. Still, it felt too quiet.

Quick footsteps approached and Elise spun around. Without speaking, Septa overtook her and darted up the steps in front.

Elise looked up at Septa's retreating figure. It was just the two of them tonight, with Raynor and Max waiting for them back at base camp. Raynor had been Elise's initial choice for the mission, but she had looked so tired by the time early evening came that Elise reluctantly made the decision to ask Septa to accompany her instead. She glanced around again; she wouldn't allow herself to worry about the lack of guards until it became necessary. She'd learnt in the first year of her training that if she prepared for too many scenarios, she left herself open to misin- terpreting the current one.

Taking two of the narrow steps at a time, Elise ran up to the towering oak doors. Raynor had already managed to steal a key card from a museum host in the Emporium that morning, and so they presented no obstacle. Septa silently pushed the door open and stepped inside.

Keeping tight to the walls, the two women headed towards the rear of the building where the admin offices were located. The museum was deserted, and they passed without incident. Despite this, Elise's sense of unease grew. It had been two years since she had been captured by Marvalian in Cytosine, but though she hid it well, the fear of incarceration always hung over her. Given her previous experience, she did not think it was unhealthy.

When they entered the administration section, Elise slowed slightly to allow Septa to rush ahead to the largest of the offices, relying on her predictable habit of always wanting to be first.

'I'll check the next room,' Elise said to the door closing behind Septa.

Instead of moving to the next office, Elise carried on down the corridor. If the museum was laid out in the same way as Thymine's, then the room she was looking for would be four doors up on the right. As she walked, electric lights snapped on above her, but there was no other sound or movement. She was alone. When she reached the door with a sign that read 'Olivian: Museum Director', Elise pressed the key card Raynor had swiped up against the electric lock, but nothing happened.

Moving farther down the first-floor corridor, she reached one of the large windows and pushed it open. After pausing to listen again, she pulled out a small box from her trouser pocket, no bigger than her thumbnail. When she flipped open its lid, a tiny winged camera emerged from the box and made a steady, vertical ascent. Following her hand signals, it began recording everything in a three-hundred-and-sixty-degree radius, dutifully floating out of the window and along the outside of the building until it reached Olivian's office.

There were no open windows; that would be too easy. Instead, Elise peered at the camera's feed on her screen, and directed it to the minute, hexagonal-shaped ventilation holes at the top left of the stone walls. The camera followed her instructions and whirred through one of the small holes until it pushed its way through the dust and grime and circled into the Potior's office. It automatically flew towards a chair where it settled, ignoring Elise's instructions to carry on to the large elm desk at the rear of the office.

Elise sighed in frustration as the camera laboriously wiped its wings against each other, cleaning the debris from them. The museum director's desk was so close, and it could reveal so much, but investigating a Potior was against Maya's orders so she had to work as quickly as possible. The camera was now scraping its millimetre-long legs against the chair to remove some fluff.

Elise flicked her gaze down the corridor. She was still alone, but thoughts of waking up in the containment centre in Cytosine crowded her; she could almost feel the wires attached to her forehead, the pain deep in her belly when she tried to move. The memories always came to her when she most needed to remain calm. Returning her attention to the camera, she tried once more to direct it to the desk, tapping the air twice with her index finger to signal the speed she required. Finally, it obeyed.

On the desk was a Pre-Pandemic research paper, instantly recognisable as it was printed out on sheets of paper like the ones Samuel used to have back in his office. Elise focused the camera on the spidery writing in the corner:

Homo necesse? – Would signify their import.
Homo benedictus? – No, religious connotations that don't
apply now.
Homo guanine? – A nod to the tradition of naming
after place of their discovery/creation, better for us to
suggest this first before Adenine or Cytosine.

Elise stared at her screen, the implications of what was written beginning to surface, before a soft sound behind her caught her attention.

She turned around to see a figure crouched low in the shadowed corridor against the floor, lizard-like, its hand outstretched.

'You'll have to do better than that to sneak up on me,' Elise said, as she returned to staring at the screen.

Septa straightened. 'I was merely practising. Anyway, I came to tell you that we have to leave. The canteen workers are awake.'

Elise peered at the sky through the window. Dawn was coming. Reluctantly, she signalled for the camera to make its way back through the ventilation holes. She could review the recording later – there was no more she could do in Guanine for the moment.

'Stand down, Max,' Raynor said, when Elise and Septa walked into the glade. 'You won't have to put on your best running shoes today.'

'Find much?' Max asked, lifting his head from his sleeping roll.

Before Elise could open her mouth, Septa was speaking. 'Only that the Potiors have been trying to bring back another species of human.'

Elise grabbed Septa's arm and spun her around; she hadn't mentioned this on their walk back. 'What was their name? Was it Homo guanine, necesse or benedictus?'

Septa snatched her arm back. 'No, you bloody weirdo. It was Homo denisovan.'

'Are they the new species?' Elise asked, the urgency clear in her voice.

'Again, no. What on earth are you going on about?' Septa said, staring at Elise. 'They're old like the Neanderthals. I was reading about them in the office. They created two of them a couple of years ago but never shipped them out to the other bases as they don't think the cloning took properly. Contamination or degeneration of samples or something ... From what I was reading, their ancestors' remains were first discovered in the Denisova cave in Siberia, which is a region of Zone 1. That's why they're called Denisovans, and they were in existence around the same time as both the Sapiens and Neanderthals.'

'Stars,' Raynor said, glancing up to the sky. 'After what they did to those poor Neanderthals, can't they just let other species have a bit of peace?'

'So, was that what they shipped over to Adenine a year ago?' Max asked.

He pushed himself up from his sleeping roll and rubbed his face with both hands.

'Yes,' Septa said.

'No,' Elise said at the same time.

Septa bristled. 'Of course it was.'

'You said yourself that they hadn't sent them out to the other bases because the cloning hadn't been successful. Why would they do it now?'

'For a multitude of potential reasons. The Denisovans got better, or the Directors thought a change of environment would help, or the Potiors just wanted them in Adenine. Who knows how their brains work?'

Elise sat down. 'Well, I found something too. And it suggests something even more worrying.'

'This'll be good ...' Septa muttered.

'I think the Potiors are creating a *new* species of human, rather than focusing on bringing back others that went extinct. I saw a list of potential names for them. There was Homo necesse, which I think might mean "Necessary Man", Homo benedictus ...'

Elise paused. She had no idea what benedictus meant, having never heard it used before or anything close to it.

'It means "blessed",' Max said, not quite meeting her eye. 'We had to learn some Latin in school ... It was a Pre-Pandemic religious term. It would make the new species "Blessed Man".'

Elise nodded. 'The last one was Homo guanine. So, Man from Guanine. I think they wanted to suggest it before Adenine or Cytosine had the same idea. Samuel once told me that lots of extinct species were named after where they were found—' She stopped briefly as she thought of Samuel. Embarrassed at her reaction, she carried on quickly, 'Neanderthals were named after the valley where they were first found.' She ran her hands through her hair. It was short again and it made her think of Seventeen. 'Stars, what gives them the right?'

'Max, did you know anything about this?' Raynor said sharply.

'No, of course not. As I've said a million times before, I was only nineteen when I left – a child in their eyes. They expect us all to stay in education until we're twenty-five. I knew very little of their grand plans.'

'We'll have to tell Maya as soon as we can,' Raynor said. She reached over to the fire to heat some water. 'When's our next meet-up?'

'Not for a few weeks,' Elise said, suddenly feeling exhausted.

'I don't believe it,' Septa said firmly. 'A few names with no context doesn't mean anything. And even if it does, it doesn't mean they've actually done it.'

Elise stared up at her. Septa had a point, but she wasn't going to give her the satisfaction of actually admitting as much.

'Either way,' Elise said, 'we'll report to Maya and let her decide. She'll have intelligence coming in from the other research teams too and may know more than we do. Whatever the truth of what they're creating is, we have to look at the bigger picture. If we get rid of most of the Potiors, we can free all the people and animals they've trapped in the museums. They shouldn't be caged either. Nothing should be.'

'There is no bigger picture,' Septa said. 'We should be looking to Uracil, protecting what we've got.'

Elise raised her head. 'There is! And we can't just ignore it. I know that, because back in Thymine, when I started working with the Neanderthals, the Potiors and Medius always told me *not* to think about the "bigger picture". Instead, I was told to concentrate on the day-to-day things. I've since worked out that it's best to do the exact opposite of what the Potiors want of me. No offence, Max.'

Max shrugged but didn't seem to take Elise's comments personally. 'That's all well and good, but I don't know what Maya and the Tri-Council are thinking. We're too small, too weak, to take on the Potiors.'

'I have to agree with Max,' Raynor said. 'It's the wrong decision to go against the Potiors. They'll want their revenge.'

Max frowned and the group fell into an uncomfortable silence.

'It's Adenine next, isn't it?' Elise asked, trying to break the tension. 'When will we be setting off?'

Raynor cleared her throat and spat on the ground. 'About that. We've had word that there's been a change in the itinerary. A runner came in with a message whilst you were out. And you're not going to like where we're being sent.'

'Just tell me,' Elise said, looking up.

'We've been ordered to go to the museum in Cytosine. And Septa's in charge of this one.'

CHAPTER 5

* *

Twenty-Two

The next morning, Ezra brought Twenty-Two's breakfast to her cabin since she did not feel ready to join one of the large tables in the central hub of Uracil. Not for the first time, Twenty-Two missed the simplicity of her pod back in the museum in Cytosine, back when Fintorian had been there and everything had been predictable. As Ezra busied himself getting down some plates for them, Twenty-Two peered out of her window at the near-deserted walkways.

'Is there something you want to say?' Twenty-Two asked, after they had eaten in silence for a few minutes.

Ezra finished off the last corner of his toast. 'It's this job of yours. Are you sure you should be doing it?'

Twenty-Two continued to methodically eat her own toast in a symmetrical pattern, as she had done since she was first introduced to bread: left bite, right bite, middle split into two and portioned to each side of her mouth. Waiting for Ezra to say more.

'It's just that working for the Tri-Council was what caused all the trouble for you last time,' Ezra continued.

'Do you think I am not right for the job?' Twenty-Two signed, before tidying her plate away.

Ezra stood up from the floor, his freckled face frowning in concern. 'No, no, it's not that. I just don't understand why he asked you. Honestly, you'd be the last person I'd want working for me if I was on the Tri-Council.'

Twenty-Two whipped around. '*Why?*'

They rarely lost their tempers with each other and the force of her response made them both pause for a moment.

Ezra stood his ground. 'Well, you did, sort of, kill the last person you worked for.'

Twenty-Two thought about it. It was true that no one knew of her promise to Kit. She had sworn on her ancestors' lives not to pass judgement on anyone in this manner again without discussing it with Kit first. It was, therefore, understandable that people might believe that she could follow a similar course again.

'You are right,' Twenty-Two responded. 'He doesn't know that I won't do it again, so why would Michael want to work with me now?'

Ezra bobbed on his feet. 'That's what I'm saying. It don't seem right to me. And I don't really understand why you would want to work for him anyway.'

'You do not trust him?'

'No, I just don't know why you'd want to put yourself so close to the Tri-Council again.'

'So I can watch them. And show everyone that I'm accepted by Uracil.'

Ezra frowned.

'What is it?' Twenty-Two signed.

Ezra looked at her. 'Always start with honesty. That's what you say to me, isn't it?'

Twenty-Two nodded. She knew her own words.

'I don't want to discourage you, but I don't think it's going to be as easy to be accepted by Uracil as it was to get a job with Michael. People ...' He paused signing, so he could scratch his head. 'People around here still talk about what you did to Faye. They're not too keen on folk pushing people off walkways. Even if they have served their punishments ...'

Twenty-Two lowered her hands and nodded, some of the excitement about her first day draining away. Clearly it would take more work to be accepted by Uracil.

Ezra accompanied Twenty-Two to Michael's platform before setting off to his own place of work. For the past year, and with Georgina's encouragement, he had been studying child development at Uracil's school. With its younger population expanding, teachers were in high demand and more positions were opening. When he had qualified last month, he had requested a job working in the pre-school with Uracil's youngest residents. Twenty-Two couldn't think of a better person to take care of Uracil's fledglings.

As Twenty-Two and Ezra traversed the wooden platforms high up in the tree branches, she kept her head down and didn't make eye contact with anyone she passed. It was still early in the morning, but Uracil had already begun to wake up. Eyes firmly down, she noticed the feet that approached seemed to change course once they came close to her; they would press into the sides of the wooden barriers or stop altogether until she had passed. As she watched those feet, she was not encouraged by their movements. It seemed Ezra had been right.

'Are you sure you'll be okay?' Ezra signed as they stopped outside the large platform where Michael would meet the day's visitors.

'Yes,' Twenty-Two replied.

She studied his freckled face. He didn't look convinced.

'Why don't you come and work in the school with me? You'd get to see Bay every day,' he signed.

Twenty-Two considered her response before answering. 'Because, as I said before, I think there is more work for me to do with the Tri-Council. Perhaps the stars want me to watch over Uracil again.'

'Will you come and find me if anything gets weird?' Ezra asked. 'Promise me you will?'

'Promise,' she signed, before waving goodbye to him.

Twenty-Two made her way to the platform and waited for Michael to arrive. She didn't have access to his morning appointments yet, so she couldn't prepare. As she sat, her thoughts swirled. She hoped that Michael hadn't asked her to work for him to make an example of her to the residents of Uracil. She felt flustered at the thought. Before she could spiral any further, she reminded herself that she had survived her last months in Cytosine, with no one but Dara, and barely enough food to scrape by. If she could live through that, then she could survive a few weeks of being ridiculed and mocked. She would just have to become used to unwanted attention; it had to be better than no attention at all.

At five minutes to eight, Michael's laboured steps could be heard. Twenty-Two turned to face him. He was already staring at her from way across the platform, his hair standing out in different directions, as if it couldn't collectively decide which route to take.

When he got closer, he raised a sandy eyebrow. 'You're here.'

'You wanted me to be, didn't you?' Twenty-Two signed.

'Yes, I did. I just wasn't sure whether you'd turn up.'

Twenty-Two looked at him steadily. 'If I make a promise, I stick with it.'

Michael gave a half-smile. 'So I've heard.'

He sat down wearily and faced Twenty-Two. 'Today is not going to be a typical one. I had hoped we would be able to start off with something more standard, but something has happened this morning that needs to be dealt with straight away.'

Twenty-Two leant forwards.

'Have you ever come across the Commidorant List?' Michael asked.

Twenty-Two took a moment to search her internal catalogues while she settled on her usual seat in the carved oak tree. 'No, I have not.'

Michael didn't seem perturbed by her answer. 'It's a list containing the names of members of a rebel group who call themselves the Commidorants. They're made up of Sapiens who believe that they should live separately to the Medius. They have members in all of the bases and have recently taken to extreme methods to make their point heard by the Potiors.'

Twenty-Two nodded as she briefly considered this information. She did not really care if some of the Sapiens in the bases wanted to live separately to the Medius; it did not concern her. Did she believe that the Neanderthals should have to live separately to the Sapiens? No. She would miss Ezra too much. But if other Neanderthals wanted that, they should be able to choose.

'One of them has managed to locate Uracil. He arrived an hour ago,' Michael continued. 'We have a policy of considering requests for refuge from people who find us, but this one's different as his name's been registered on the Commidorant List.'

He leant back in his seat. 'Considering his request will be our first thing to deal with today. We've moved all other appointments back so we can see him first. Raul and Flynn are on their way. We conduct all of the important business together now.' He smiled. 'I'm carefully watched.'

While Michael waited for the others to arrive, Twenty-Two busied herself laying out cooled coffee and chilled spring water for Raul and Flynn. She hoped their tastes had not changed from the last time she had met them.

Ten minutes later, when the familiar figures of the two founding members of Uracil approached the platform, Twenty-Two tried not to react. She had not seen them since the day of her incarceration, and much had changed in them since then. Their approach was slow; Raul had a slight limp and clearly favoured his left leg. He carried a knobbed wooden stick in his right hand, which he leant on for support. They were both still swathed in unnecessarily voluminous amounts of cloth, but Flynn's attire did little to help hide the weight he had gained in the past year. Twenty-Two wondered how the two leaders could have changed so much in the relatively short amount of time.

Aren't the Medius ones supposed to stay young?

Once Raul was seated, he leant forwards and rested both hands on the head of his stick. Twenty-Two could not help admiring the smoothness of the carefully sanded and varnished walking stick, its neat metal tip producing a decisive tapping noise as it met the floor. As she stared at it, she wished that she owned such an item.

Remembering herself, she took a seat farther away with Raul and Flynn's assistants. Raul's assistant, a neatly dressed man of middling years, nodded curtly to Twenty-Two and then continued to stare at the Tri-Council. Twenty-Two returned the gesture.

She glanced over at Flynn's assistant, a young, pale, Sapien-looking woman who was so slight that she hardly seemed to be there. The pale woman glanced over at Twenty-Two and cleared her throat as a sort of greeting, her face reddening. Twenty-Two was not used to this type of salutation, so she tried to clear her throat in response. A sort of grunting noise emerged, which Twenty-Two didn't like. It would have to do.

Flynn glanced over at the three of them. 'We're ready. Petra, will you go and collect him?'

The pale woman nodded and scurried to the edge of the platform, her head bent low.

She returned with a man who was so hunched over he appeared much shorter than he was, two guards trailing behind him. As the man passed Twenty-Two, he glanced towards her, and her breath caught in her throat. He had been so badly beaten that his left eye drooped slightly, and the corner of his mouth bulged with swelling that hadn't yet settled. Ripe bruises were layered over fading ones and deep marks laced around his wrists. Part of the top of his ear was missing; it was not a ragged wound but a straight, almost surgical cut. His clothing was torn, and he wore only one shoe. He was one of the sorriest sights Twenty-Two had ever seen. She wondered whether everyone who arrived in Uracil had been damaged in some way.

Michael stood and ushered the stranger to a seat. 'Have you seen the doctor yet?'

'Yes, I saw her half an hour ago.'

Petra gave a small gasp. The man's response showed that several of his front teeth were missing.

Flynn studied the man. 'How did this happen? If it was the Protection Department, we need to know straight away; they may have followed you.'

The man coughed and winced at the effort. He rested his hand over his ribs. 'No, no, it wasn't them. Don't worry. It was some of my former associates. They ... ah ... they thought that I'd betrayed another member of our group. Decided to beat a confession out of me.'

'And did you?' Raul asked, leaning forwards on his stick. 'Did you betray your fellowship?'

The man straightened up. 'No, never. I believed in what they were trying to do. I believed in everything. But after a beating like that ... well, you'd say anything to make it stop.'

A tear slid down his cheek and all of the Tri-Council looked away for a moment. Twenty-Two leant forwards and watched the progression of the tear, a physical response to pain and sorrow that she could never replicate.

'How did you find us?' Michael asked.

The stranger seemed to consider the question before answering. 'I'd heard an old wives' tale, back when I was a boy, of another settlement on an island. I didn't believe it, but it did give me an idea of where it might be safe to hide away from the other bases.' The man paused as he coughed again. 'When I escaped, I walked north for a few days – the settlement I'd come from is not too far south-east of here. I made a raft and tried a few nearby islands but none of them were suitable; not enough cover or food. When I tried this island next, I was picked up by your guards within five minutes.'

Raul and Flynn exchanged glances.

'That's how I found Uracil,' Michael said. 'Back when I was fourteen.'

Twenty-Two stared at Michael; she wanted to hear more.

Michael looked down at his screen. 'I see you're from Thymine, "Purpose and Productivity," eh? Same as me. Can I ask—?'

There was a commotion by the edge of the platform and raised voices.

'But it's not your turn!' a man shouted.

Twenty-Two stood to intervene but stopped when a whirl of gauze came running towards her.

'*Is it true?*' Georgina shouted, ploughing her way into the centre of the platform.

Twenty-Two froze as she tried to decide what to do.

Georgina whipped around as she searched all their faces, her eyes finally resting on the newcomer. She let out a cry when she saw him.

All three members of the Tri-Council stood.

'Georgina, you can speak on your brother's behalf when we have finished interviewing him. He has seen a doctor; he will recover with medical attention and some rest,' Flynn said. 'Please go and wait outside. Right now.'

'*Speak on his behalf?*' Georgina said, visibly shaking. '*Speak on his behalf?* I wouldn't give surety for him if his life depended on it!'

Twenty-Two stared at her friend. She hadn't even known that Georgina had a brother. She had never spoken of him.

Georgina's brother pushed himself up from his seat. He couldn't look away from the raised burgundy scar that traced its way from Georgina's eye to her chin. 'Sister, I know I owe you an apology—'

Georgina snorted. 'An apology? A bloody *apology*? That's not going to work this time, Lewis.'

Raul sat down abruptly and sighed. 'All families have their differences ... everyone is human. Let us decide first if he can stay. That is not your decision to make; it has to be dealt with objectively.'

Georgina spun round. 'With all due respect, this is not a matter of mere differences.' She pointed at Lewis. 'He used me. He blackmailed me. He made me seduce people that made my skin crawl. He forced me to betray my friends. He hit me and threatened to kill me. And he dares to call me *sister*.'

Lewis hung his head. Everyone stared at him.

'It's true. Everything she says is true,' Lewis said, after a moment.

Raul's eyes widened.

Lewis looked up. 'What I did was wrong. I should never have used Georgina in that way. I convinced myself it was justified because I was doing it for a cause I thought would free us all. Disrupt the museum and get the Potiors' attention. It all led to nothing anyway. A few animals let loose in the museum. The Potiors covered most of it up, along with the death of Fintorian. None of the Sapiens even heard about it.'

Twenty-Two felt a pain shoot through her chest at the mention of the man she had once held in such high regard. Fintorian, who had been the closest thing to a father she had ever known. She longed for the days when it had all been simpler.

She went and stood by Georgina's side and assessed this man who had wronged her friend. Regret was radiating from him.

'If I could change it all, I would,' Lewis continued. 'Please give me a chance to show that I wouldn't make the same mistakes again.' Another tear fell down his cheek. No one looked away this time. 'Please ...'

Lewis covered his face with his hands and turned from them. 'I've learnt and will continue to learn. But I understand if you decide I can't. Please, just give me a chance to heal and then I'll leave.'

The Tri-Council looked at each other.

'If he leaves now it'll be a death sentence,' Michael said. 'And we'll have to give him a memory blocker either way.'

Raul shifted in his seat and gave the smallest of nods.

'If you stay, you will be judged for your crimes against Georgina,' Flynn said. 'And you will be incarcerated, here on this island, while we decide what to do with you. Medical attention will be provided while you await our decision.'

Georgina's eyes flashed. She turned to Flynn. 'Don't trust him. Never trust a word that comes out of his mouth. He's incapable of change.'

'That may be so,' Flynn continued. 'But that is our decision to make, not yours.'

'Twenty-Two, please go and get the guards,' Michael said.

Twenty-Two nodded and padded to the edge of the platform where two guards were trying to calm down the residents in uproar after watching Georgina usurp their appointments. Twenty-Two beckoned the female guard over, who, in turn, nudged her colleague to get his attention.

When the other guard turned, Twenty-Two waved at him. She had not seen him in eighteen months and her visitors had avoided answering any questions about him, only telling her that he was busy training to protect Uracil. Twenty-Two scrunched her eyes, happy to know that Luca was still in Uracil and safe.

Luca did not return the greeting. Instead, he only gave her a curt nod. There was no warmth in his eyes. His hair was still closely shaved; he didn't physically look any different, but his manner had hardened. There was no smile for anyone.

She watched as Luca walked past her, jaw clenched, not even glancing in her direction. She felt a tightness in her throat; Luca was obviously not her friend any more. He must have disagreed with what she did to Faye. Twenty-Two could not understand this. He had always been one of the most decisive members of their small circle of friends; she would have thought that he would understand her desire to take action.

Twenty-Two stared at his back, willing him to turn around as they returned to the platform.

'Jenna, could you take him to Cabin Four,' Raul said to the female guard. 'Make sure the doctor comes this evening to check on him again as well.'

Jenna nodded and Luca approached Lewis. He stopped before the prisoner and gave out a low whistle. 'They did you over proper and good. Sure you deserved it too.'

'Just get him to the cabin,' Jenna said.

'He's the scumpot that nearly got us all killed.' Luca glanced at the Tri-Council before his gaze settled on Georgina. 'I assume you told them what he did to you? Eye for an eye, I say.'

'I'm so sorry ...' Lewis trailed off as he watched Luca clenching his fists.

His glowing blue guard's gloves began to turn amber. Lewis flinched.

'That's enough, Luca,' Michael snapped. 'You escort him, Jenna. And then make sure someone else other than Luca is set to watch him.'

Jenna nodded and beckoned at Lewis to follow her. She turned to Luca. 'Come on, "eye for an eye", I'm stationing you at the other end of the island so you don't get any ideas.'

Twenty-Two watched as the three of them left the platform, then went over to Georgina. 'Are you okay?'

All of Georgina's anger and indignation had slid away and been replaced by a frailty Twenty-Two rarely saw in her. 'I came here to escape them, escape my cruddy family, and here he is. I might as well have stayed in Thymine.'

Twenty-Two studied Georgina. 'That is not true. You have Tilla here, and you can live with Bay. That wouldn't happen in Thymine.'

Georgina sighed. 'I know. I'm just being dramatic. Must be Tilla's influence. I just wish he wasn't here. I never wanted to see him again.' She absent-mindedly traced the scar that zig-zagged its way across her cheek. 'Anyway, I should go.'

Twenty-Two didn't take her eyes from Georgina's retreating figure until her friend rounded the corner of the oak tree and was out of sight.

The rest of Twenty-Two's day was taken up with helping Michael catch up with his delayed appointments. Most of the residents she met either shrank from her gaze or gawped at her. There was no in between.

When she had finished, Twenty-Two was pleased to see that Kit was waiting for her. With the sleeves of his shirt rolled up, he nodded to the few people who passed him and even scrunched his eyes at one. They did not stare at him and instead reciprocated his greetings before continuing with their journeys. He must have worked hard over the last eighteen months to be accepted by Uracil. She wondered if any amount of hard work could help her achieve the same.

'How was your first day?' Kit signed when he saw her.

Twenty-Two studied his countenance before answering. He was still as difficult to read as he had always been. Unlike the others, he rarely used facial expressions or gestures alongside his signing, which could make him difficult to interpret.

'Luca isn't my friend any more. And Georgina's brother, Lewis, is here.'

'I see.' Kit nodded to an older woman who passed him before turning to Twenty-Two. 'Come on. Shall we go and get some food? I think we have some things to discuss.'

Twenty-Two kept her head down and tried to block out the noise of the other residents as they collected their meals from the communal dining area, before walking past the long benches of diners and returning to her cabin.

'You know you will have to start eating downstairs again soon,' Kit signed as they settled on her furniture-free cabin floor.

She looked around and admired the space. It was so much better now that there was room to move, room to breathe.

'I know. But I hate the way they stare. They don't do that to you.'

'Not as much as they used to, no – but it took time and I had to make an effort with them. It did not just come to me.'

Was it worth the exchange? Months of feeling awkward and uncomfortable for the possibility of some degree of peace afterwards? Perhaps.

'Why does Luca look through me now?' Twenty-Two signed. 'He was pleased that Lewis had been hurt. He said, "An eye for an eye." In the books that I have read, that means if you hurt someone you should be hurt in return. If he believes that, then why would he not agree with me killing Faye when she had killed other people first?'

Kit put down his empty plate. 'You are right; Luca has always believed that. But you have not considered one other point.'

Twenty-Two leant forwards.

'He thought he was in love with Faye,' Kit continued. 'I think it was most likely closer to infatuation than love, as he did not spend very much time with her, but only he knows the truth of it. Perhaps he could still love her while only peeking through the tree branches that separated them.'

Twenty-Two's eyes widened. 'In love with Faye? Why would he love someone who would never love him in return?'

'We cannot always choose who we love.'

'But he must have known she would never think of him like that!'

'Why would she not think of him in that way?' Kit asked.

'Because he is short and often has no hair.'

Kit scrunched his eyes. 'I would not say that to Luca if you hope to make him your friend again.'

Twenty-Two glared at Kit. 'I'm not stupid. I know that people do not want to hear negative truths about their physical appearance. I make a point of not commenting on people's looks as there is little we can do about them.'

Kit nodded. 'I am sorry. I was just teasing you.'

Twenty-Two accepted his apology.

'Did you know Lewis when you lived in Thymine?' she signed after they had eaten in silence for a few minutes.

'Yes, he was going to be Bay's new Companion. He was chosen over Luca.'

'He seems to be a very bad person. What he did to Georgina was very wrong. That is not how you should treat a sister. Or anyone.'

Kit sighed. 'You are not still keeping your "Bad Person" list, are you? I thought you had finished with that.'

Twenty-Two ignored his question. It did not sound like one that required an answer.

'Was it true what Georgina said? What he did to her?'

Kit studied Twenty-Two before answering. She used the time to think about Luca and ways to make him her friend again.

Perhaps I could find him someone new to love?

'Yes, what she said is true. But some people are capable of change. And remember he has no power now. The more power someone has, the more responsibility they have to use it wisely.' He stared at Twenty-Two. 'Anything done to him when he is weakened, when he is possibly on the verge of becoming a better person, could never be justified. If Georgina did something to him, it would be for revenge. And if you did anything to him, it would be unforgivable. These things have a way of escalating until the original act is forgotten and people are just at war. We are better than that.' Kit leant back against the cabin wall. 'We have to be, or there is no point to us coming back.'

When she was alone again, Twenty-Two circled the inside of her cabin while she mentally scrolled through her 'Bad Person' list. Kit didn't have to know she still kept it. She reassured herself that it was a 'bad person' list, not a 'take revenge on' list. A list was not the same as an act. She kept the list in order of when she had met them, rather than by the scale of the deed that had brought them to her attention. Pondering the names, she carefully updated the list and scrolled through it again.

1. Marvalian
2. Hadrian
3. Guard with ponytail
4. Guard with left eye lower than right
5. ~~Faye~~
6. Cedric

One more name wouldn't hurt. Would it?

7. Lewis

CHAPTER 6

Genevieve

'Serenity. Isn't that what everyone wants?' Genevieve said, reading from her screen.

She glanced up at Mortimer, eager for his response. She had been given her new assignment yesterday and had begun working on it immediately. Genevieve liked to think of herself as a woman of words, but this particular task was proving more difficult than she had anticipated.

'Do you think they'll know the meaning of "serenity", dearest daughter?' Mortimer asked.

Genevieve tapped her screen and looked up the comprehension level of the word.

'Yes, they should do. It's only a level-five word; it should resonate with most of them. Even if they don't know the exact meaning.'

Mortimer rubbed his clean-shaven chin. 'How about: "Fulfilment. Isn't that what everyone wants? Imagine your children achieving their potential every single day."'

Genevieve swung around in her chair to face him as she pondered the suggestion. 'Yes, it could work. I'm just not sure what I should suggest as the new name of this species.'

'Well, it would have to follow on from the other names ...' Mortimer responded.

'Homo potior, meaning "Superior Man",' Genevieve said. 'Then Homo medius as "Middle Man" and then the Pre-Pandemic Homo sapiens or "Wise Man".'

She considered the matter as she stared out of the window. It would have to be something encouraging, not derogatory; the Sapiens would have to feel it was a worthy role to bestow on half their children. In a flash of inspiration, she had it.

'How about Homo vitalis, which would loosely translate to "Vital Man"?'

'Why, that is quite inspired, my dear. Yes, I think it could work.'

'I can always put it forward and if they don't li—'

Dina entered the room and Genevieve slipped her screen under a cushion.

'Did you want some tea? Some light sandwiches, maybe?' Dina asked, looking at them both.

'No, we are fine for the moment,' Genevieve said. 'Thank you for asking and please close the door behind you.'

She waited a full minute after Dina had left before speaking. 'She keeps on doing that, doesn't she? Bursting in on us when we're alone?'

Mortimer nodded and spoke so his words were barely audible. 'I'll deal with it. Find out where she came from, where her allegiances lie.'

Genevieve's servants were not her allies, and certainly not her confidantes. She hadn't always lived with this level of assistance, and the feeling of being watched had never sat comfortably with her. Genevieve was always on her guard; she had to be careful about what the servants saw and what they overheard. Houses were hard to soundproof; ears could be pressed against doors. Even as master and mistress of their home, Mortimer and Genevieve were forced to live their lives predominantly in the open. Secrets were difficult to keep.

Genevieve closed her eyes and listened intently. Dina had gone.

She went back to her screen. 'How about: "If you could choose anything for your children, wouldn't it be contentment?"'

'Too many "C"s; it's practically alliteration.'

'Alliteration makes it resonate, makes it memorable.'

'But is also open to alteration,' Mortimer said. '"If you could choose anything for your children, wouldn't it be compliance?"'

'And we wouldn't—'

Genevieve pulled the screen to her chest and raised an eyebrow towards the door. From the other side, she could hear the unmistakable sound of Thomas's raspy breathing. She waited for him to knock.

'Yes, what is it, Thomas?'

'There's someone to see you,' he gabbled from outside the room.

'Well, come in and explain why a mere visitor has you so panicked,' Mortimer called out. 'You didn't start hmming at them again, did you? You know that always unnerves people.'

Thomas opened the door and took a step towards them before whispering, 'He says, hmmmm, he says, hmmmm …'

Mortimer eyed Thomas. 'Stop hmming and just spit it out.'

Thomas took a deep breath and stared intently at his shoes. 'He says he's from the Premier's Residence!'

Mortimer and Genevieve jumped to their feet and exclaimed at the same time, 'Well, show him in, then!'

As Thomas rushed from the room, they looked at each other. Words were not necessary. They both took deep breaths and sat again, this time facing the door, smiles ready to jump onto their features as required.

When the door opened, they both turned towards it casually, Mortimer in the middle of a pleasant anecdote.

'So, I said to her— Ah, we have a visitor, Genevieve.' He waved at the Medius messenger. 'Do come in.'

A spectacled man with a neat moustache took one step into the room; it was clear he was not staying for long.

He turned to Thomas, who was still holding on to the door, slightly slack-jawed as he stared at the unusual visitor. 'Please leave us.'

Thomas's eyes focused and he remembered himself. 'Sorry. Yes, hmmmm, I'll be off, then.'

His footsteps could be heard hurrying down the corridor to the large kitchen. Everyone in the household would know of the visit within the next ten minutes. The servants of the surrounding neighbours would know in under an hour.

'The Premier has requested your presence at a conclave next week,' the messenger said.

Genevieve stared at him. He was definitely addressing her.

'A conclave? Who else will be attending?' she asked, trying to make her tone sound light.

The spectacled man stared at her. 'It would hardly be a conclave if you knew all the attendees, now, would it?'

'No, I guess not,' she said.

She had never been invited to a conclave with the Premier before. She had attended general conferences where he addressed a large audience but nothing so intimate as a private meeting.

The messenger relayed the time and she entered them into her screen so there would be no chance of the appointment details being mislaid. 'I will, of course, be there. Is there anything else you need to tell me?'

'Only that your attendance is mandatory.'

'I will be there, no matter what circumstances the day may present.'

The spectacled Medius nodded before turning and leaving.

Genevieve leant back in her chair as she pondered the invitation. There was nothing sinister in the request; she knew perfectly well that if she were in trouble there would be no scheduled meeting. She would just be taken – and methods to solicit accurate responses would be used. No, this was something quite different.

She turned to look at Mortimer. 'We are moving up in the world.'

Genevieve checked the place settings and cutlery, while Mortimer rearranged the small posies of flowers that ran down the length of the table. They were ready.

Twenty of them would be dining tonight and she knew it would go well. She and Mortimer were natural hosts and it was rare for a guest to leave their home hungry for good food or good company. She had the fortunate disposition to be liked by most of her peers without having to try too hard to gain their admiration; aside from the few who begrudged her heady accession through the ranks of the high-end Medius, of course. Not many topped her now.

'Perfect,' Mortimer said, after nudging one of the vases of lilac asters slightly to the right. On his nod, Genevieve lit the candles along the length of the table – she had timed the start of their evening with twilight. The days were beginning to draw in following the impossible heat of summer and she liked to mark the change of season in these small ways.

They both smiled towards the door as it opened.

'Ah, Sylvia, do come in,' Mortimer said, as he ushered the first of their guests to the drinks cabinet. 'What a pleasure it is to see you. My, gold really is your colour!'

Alone or in pairs, their guests arrived. It was a casual affair and formalities were dispensed with; everyone milled around greeting each other and swapping updates until Dina slipped into the room and nodded to Genevieve.

'The food is ready, my friends,' Genevieve said. 'As always, help yourselves, and don't hesitate to have seconds. I know I won't.'

There was an appreciative murmur as the guests sat down. Plate after plate of steaming food was brought out by the servants and placed along the table; guests were encouraged to serve themselves and take as much or as little as they wished. There had been a noticeable drop in temperature that day and everyone helped themselves liberally to the warming fare. Conversation continued over the noise of eager cutlery. After the first courses were finished, Genevieve swapped seats with Mortimer and a couple of the guests moved around the table as well.

'I hear you've had a visit from one of the Premier's messengers,' Sylvia said to Genevieve when she settled down next to her.

'I have indeed,' Genevieve said, taking a sip from her drink.

Her news would have coiled its way around most of the Medius district by now.

'Can you ...' Sylvia whispered. 'I mean, could you ... could you share what it is about?'

Genevieve picked at a piece of fluff starting to ball on her angora jumper. 'You know that wouldn't be possible.'

'Yes, yes,' Sylvia said, tapping at the crystal glass. 'Quite right. The Premier's business is his alone. May the stars bless his reign.' A sparkle entered her eyes. 'I hear that the screen-tappers down at the Office of Production have been told to double their efforts. Apparently, they can't keep up with logging Thymine's output. Who would have thought that Thymine would surpass its quota for the quarter again?'

At the mention of Thymine, Genevieve felt light-headed. Unwanted thoughts threatened to push up to the surface; without hesitation, she cast them from her mind.

When she spoke, her tone was light. 'The production-pluggers shouldn't be underestimated. They may be dull but, by the stars, they rarely fail us!'

Another of the guests, Briana, leant over and arched an eyebrow towards Genevieve. 'Well ... sometimes they fail us.'

There was silence for a moment. Sylvia stared at Briana and Genevieve remained still, hoping for Sylvia to intervene and chastise Briana in her place.

'Genevieve had nothing to do with that and you know it. She was cleared of all possible connection,' Sylvia said.

Briana shrugged and Genevieve decided never to invite her to one of their parties again. Despite Briana being clearance grade sixteen in the Innovation Department, Genevieve could not stand insolence, especially when it was served up at her own dining table.

After Briana moved farther down the table, Genevieve spent a happy half-hour being gently prodded by Sylvia for further information about the Premier's invitation. Despite the exertion of making sure that she let nothing important pass her lips, Genevieve enjoyed talking to Sylvia, who was insatiably curious. During their conversations, Genevieve found she often picked up valuable bits of information that she wouldn't normally have access to.

As the servants began to clear away the food, Genevieve motioned for Dina to come over. 'Make sure all of the staff have equal portions to take home with them.'

Genevieve always over-ordered when they had these parties so that the servants could benefit from the evening as well. She knew how restrictive the Reparations that the Sapiens lived under were, and that there were never many spare tickets for the more interesting types of foods that were available to the Medius. There were never spare tickets for much of anything really.

'Yes, ma'am,' Dina said. She did not show any sign of pleasure and was comfortable meeting Genevieve's gaze.

Genevieve stared at her before smiling. 'That will be all.'

Dina's manner left her with an unsettled feeling; she would have to check with Mortimer on what he had found out about her.

At the end of the evening, as Genevieve served coffee to whomever wanted it, one of her quieter guests motioned for her to join him. Elijah was sitting by himself in a large armchair in the corner of the room. Despite the comfort that the chair could provide, he clearly could not relax into it; he was sitting on the very edge of the cushioned seat.

Genevieve decided to progress their acquaintance by sitting on the arm of the chair rather than taking the opposite one. Elijah was handsome, even beyond what was expected of a Medius, and she found herself drawn to his slightly wide-eyed approach to the evening.

Elijah shuffled to make room for her, and Genevieve decided not to unnerve him any further by shifting closer to him.

He glanced over her shoulder. 'I wanted to talk to you about the project you were told about a few days ago. At the museum.'

Genevieve hid her surprise by smoothing down her jumper, the delicate loose strands dancing at her touch. 'I shouldn't really be discussing these matters outside of an official capacity.' She gave him a smile so he would know that she wasn't cross. 'You know that, don't you? Tell me, when did you get your job as a researcher at the museum? A coveted position, I am sure.'

Elijah glanced over her shoulder again. She didn't know what he was so worried about; all the guests were at the other end of the room and no one could hear their conversation over the hum of the evening coming to an end.

'But you know what they're planning on doing, right?' Elijah leant even farther forwards in his seat and peered up at her. 'To the Sapiens, to the population. Don't you think it's a step too far?'

Genevieve realised that she had made a mistake by initiating this easy intimacy with him. They all walked a thin line and Elijah was veering away from it. She could not be seen to be failing to report her suspicions, or, worse, be suspected of accompanying him on his journey. Control of oneself and one's thoughts was essential in this life; you never knew what would appear on the surface.

She rested her arm gently on his shoulder and turned her back to the rest of the room. She looked directly at him while she spoke, her voice calm but firm. 'Do not speak to me of this again. I will give you one chance and put it down to the wine.' She paused to see if her words were having the required effect. 'Try not to think of these things. We all have a job to do. Just get on with yours.'

Elijah stared up at her and blinked. 'Yes. Thank you for your hospitality, but I have an early morning meeting ...'

She watched him as he made his way to the door. He didn't say goodbye to anyone and was so agitated that he knocked into one of the chairs that had been abandoned far from the table.

She suspected that he would be picked up by the Protection Department within the week.

CHAPTER 7

* *

Elise

Elise was standing in a place she didn't want to be. She had been captured before she could complete her last mission in Cytosine's museum nearly two years ago and it seemed that the Tri-Council hadn't wanted to risk another operative since. But now here she was, back in the place where she crashed out of one life and into another. Only this time she wasn't with her friends; she was with two colleagues she didn't entirely trust, on a mission led by Septa who she certainly didn't trust.

'It's nothing but arrogance if you ask me,' Raynor said, looking around the museum's foyer. 'Why fanny around bringing back animals when you're just going to cage them? At least set them free to wander – there's enough bloomin' space out there for them now. Why not fix this world instead?' She leant back against the reception desk. 'It's nothing but todger-waggling.'

Elise had never really thought about the Potiors' real reason for bringing back the extinct species of animals. She had been taught in school that it was done to reverse the wrongs of the Sapiens, but that didn't ring entirely true now with everything she knew. The Potiors would have had other reasons as well.

'Who cares what their reasons are?' Septa said. 'Let's get a move on so we can leave this place. I don't like that I can hear – but not see – a thousand animals that can eat, bite and sting me.'

'I think it's this way,' Elise said, nodding towards a double door.

They crossed the darkened atrium and Elise pushed her way through the first set of swinging doors. They walked in silence for fifteen minutes before reaching the corridor that held Lab 412. Her whole body tensed and she rested her hands on the push knives strapped around her thighs. Her mind did not remember any of that day – the pill she had swallowed had made sure of that – but it seemed her body did, and it was trying to protect her from moving any farther forward. She had to force her feet to carry on walking down the corridor.

Trying to still her racing heartbeat, she felt the threat of a panic attack circling her, waiting for an opening. *Breathe. Concentrate on your breath. Just like Maya taught you. In … out … in … out … It won't happen again. It can't happen again.*

She began to regain control and the panic subsided.

'Right, let's get in there,' Septa said, when they reached the lab door.

'You know it's just me who's supposed to go in,' Elise responded, staring at the door while willing herself to remember something, anything, about that day two years ago. 'Maya's orders.'

'Well, I'm leading this mission and I say we all go in,' Septa said.

'Last time I checked, mission leaders don't outrank the Head of the Infiltration Department,' Elise said, still staring at the door. She ignored the small voice inside her, reminding her that

89

it wasn't long ago that she had been investigating a Potior in Guanine against Maya's orders.

'And if you insist on pishing all over Maya's orders, don't think I'll be keeping quiet about it,' Raynor said, leaning against the wall. 'Maya's about as much fun as a cold shower on a wet Tuesday, but she'll have her reasons for it. And they'll be good ones.'

Septa reddened. 'Just get in there. And release the camera immediately so I can see the feed. No dawdling.'

Elise nodded and pushed open the door.

To her relief, the room was empty; despite the fact that all had been quiet when they'd listened in, a small part of her had half been expecting it to be filled with guards and a Potior museum director. Following Septa's orders, she flipped open the box for the camera and watched as it began to circle the room.

She stepped to the right of the door. The room had three glass walls, and behind the left one, three blinking eyes with suckers around the edges flashed into her line of sight. She had never seen anything like them before – they were wrong, unnatural. Elise concentrated on staring at the far end of the room, through the glass into the pod that appeared to be empty. To her right, a large furry leg reached up and tapped against the window. She tried not to imagine how big the animal that possessed such a leg must be. They must have been made from the DNA of several different animals – nothing sat right with them – and her stomach turned as she thought about how little they had to do with the stars. Instead, they were the children of the Potiors.

And then it came ...

A trickle at first, an emotion she couldn't place, followed by a sense of déjà vu. The whisper of a memory seemed to hover at the edge of her vision, but it pulled away when she turned to look. Finally, she caught it.

Elise pressed herself against the wall next to the door and stared at the blinking eye and tapping leg across from her.

She had been here before. She had stood right here and seen these creatures, which meant that they had been here for over two years. They had been trapped in this room with no contact with the outside world. Her initial disgust slipped into pity. If they had been allowed to exist for over two years then they were valued by the Potiors and had a purpose that Uracil was unaware of.

She turned to the door, and another memory washed over her.

The door to the lab swung open. A Potior with straight blond hair walked in and past her, followed by a tall man who was clearly a Medius. Five guards traipsed in after them and stood with their backs to Elise. Concentrating on her breathing as Maya had taught her, Elise slowed her heartbeat. She started to inch towards the door, so she could push it open and slip outside. At the same time, she lifted the bracelet to her mouth, just as she had been instructed to do.

She tried to hold on to what she was feeling; she tested it and rolled it around her head. In that moment she had been scared, but deep down, she had been at peace. Happy even. Before she had entered this room, there had been a lightness in her step, a sense of purpose built on hope, not vengeance. She felt a rush of strength that she had lost along the way.

Just steady your heartbeat; three more steps and you'll be by the door. Do this for your family. Do this for Samuel. Flip open the bracelet lid, rest the pill on your tongue. Don't worry; you won't have to use it. It's just in case. One more step now, almost there . . .

Elise waited, but nothing more came. After that there was only darkness, and the containment centre. It was enough. She remembered a small part of who she had been before she had lost herself. Before she had been taken. She'd had purpose in her work, and been excited about the life she was on the verge of leading.

And she remembered how she'd felt about Samuel. How she'd loved him, and he had loved her in return.

The camera finished its recording and began to leisurely circle Elise's head, waiting for further instructions.

Where would she be now if she hadn't been captured two years ago? If she had pushed open those doors, left the museum and joined her friends outside Cytosine?

A sob slipped out. She ignored it; now wasn't the time. She had to get out of the museum. Back to this life.

Clicking her fingers for the camera to follow her, she opened the door.

She stared at Septa and Raynor. 'Let's go.'

Three hours later, after Elise had dropped in on Eli at the crematorium again, they made their way into the base camp. Septa ambled over to Max, who was lying on his sleeping mat, and gave him a nudge with her foot.

'Get off,' Max grumbled.

Raynor crouched down next to him. 'It's the Protection Department. We've come to arrest you. You've betrayed your kind and spent far too much time with the short people.'

'No, it's not,' Max mumbled into his arm. 'I knew it was you three a couple of minutes ago, so I lay back down again.'

'Liar. How could you possibly have known it was us when it's still dark?' Septa asked, still standing next to him.

'I could smell you.'

'*What?*' Raynor exclaimed. 'You could *smell* us?'

Max sat up slowly. 'Heightened sense of smell, Madam Ray. And if I'm not mistaken, Maya will be joining us in approximately ninety seconds ...' He held his head up and gave a sniff. He then pointed behind him. 'From that direction.'

'Ugh. That's disgusting,' Septa said.

'Maybe it's you that is disgusting,' Max said, wrinkling his nose.

A look of worry crossed Septa's face and she stalked over to her backpack.

Elise turned towards the direction Maya was supposed to emerge from. There were no unusual sounds, but she knew that was no indication that Maya wasn't there. She was too careful for that. Elise started walking in the direction Max had indicated, letting her backpack drop to the ground.

Maya. She must have known.

Elise began to run. She ignored Raynor's calls and broke into a sprint, winding her way through the trees.

Without warning, a figure stepped out in front of her. She swerved to her left and stopped dead in front of Maya.

'Were they real? Were those memories real?' Elise demanded, her voice slipping as she tried, and failed, to keep her composure.

Maya didn't move past Elise. Instead, she looked at her like she had done on the first day they met, quietly assessing her, noting what was needed.

'Yes. I have no reason to suspect they were not real.'

Maya stared at Elise and clasped her hands in front of her.

'I was hoping you might get a snapshot,' Maya said. 'I'd heard it was possible if you were put in exactly the same place, under the same circumstances as when you swallowed the blocker pill.' She gently touched Elise's shoulder. 'But you couldn't know about it, or you would search for those lost memories, create false ones in their absence.'

Elise took a step back, unsure how she felt.

'I was happy,' Elise said.

'I know. But I wanted you to see it for yourself.'

'And they took that from me.'

'They did. But you can be happy again. What they did to you in there was so very wrong—'

Elise raised her head. 'It wasn't just me they did it to. It was Ezra as well. All of us in there were stopped from having children.'

She thought of the now-faded scar across her stomach. Discovering it had been her first memory after waking up in the containment centre. She had believed the lies they had told her – an emergency appendectomy. She had even been grateful that they had saved her life; she hadn't known that they had taken the chance of creating any future lives from her.

Samuel had known what they had done. Even before Elise did. All the operatives knew. They'd heard rumours of what went on in the containment centres, that the Potiors curbed the undesirable population without their knowledge or consent. A few days after she had arrived in Uracil, Maya and Samuel had arranged for Elise and Ezra to have a medical check, firstly with Georgina, then afterwards with a doctor. It was Georgina who had broken the news to Elise – the operation she'd had in the containment centre was not an appendectomy, but sterilisation. Georgina had sat with Elise every night as she struggled to process what this meant, as she flipped from denial to desperate anger to some form of acceptance.

'The doctor in Uracil said they might be able to reverse it with the right equipment,' Maya said, taking a step towards Elise.

'Might ...' Elise said.

'There's still a chance,' Maya said.

'I told you before; I never really wanted children. And that's not the point!' Elise could hear her voice rising. 'No doctor can reverse that they operated on me without my consent and took away my ability to choose. And they've done the same to thousands of others over the past hundred years, without them knowing or giving permission. And they justify it by saying it's for "population control". Show me a place where the people who have all the power step forward and volunteer for these things? But it doesn't happen that way. It's always the Saps like me who get it.'

Elise scrabbled to remember how she had felt in that room a few hours ago. The peace. The joy. She looked around her, desperate for something to distract her, something to focus on.

'Did I do the wrong thing?' Maya asked quietly. 'I thought it might help. I thought the knowledge of how you felt before this might help ... bring you back.'

All of Elise's strength fizzled away. 'It was the right thing to do. I should know how I felt when I stepped in that room. It helps to remember who I used to be and how much I've changed. It's just ... a lot.' She looked up. 'Have you heard from Samuel?'

Maya didn't react to the question. 'Not for a few weeks. I could send a message to him if you wanted?'

Elise thought about it, then sighed. 'No, he needs to find his dad. Come on. Let's get back to the others. We need to move camps.'

That evening, once they had walked ten miles north of their last base camp and eaten, they settled down to watch what the camera had recorded in Lab 412. Elise stared at the images on Septa's screen, hardly blinking as the camera circled the room with glass walls.

'Stars, what *are* those things?' Max said, as the suckered eyes flashed into view and then disappeared again.

'Nothing natural, that's for sure,' Septa responded.

'The Potiors have been playing at creation again,' Maya said, her eyes never leaving the screen. 'But I can't imagine why.'

Elise stared at the recording, willing her other memories of that room to play over the top. But there was only Elise on the screen, edging towards the door and staring at some unseen presence in the middle of the room.

'Wait until you see the giant, furry leg on the other side,' she said, trying to bring herself back to the present.

'Abominations, the lot of them,' Raynor said.

'Was there nothing in the third pod?' Maya asked. 'The one at the end.'

'It appeared empty,' Elise replied.

The camera was now slowly making its way along the length of the pod at the back of the room.

'There!' Maya said. 'Stop there. Rewind. And zoom in.'

'It's nothing,' Septa said, as she started to fast-forward the images.

'Do as I say,' Maya instructed, her eyes flicking over to Septa.

Septa followed Maya's order and everyone apart from her leant in.

Elise studied the image on the screen and a figure slowly came into focus. There was nothing unusual about the physiology of the occupant of the last pod, no thirteen legs or detached sensory organs. He turned his head and stared over his shoulder, right at the camera. Isolated in a lab full of the Potiors' creations was a lone Sapien-looking man.

Maya turned to Elise. 'Why didn't you find out more about the man in the pod? Were you worried it would take up too much time?'

Elise felt like she had been punched. 'Is that what you think of me?'

Maya was silent.

Elise tried to calm herself before responding. 'I didn't know there was anything or anyone in the third pod. I was standing by the door the whole time. And you know why I wasn't walking around.'

Maya rubbed her forehead. 'I'm sorry. Of course you were.'

Elise turned and stared at Septa. 'You were watching the feed; you would have seen him. Why didn't you say anything?'

Maya's head snapped around to Septa. 'You were watching the feed?'

Septa leant back on her hands. 'Half watching. I wasn't really following everything that was happening.'

Raynor snorted.

'You saw him, didn't you?' Elise said. 'You left him there, left him *imprisoned* in there, without finding out if we could help him.'

'No, I didn't,' Septa said, raising her voice. 'And we couldn't have rescued him anyway; it was an information-gathering exercise only.'

'Alright, that's enough,' Maya said, staring at them.

'We have to go back,' Elise said. 'See if we can find out why he's there, whether we can help him.'

'No, you can't,' Maya said. 'You know the rules. Once an operative leaves a base, they can't re-enter for at least a month. It's too dangerous. If one of their cameras recorded you, they'll be looking out for you.'

'I'll go back,' Max said. 'I didn't go in the first time.'

'There's a reason you didn't go in with us,' Raynor said. 'They'll be all over you in a second if they see you. There's only a thousand Potiors and I'd bet a month's tickets that they know exactly where every single one of you should be. If they see you, they'll try to identify you. You were supposed to have died four years ago.'

'I'll go,' Maya said. 'I've got something else to do first, but once I'm finished with that, I'll camp out here for a few days and then go into Cytosine by myself. See if I can find out more about what the Potiors are doing and try to assess whether we can bring this man out at some point.'

'You won't be able to bring him out,' Raynor said. 'Stars knows how long he's been in there by himself. He'll be as mad as a caged squirrel.'

Elise felt sick. He could have been there the first time she visited the museum two years ago. If she hadn't been captured, she could have tried to rescue him back then. She wasn't the only one whose future had branched out in a different direction that day.

'That may be,' Maya said, rewinding the video and watching it again. 'But we have to at least try.' She looked up. 'Tell me, what did you find in the museum in Guanine? Did you discover what the Potiors shipped over to Adenine a year ago?'

'I found out that they brought back another extinct species a couple of years ago,' Septa said. 'They are called Denisovans and lived in Zone 1 around the same time as the Neanderthals. That must be what they shipped to Adenine.'

Maya smiled. 'That's brilliant work, Sep—'

'There's another possibility,' Elise interjected. 'I think they've created what they're considering a new species of human. I found a list of potential names for it. I imagine it won't actually be a new species of human, just genetic modifications that they pass off as a new species like they do for Medius and Potiors, but either way, it's very worrying.'

Maya frowned. 'I agree. Whatever the scientific truth, if the population is told that it's a new species it would have a huge impact on the bases.'

'We don't know any of this for sure,' Septa said. 'A name doesn't mean anything.'

'True,' Maya responded. 'But it's also not to be ignored. Neither possibility is.'

Elise rubbed her forehead; she was so very tired. 'I can't stop thinking about that man back in Lab 412.'

'What happened to the "bigger picture" you keep going on about?' Septa said.

'What happened to *you*?' Elise snapped. 'Did you ever have any kindness or compassion in you, or have you always been this cold?'

'You're not as perfect as you think,' Septa retorted. 'You sent Samuel packing. I heard he couldn't take it any more, had to get as far away from you as he could.'

Elise lurched for Septa. 'That's not true!'

'That's enough!' Maya said. 'I'm sending you all back to Uracil. You need a break, a bit of quiet before your next mission.'

Elise's head snapped around. 'Please don't send me back. I'm of no use there. None of us are.'

'Speak for yourself, girly,' Raynor said, as she poked at the fire with a twig.

'I don't want to go back to Uracil either,' Max said. 'It's boring up there; I'd rather be out here.'

'You don't want to go back to Uracil because Theo will be waiting for you,' Septa said, eyeing Max. 'Following you around everywhere. "Oh, Max,"' she said under her breath before turning to face him, her hands clasped underneath her chin. '"When will you settle down? Start thinking about our future together? I miss you sooooo much, my Maxywaxy ..."'

Raynor laughed.

Max looked sheepish. 'I told him not to call me that in public ... '

Raynor took pity. 'There are far worse pet names than Maxy-waxy ... One of my previous beaus used to call me Thunder Lungs—'

'Please,' Elise said to Maya, ignoring the others. 'We can do so much more out here. What was our next mission going to be?'

Maya looked at each of them. 'Do you want to stay out or go back? Raynor? Septa?'

'I'm for staying out,' Raynor said.

'I'd rather stay out,' Septa said. 'Run some more missions.'

'Fine, stay out for one further project,' Maya said. 'But first I'm going to take Elise with me for a couple of weeks. I'll send her to meet up with you afterwards and then I'll go to Cytosine and check on that man we saw in the recording. The rest of you should take the next three weeks to rest and restock your supplies before you begin this final mission. Once you've finished, you are to return to Uracil immediately. Particularly you, Raynor: you haven't been back for nearly two years.'

Septa opened her mouth to speak but clamped it shut when she saw the look Maya shot at her.

'Where will our mission be?' Max asked.

Maya smiled. 'You might like this one, Max. Next is Adenine.'

CHAPTER 8

* *

Twenty-Two

Twenty-Two had thought about her conversation with Kit for several days. She had been given a second chance at living, and the weight of what she should do with it was pressing on her. She knew that her instinct was to protect others, be useful, spend time with her friends. But this had gotten her into trouble in the past, so perhaps she needed to find something else to focus on.

Why had she been happy when she was much younger? She considered it from every angle, prodding and poking at her childhood, testing the robustness of her memories. It took a while before the answer came to her: it was because she had belonged. She had been exactly where she had thought she was meant to be, even if she now knew differently. When she dug down farther, she realised that she wanted to feel part of her surroundings, like one of the stars nestled in the sky above. She yearned for that settled feeling she had known, back when she was a girl, before her small world had begun to implode and then expand at a rate she could not keep up with.

Twenty-Two knew she could not bend the whole of Uracil to her will and make them accept her as she was. So, reluctantly, she decided that it was she who would have to change. Just like

Kit had, she would make the effort with the residents of Uracil, put up with the stares, grimaces and the general uncomfortableness, in exchange for the possibility that one day there would be an end to it. Firm in her decision, she promised herself that she would start today.

Once she had washed and dressed, she made her way to Ezra's tree house. It was still early, so she didn't pass many people, but instead of walking with her head bent as usual, she kept her eyes firmly ahead and gave a little nod of greeting to everyone she passed. No one returned the gesture. The lack of acknowledgement hurt, but she reassured herself that it was only her first day; perhaps tomorrow one of them would mirror her greeting.

Knocking on Ezra's door, she waited for him to answer. There was no sound from inside and she wondered if he had already left for his duties at the children's nursery. Instead of retreating back to her room, she tapped at the door again, louder this time, and was rewarded by the cacophony of Ezra rolling out of bed and stumbling towards the sound of knocking.

When he slid back the door and saw it was her, he pulled at his pyjama top with both hands in an effort to straighten it. 'Are you alright? Is it your job?'

'No, everything is fine. Nothing like that. I was just wondering if you wanted to come down for breakfast?'

Ezra's eyes widened but he grinned. 'Sure thing. Just give me five minutes to get dressed and then I'll be with you.'

As she waited by the front of his tree house, she felt her thoughts drifting. It was this ability to pass time without actively engaging with it that had helped her survive the isolation she had grown up with. Now, instead of escaping the present, she made an effort to pull herself back to the sensation of her bare feet standing on the soft wooden planks that gently dipped outside the door to Ezra's tree house. She looked up and down the walkway and nodded to a couple who passed. The man had his arm around the woman's shoulder and the woman's arm was looped around his waist. Twenty-Two wondered what it would feel like to have someone walking with her that way. She imagined it would be comforting, to be in step with another. She nodded at the couple again and scrunched her eyes. The woman looked away from Twenty-Two and the man flinched.

It's still only the first day.

After they had collected their breakfast, Ezra started to walk towards the empty bench in the farthest corner, but Twenty-Two grabbed his sleeve and tugged at it. She scanned the tables for anyone she recognised, and her gaze fell on Elise's parents and brother, sitting at the end of the bench under the sycamore tree.

Nodding to Ezra, she weaved her way over and put her plate on the edge of the table. 'Can we sit with you and talk maybe?'

Elise's mum smiled up at them and moved down the bench. 'Of course you can! Is everything okay? Did you need to speak to us about something specific?'

Twenty-Two sat down next to her and Ezra joined farther down the bench. He grinned at Elise's brother and dad.

'No, nothing specific. I just thought we could talk while we ate. Like the others do,' Twenty-Two signed.

'Well, we're still pretty new here, so we could always do with more friends. Can't have too many in this world, eh? I'm Sofi, by the way, and this is my husband, Aiden, and son, Nathan.'

Twenty-Two looked over at them but they were both signing to Ezra.

She nodded and gave a little grunt like Petra had when she first met her. Twenty-Two remembered their names from their first meeting, but understood the formalities required in such situations. 'I'm Twenty-Two.'

Sofi laughed. 'You don't need an introduction.'

Twenty-Two frowned. 'I suppose everyone here knows about what happened with Faye.'

Sofi put down her cup and looked directly at Twenty-Two. 'Not because of that. I know you because you're special; you've been brought back from the past.'

Twenty-Two tried to think of something else they could talk about that didn't involve her resurrection. The weight of responsibility she felt for being chosen in this way was always at the back of her mind.

'Do you know Georgina's brother, Lewis? You both lived in Thymine, but I don't really know the scale of the place and whether you knew all the other Sapiens.'

Sofi rolled her empty cup between her hands before putting it down again. 'I know of Lewis but haven't met him before.'

'What do you know of him? He did terrible things to Georgina so he seems to be a very bad man.'

Sofi nodded. 'I knew very little about him back in Thymine, but Elise told me what happened with Lewis when she came to collect us and take us to Uracil. I hadn't seen her for so long; it was awful to find out what happened to her when I wasn't there to help.' She paused, remembering. 'I'll never forgive Lewis for what he did to Elise and her friends. What happened changed her – took my girl away from me. Sometimes I don't even recognise her now. Even the way she speaks has changed; she doesn't sound like someone from the Outer Circle any more. It's as if I'm talking to a Medius sometimes.'

Twenty-Two already knew that Elise had changed, Georgina worried about it too. Kit's Companion hardly ever laughed any more. Whenever Elise came back to Uracil, it was as if only part of her had returned and her thoughts had remained elsewhere.

'Her speech is probably because of Samuel and Georgina,' Twenty-Two signed. 'She used to spend a lot of time with them.'

'You know Samuel?' Sofi asked, her eyes widening. 'We only met him once – when he broke into our house. Aiden nearly finished him off with a saucepan. He'd left Uracil by the time we arrived.'

'Yes, I know Samuel. He killed the Potior who raised me. But I have forgiven him.'

Sofi looked flustered. 'Elise won't speak a word about him, although I know something went on there …'

'They were in love,' Twenty-Two recounted, pleased that she could add to the conversation. 'And then Elise lost her memories just before she went into the containment centre with Ezra. So, she forgot that she loved him.'

'Oh. Well, that explains a few things … but then raises a lot of other questions too,' Sofi signed, before staring up at the tree canopy. 'My poor daughter …'

Twenty-Two considered how to restart the conversation. She realised that having people in common was helping it flow. 'Did you know Michael too? He said he was from Thymine.'

'Michael?' Sofi gave a half-smile. 'Yes, I knew Michael. He left Thymine years ago and we all thought he had died. It was a huge surprise to come here and find we were wrong. This whole place has been a surprise really. I'd always prided myself on knowing a lot about the way this world works ... Turns out I was a bit overconfident in myself. Oh, well. We can only learn ...'

'Why did Michael leave?'

'Oh, yes. His mum was killed by a guard in Thymine, about twenty years ago. There was a terrible outbreak of meningitis and when Michael got ill, his mum was beside herself with fear and grief. She'd already lost all her other children. So she went to the centre of Thymine and asked for help. In return, she was struck by a guard; she hit her head when she fell and died at the guard's feet.'

These Sapiens and Medius, cruelty always traces its way through their stories.

'What happened after she died?' Twenty-Two signed. 'How did Michael get to Uracil?'

'We all clubbed together and donated tickets for him to get the medicine he needed. But when the riots happened, he slipped away, left Thymine. Back then we had no idea it was possible to survive outside the bases.' Sofi refilled her empty cup and stared at it. 'All those years we thought we needed treated water, and look at us now. Drinking boiled stream water. If only we'd known back then, things could have been very different.'

Twenty-Two considered the word she had never heard or read about. 'Riot? What's a riot?'

'What a question! How to explain it?' Sofi signed, before taking a sip of water. 'It's when people come out of their homes, take to the streets and cause disruptions because they can't take it any more.'

'Can't take what any more?'

'Life for Sapiens in the bases: the poverty, the hierarchy, the unflinching rules, the judgement, the separation, scrabbling around for tickets, worrying about what will happen if one of you gets sick. It's all too much to ask people to accept, but the Potiors do.'

Twenty-Two stared at Sofi. A riot seemed like chaos to her. Matters could be dealt with much more simply by one person.

Sofi seemed to read Twenty-Two's expression. 'They're not the ideal outcome. I wouldn't wish them on anyone, but they happen from time to time, usually when people have been pushed too far. And their outcomes are chaotic and unpredictable.' Sofi glanced over to her husband. 'Aiden lost both his brother and sister after the last riots in Thymine ...'

Ezra bounced over to them. 'Aiden's said he'll help train me to fight!'

'Well, just a few moves,' Aiden signed once he caught sight of Sofi's frown, which travelled down the length of the bench.

'I could show you how to use a sling if you want,' Nathan signed to Ezra.

'Like Elise uses?' Ezra's grin took over the whole of his face. 'Please! Who'd have thought it? Ezra from the orphanage learning sign language, being friends with a Neanderthal, and to top it all off, I'm going to learn to fight like the best in Zone 3.'

Twenty-Two automatically frowned but wasn't sure why. 'Can I learn to fight too? Maybe with a spear like Kit?'

Aiden looked flummoxed. 'I don't know how to make you a spear. I'd say my speciality is using everyday objects to complement hand-to-hand combat. Kitchen implements and the like.'

Twenty-Two thought about it; she'd never really been in a kitchen. 'Maybe you could help me fight with my hands instead?'

Aiden glanced at Sofi, who gave the smallest of nods. 'I don't see why not. I'd like to know what you can do as well – I've always wanted to spar with a Neanderthal. See if you are as strong as you look.'

Twenty-Two scrunched her eyes at him and Aiden returned the expression with a wide grin of his own.

'I'm sorry that Lewis is in Uracil,' Twenty-Two signed to Georgina the following day.

They had taken Bay and Twenty-Seven for a walk outside the base. Georgina was determined that both children would see the outside world and not think of Uracil as just another museum. Several times a week, she could be found striding over the hills surrounding Uracil, leading two little figures to investigate some rock pool or pond she had discovered.

'I'll just have to try my best at his sentencing hearing,' Georgina signed. 'Try to convince them that he can't be trusted.'

'At least you won't have to see him,' Twenty-Two signed. 'Perhaps he won't even survive; his injuries looked very bad.'

Georgina snorted. 'He'll outlive us all. His desire for self-preservation outweighs everything else.'

She paused for a moment to let Bay and Twenty-Seven catch up. They were some distance behind, having stopped to stare at something in the bracken. Twenty-Seven raised his head and waved at them to join him; they both hurried over. The two young Neanderthals were holding hands as instructed – Twenty-Seven took his job not to lose Bay very seriously.

'What is it?' Georgina signed to him.

She scooped up Bay, who was rubbing her eyes – Georgina said this was Bay's version of crying.

'Under there. Is it dead?' Twenty-Seven signed.

Twenty-Two pulled back the bracken and knelt down. There was a small bundle of fur curled up, no bigger than her hand.

She looked at Georgina. 'What is it?'

Georgina peered closer. 'I don't know. I can't see it properly.'

Just then, the bundle of fur raised its pointed face and dropped it again, pushing its nose back under its bushy tail.

'I don't know what it is,' Georgina signed. 'But it's only a baby and doesn't look very well.'

Twenty-Two stared down at the helpless creature. 'Where's its mother?'

'Nowhere to be seen,' Georgina signed while looking around. 'Look, let's continue with our walk. If it's still here when we get back, we can decide what to do.'

For the next hour, Twenty-Two could think of little else but the baby under the bracken. She tried to make conversation with Georgina, but found herself constantly worrying that it had been found by an eagle or a fox. When they eventually looped back round again, Twenty-Two found herself walking faster as she returned to the same spot.

Pulling back the bracken, she was pleased to see the baby was right where they had left it. Crouching low to the ground, she waited impatiently for Georgina to catch up.

'It's going to die if we leave it out here,' Twenty-Two signed. She could feel herself becoming more agitated as she glanced around for any potential predators.

'Please, Mummy,' Bay signed to Georgina, still rubbing her eyes.

Georgina sighed. 'Well, we could take it to Jerome, if I can remember the way. He lives near here, I think. I don't normally walk to him from this direction.'

Before Georgina could change her mind, Twenty-Two tentatively lifted up the baby. She expected some resistance, but it was so weak it only made a small mewing noise. She pulled open her empty foraging bag and popped the animal inside, careful to make sure that she left the top open for air. Following Georgina, she carried the bag in both hands, stretched out in front of her, and didn't take her eyes from it the entire journey. She willed its occupant to stay with her and away from the stars.

They were hiking up the mountain that Twenty-Two thought looked like a pointed party hat, when Georgina suddenly veered to the right.

'It's along here, I think,' Georgina said, as she switched to carrying Bay with her other arm. Twenty-Seven peered down the side of the stony pathway with a look of apprehension, his fists clutching Georgina's trailing scarf.

Continuing, they followed the bend round the mountainside until they came to a small, grassy paddock contained by a knee-high fence. Twenty-Two scrunched her eyes. The unexpected enclosure was positioned directly in front of a cave mouth and she could immediately see the advantages of it facing the sun. A handful of rabbits, one hare and a few other animals Twenty-Two couldn't name were running free on the grass and there appeared to be more in variously sized cages; she strained to see what was inside and Twenty-Seven copied her.

'Jerome is ... a bit different,' Georgina signed, raising her eyebrows. 'Actually, I might need to adjust that to downright odd. He spends a lot of time alone and doesn't have great social skills, but he's excellent with animals.'

Twenty-Two moved the satchel containing the small animal into one hand so she could sign. 'Why doesn't he live in Uracil?'

'He doesn't want to. I think he once did, but that was long before we arrived,' Georgina responded. 'He still gets his supplies from us and in return he takes in any injured animals we find and tries to heal them until they can go back into the wild. I bring him medical supplies every few months. He can be a bit abrupt, so it's not one of my favourite jobs, but I think what he does is worthwhile.'

Georgina moved to the mouth of the cave. 'Hello! Jerome? Are you in there?'

There were a few scuffling noises and then from the darkness of the cave emerged a man with the longest, whitest beard Twenty-Two had ever seen; it was plaited and the bead that secured the final twists hung below his stomach. His eyes darted between them all before they finally rested on Twenty-Two.

'My, my, what have we got here?' he said, looking directly at her.

His gaze wasn't unkind, more inquisitive. She held out the foraging bag with the animal still inside.

'This is my friend, Twenty-Two,' Georgina said. 'We found a young animal in the bracken near the largest of the lakes. I think it's been separated from its mother.'

Jerome took a couple of steps towards Twenty-Two and gestured for her to hand over the bag. He continued to stare at her brow ridge. 'I've never seen one of your kind before.' He looked uncertainly at Bay and Twenty-Seven. 'They won't be touching anything, will they … ?'

Georgina bristled and Jerome stared at her reaction.

'Oh, I'm not saying that because they're Neanderthals,' he said eventually. 'I ain't speciesist. I'm saying it because I don't like children. The children at Uracil were always prodding and poking at my animals, they were. I couldn't stand it … grubby little fingers and loud, squeaky laughs …'

Jerome shuddered and shrank away from his visitors.

Georgina tried to smile. 'They won't touch anything. If you could just take a look inside the bag, and then we'll be on our way.'

Jerome peered eagerly into the bag that Twenty-Two had passed to him. 'Oh dear. She's not in a very good state, now, is she?'

He gently lifted the animal out of the bag and cupped her in both hands. 'She'd be scratching me and hissing if she was fit and well. Good job you brought her here.'

'What is she?' Georgina said as she placed Bay on the ground.

'She's a pine marten. Elusive little fellows. Don't often see them in the fur, so to speak. Usually only know they've been a-visiting by the droppings that they leave.'

'Is she a baby?' Georgina asked.

'That she is. They call the babies "kits".'

Twenty-Two scrunched her eyes as she thought of seeing her friend later and telling him she had found another Kit.

'She must have left her den too early and lost her way,' Jerome said, lifting up one of her paws and inspecting her claws. 'Her mum might've had four others to look after and not wanted to risk chasing after this one. She needs feeding up until she's big enough to go off by herself.'

He turned to the cave mouth. 'I have just the thing ...' he muttered, stroking the pine marten's tail. 'Jerome will take care of you. We'll grow you big and strong. A pine marten to be proud of ...'

'Sorry, Jerome, but we have to be getting back to Uracil now,' Georgina called after him. She looked down at the scowl on Twenty-Seven's face. 'Yes, we do. It's nearly dark,' she signed to him.

Twenty-Two also didn't want to leave but managed to keep a scowl from her features. She looked around at all the animals. They were in various states of health, but they were obviously well cared for. Could she learn to help them as Jerome did? The people of Uracil didn't want her assistance, but perhaps the animals would.

'That's fine by me. See you in a couple of months' time,' Jerome called out.

Twenty-Two signed to Georgina quickly before Jerome disappeared into the cave.

'Wait!' Georgina called out. 'Twenty-Two would like to know if she can come back and help some time.'

Jerome stopped in the cave mouth. He turned slowly and looked Twenty-Two up and down. 'How old is she?'

'She's just turned sixteen,' Georgina responded, answering for Twenty-Two. 'And as measured as they come.'

Twenty-Two scrunched her eyes at the compliment.

'Well, as long as she promises not to touch anything unless I tell her to, she can come next Sunday. If it pleases her.'

Twenty-Two nodded in response as she took Twenty-Seven's reluctant hand to begin the long trek back to Uracil.

The next morning was the second day of the weekend and Twenty-Two revelled in having a further day to do just as she pleased. Shortly after dawn, as arranged, she met with Ezra, Aiden and Nathan in the glade north of Uracil.

Nathan had set up four cans at the far end of the open ground. Standing at the other end, he was using a sling to fire stones at each one, seamlessly reloading it between swings. It was fascinating to watch and Twenty-Two stood for a moment to admire his skill.

She knew Nathan was around twelve years old, but he was already taller than Ezra. Twenty-Two decided that this would have made him popular back in Thymine – in her experience at the museum, she had observed that Sapiens held height in high regard. Nathan had a quiet focus that Twenty-Two had rarely seen in someone so young. She was used to the younger residents of Uracil cavorting their way around the walkways high up in the branches; goading one another to take the zip wire without closing their eyes or racing each other through Uracil's sawdust centre. Nathan did not seem to have this lightness to him and Twenty-Two wondered whether he missed his childhood.

Aiden turned around and saw her watching Nathan. 'Pretty good, eh? Pure talent. What I'd give for those reflexes. He can fight too. As quick as they come.'

Ezra bounced over to them and Nathan followed.

'Nathan's going to teach me to use the sling,' Ezra signed. 'Says it's a better weapon for smaller people like me.'

'How long did it take you to learn?' Twenty-Two signed to Nathan, who looked sideways up at his dad before responding.

'It took a few months to get the hang of it,' Nathan signed. 'I had to practise out in the woods back in Thymine, where no one could see me.'

'Elise gave him the sling for his birthday,' Aiden signed, frowning. 'We didn't know anything about it. They kept it secret from us.'

'You know why we did that, Dad.'

Aiden ruffled Nathan's hair before signing, 'I know, son. You did what you thought was right.' He paused. 'Your sister, on the other hand, shouldn't have given it to you without speaking to us first. She put you in danger and she knows better.'

Nathan shrugged. 'You should have seen the look on Dad's face when he first saw me use it. Once I knew we were safe in Uracil, I took him out to show him what I could do.'

'Yes. "Surprised", I think, is the polite way of putting it.'

'You never know when you'll need something to help you get out of a difficult situation.' Nathan grinned and then gestured for Ezra to follow him to the other end of the clearing. 'That's what you always told Elise, Dad!'

'He is already so capable of protecting himself,' Twenty-Two signed, while she watched Nathan and Ezra scour the ground for suitable stones. 'Can you make me like that?'

Aiden took a step back as he assessed her. 'You're built differently to Nathan and Elise. I don't think you'll manage their level of ... agility.'

Twenty-Two stared up at him. 'I know. But I am strong.'

Aiden gave a half-smile. 'There's no doubting that. Let's see what you can do.'

CHAPTER 9

* *

Genevieve

On the afternoon of her meeting with the Premier, Genevieve gave herself enough time to go home at lunch and change her clothing. Creases would not do for such an important event.

Zipping up her freshly pressed dress, she stared at herself in the mirrored room. Was it right? Had she chosen correctly? She was aiming for assured yet practical, and her reflection revealed only small lines of worry across her brow. The dress hugged the right places but was not so tight that it looked as if she were trying to laud her own figure. Whatever Mortimer said, cinnamon was her colour, far surpassing teal.

As she crossed their one-storey home from her rear bedroom, she heard the front door open and close again from several rooms away. Her head snapped towards the noise. It couldn't be one of the servants – they always used the side entrance. She reminded herself that they wouldn't come for her in the daylight. Not unless they wanted to make an example of her ...

She composed herself, concentrating on settling her fluttering heart so she would appear as calm as possible. Then she turned the corner into the hallway and stopped abruptly when she saw who it was.

'Stars, Father, you nearly had me thinking—'

Mortimer smiled at her as he placed his unused umbrella by the door. 'I thought I would pop home to see that you got off alright.'

Genevieve smiled at him.

'You look perfect, my dear.'

'Thank you.'

As she busied herself putting on her long coat, he put his arm on her shoulder, which caused her to pause for a moment.

'Try to relax,' he said, so only she could hear. 'Our demise would not be decided at a meeting with a polite request for attendance. This can only have a positive outcome.'

Genevieve was surprised when she felt a tear form. She hadn't cried for nearly two years, not since she found out— She stopped herself before the thought went any farther. Compared to what she had faced before, this was nothing, and she didn't understand why this particular moment had brought tears with it. Perhaps it was all becoming too much; perhaps she was weakening.

She sniffed and tried to wipe the tear away before Mortimer noticed. He carefully looked away while she rubbed at her face.

'It takes its toll, this life,' he whispered. 'But we wouldn't be human if it didn't.'

Shaking away the fear she felt circling at her feet, she smiled broadly and with genuine warmth. Mortimer was her deeply tethered root; she had risen above the soil and blossomed for all to see, but it was Mortimer who had allowed her to do so, quietly and with little fuss.

She patted his cheek. 'Wish me luck.'

'But you don't need it, my dear.'

*

As Genevieve reached the boulevard in front of the Premier's residence, she regulated her pace. She found it nearly impossible to walk slowly – it was such a waste of time – but she did not want the guards to think that she was flustered. Always anticipating the next move, she began to roll up the sleeve on her right arm. There was no queue this afternoon and she was able to approach the guard and hold out her arm to him without a word being spoken. He scanned her wrist while she watched the boulevard. A few passing people recognised her, but that didn't matter; they all knew of her summoning by now.

Crossing the arched bridge, she looked down at the moat. It was only a few feet deep. The stone slabs beneath her felt solid, but she knew the bridge had been designed so that a small explosion, in the right place, would have the whole thing crashing beneath her. The Premier's Chief of Protection carried the detonator and it never left his sight.

As she stepped off the bridge and approached the second set of checks, she held her wrist out again. She hadn't bothered to roll her cuff down. Verification here took longer, as attendees were not only scanned, but also had the legitimacy of their appointments triple-checked.

Once her attendance had been confirmed, she was assigned a guard. He led her through an ornately decorated set of double doors without speaking. For the first time, she turned left at the main chamber, instead of turning right into the conference room. She had spent many an hour wondering what lay on the other side of that wall.

Following the guard, she passed through room after room, each with several doorways leading from it, never proceeding in a linear direction. Keeping her gaze raised as always, she glanced around her as she entered each room. Once or twice they emerged into peaceful courtyards. These appeared to be open to the sky, but upon careful inspection, she realised clear glass separated the courtyards from their views of the outside world. The Premier's residence was sealed in every direction.

After ten minutes, Genevieve knew she would have difficulty finding her way back alone. She had also decided that 'opulent' was the word for this more private part of the Premier's residence. A mirror opposite of the Sapiens' homes of penance, the Premier's residence reflected his worth with every bubbling fountain, sweet-smelling blossom and marble fireplace. It certainly didn't represent any 'kitchen table' Genevieve had come across and she silently commended whoever had thought up that ingenious segment of the Premier's public persona.

She had always been intrigued by the design of the Premier's residence but had been unable to find out much about it over the years. She was in the Disclosure Department, and these architectural details certainly didn't need to be shown to the world. She did know that behind each tailored wall was a carefully planned layer of protection. Like the bridge, there were many areas that had been primed to halt any unwelcome visitor.

With little ceremony and even less communication, they finally reached an antechamber containing around fifty other Medius. They all sat on red velvet chairs lining the walls. The guard nodded to an empty seat and then joined the other guards along the rear wall. Genevieve took off her coat and smoothed her dress under her before sitting and laying the coat across her knees. She had been blessed with the fortune of having a mouth that, when settled and at rest, looked as though she were still half-smiling. Consequently, she could scan a room and look completely at ease in any environment with only minimal effort. Leaning back, she took her time inspecting the company she now kept.

The highest Medius representatives of each office were present. As one of the five Assistant Directors of Disclosure, Genevieve was only preceded by the director of her department, who was, of course, a Potior. All of her colleagues in the same role were present and she could see that the same was true for the other departments.

She knew most of the people present by sight and nodded at the few who caught her eye. No one spoke. Most stared down at their hands or up at the ceiling. Genevieve absent-mindedly twirled the bracelet she always wore, and her gaze settled on a portrait of the Premier hanging above an Assistant Director of Education's head. Clearly believing that she was staring at him, rather than the portrait, he started to redden, but she did not look away. In the end, he leant down to adjust his shoelace to avoid her gaze.

'The Premier is ready for you,' a footman called out, rather grandly pushing open another set of double doors.

Genevieve stood and joined the swell of Medius as they made their way into the room, hanging back so that she could take a seat towards the rear. She had only recently been promoted and knew that it was better to take a position that reflected this.

When everyone was settled, they all stared towards the raised platform at the end of the room. The Premier stood in front of a lectern and was smiling at the familiar faces of the more senior Medius as they took their seats at the front.

At well over seven feet tall, he commanded the room's attention effortlessly. His skin was flawless, like all the Potiors, but his advanced years were allowed to show in the white streak running through his shoulder-length black hair. His pale skin gave the impression that he never saw daylight, and he was dressed in what could almost be considered a military outfit, as if at any moment he could be called to command Zone 3's armies.

'Thank you for attending at such short notice. I know that you are all busy with your various duties,' he said, his voice low and steady.

All the attendees beamed up at him, clearly grateful for the acknowledgement of their heavy workloads. Genevieve made sure to match their expressions.

'A time comes in every great civilisation when unrest rears its head. Chaos sits upon the shoulders of civilisation and it is our duty to ensure that it does not climb down and infect our world. The history of the Sapiens is littered with these incidents of bloodshed, but we have evolved beyond this. Peace is a marker of an enlightened and advanced society, and it is therefore imperative that order remains.'

When he paused, a few of the Medius nodded as they stared up at him.

'With this in mind, it is with great sadness that I have to inform you of a new threat to our status quo. One that must be suppressed with as little disruption as possible. We will deal with this swiftly and without the input of the masses. We shall protect them from both the force that would harm them, and the discomfort that would weigh upon their shoulders if they knew of it.'

Genevieve stared up at him, her mind spinning with implications. She had not heard of a rebellion in any of the other bases, but news of such matters took time to cross the distance between them and then trickle down through whispers and undercurrents.

'We have discovered an illegal, unrecognised settlement in Zone 3,' the Premier continued. 'Its occupants are likely to have travelled from another Zone since, as we all know, Sapiens are not allowed to leave the bases for their own protection. This number of people could not have amassed unseen from our own bases.'

A murmur rippled its way around the room. Genevieve's heart began to pound, and she glanced around for cameras. Her colleagues were as shocked by this news as she was, and several of their mouths were hanging open. An unregulated settlement was inconceivable to them.

'Fear not, for we do not believe that they have plans to descend upon us ... yet.'

The murmurs got louder, and Genevieve caught looks of both outrage and fear from a few of her colleagues.

'We must protect this peaceful nation we have built, and therefore we must deal with this swiftly. The Potiors are deciding on how best to proceed, and when we do, you must all be ready to spring into action. In the meantime, it is your utmost responsibility to suppress this worrisome news from spreading. It will only cause unnecessary upset and we must protect the lay population from this. They, as always, are our primary concern.'

People in the crowd nodded. Genevieve felt nauseous but continued to stare straight ahead. She knew she should nod along with her colleagues, but it was all she could do to keep her focus on the current moment and not let her mind flit ahead to the potential outcomes of such news. Not reacting was the best she could manage.

'I must make it clear that you are all level seventeen and above for a reason. There will be the strongest repercussions for anyone who shares or even hints at this news. Even with their most beloved.'

The Premier held his fist up in the air. 'Three first!'

Everyone leapt to their feet and matched his salute. *'Three first!'*

CHAPTER 10

Elise

Elise stared out at the blustering sea. She had only witnessed such a sight a couple of times in her life and she savoured the moment. Pulling her coat around her, she breathed deeply and let the salty air imbue her from within.

Autumn had finally arrived and she knew that soon it would be even harder to survive outside the bases. For the first time in years, she longed for a home. She thought briefly of Samuel and wondered where he was; he would have crossed a different sea, but for some reason she could feel his presence next to her. She forced herself to remember how she had felt before she had lost her memories – what was the point of them being returned to her if she pushed them away? She had been happy, and she wanted to feel that way again.

The pebbles crunched behind her and she turned to see Maya approaching, waving at her to return to the cove.

'We're all set,' Maya said, once Elise was by her side. 'There's a small sailboat we can use. Bertha will even steer us over there, but best we don't discuss our reasons for travelling in front of her.'

Elise nodded and followed Maya to the mouth of the cove. Inside the gloom were a man and woman of middling years throwing supplies into a grey-painted sailboat. Even the low-ered sails were grey, and Elise guessed this was so the boat was harder to spot from a distance.

'This is Martin and Bertha,' Maya said, nodding at the cou-ple. 'They cover the south-west coast of Zone 3 and help Uracil when we need to go a bit farther afield. They helped get Max over to Zone 2.'

'Tall one, he was,' Martin said, unknotting a length of rope.

'That's him,' Elise responded.

The man didn't turn towards her when she spoke.

It had taken them two days to walk from Cytosine to this hidden cove. Maya had explained on the way that Martin and Bertha had left Uracil years ago after volunteering to look after one of the various sailing points the Infiltration Department used to make the crossings to other shores. Elise had felt a flut-ter of envy at the quiet life Martin and Bertha led together.

'How long will the journey take?' she asked.

Bertha sucked in her breath and stared up at the sky before answering. 'Maybe two days. The wind's in our favour. A month later and we wouldn't be taking you.'

There was no apology in her tone – as if what she was saying was simply a fact that couldn't be altered or worked around.

Maya picked up her bag. 'Well, it's a good job we're here now. Shall we get going?'

Two days later, Elise stumbled off the side of the boat, not car-ing that the water reached her knees. Her stomach rolled and she bent to retch again. She couldn't believe that she still felt so unwell even now her feet were touching solid ground. After the first twelve hours of their journey, she had given up trying to shield Maya and Bertha from seeing the contents of her stomach. Maya had handed Elise water to keep her hydrated, but every time the boat rolled over a wave, Elise had again lost what Maya had tried to replace.

'I'm never doing that again,' Elise muttered, holding her bag above her head to make sure its contents didn't get soaked.

Maya hopped over the side of the sailboat with a grin. 'I presume that you want to return at some point?'

At this exact moment, Elise would have been quite happy to settle on this island to the south-west of Zone 3.

Maya turned to Bertha. 'We'll be four days maximum. If we're not back by then, return to the mainland and send word to Uracil that we've been captured.'

Elise's eyes widened. Up until now, there had been no mention of what they were doing here; apparently it would be more dangerous than Elise had anticipated.

Bertha nodded as she stared up at the sky, her attention already diverted by the forces that steered her journeys.

'Come on, Green-Face,' Maya said, smiling at Elise and revealing the large gap between her teeth. 'We need to go light a fire and dry you off.'

Three hours later, they had found shelter in a cave high on the cliff face, which they'd reached via a naturally chiselled pathway. Maya had checked the ground for debris and confirmed that the sea line wouldn't reach their sleeping place when the tide came in. Elise, unused to such things as tides and with her stomach finally more settled, had watched her with interest.

Once the fire was lit, they had draped their wet clothing around it and changed into spare outfits. Elise felt as though the damp had permeated her bones and she stared at her bleached hands while Maya made a stew out of their supplies.

'Okay. Why are we here?' Elise eventually asked, clasping the bowl that Maya had handed to her. She was hungry but she needed the warmth the bowl provided more than anything else.

'The Tri-Council wanted me to pay a visit to this island as there's a group of people who live here, and we have something of theirs.'

'People live here?' Elise asked.

Maya chuckled. 'There are whole worlds outside the Potiors' bases, ones that extend well beyond Uracil. What you know of Zone 3 is just a tiny drop in the ocean.'

Elise chastised herself for being so naive, but she couldn't even begin to imagine what lay beyond the land she had grown up in and experienced so far.

'Have you heard of the Commidorants?' Maya asked, taking a sip of her tea.

Elise shook her head. 'Not in the memories I still have. But it might have been mentioned in the months that I lost.'

'They are a group of Sapiens who have been campaigning for years to live separately to the Medius.'

'Ahh, I've met some of them,' Elise said, thinking of Holly, the young woman who had once been her best friend, and Holly's boyfriend, Lewis, who had betrayed them back in Thymine's museum.

'Well, some of them live here, having unofficially commandeered this island a few years ago. There's an even larger island farther south, which I'm sure they've also got their eye on. They set up an encampment and called it Destin. They want all Sapiens to move here and start again.'

Elise hadn't seen anything of the island except the beach and cliff edge. It was wetter than she was used to, but that didn't seem enough of a reason to dislike a place. If Sapiens wanted to live here, then good for them.

'Why bring me with you?'

'Because you're interested in the "bigger picture". But I just don't think you realise how big it gets.'

Elise thought about this for a moment. 'That's true. But it's hard to imagine what's beyond our little bases when you have nothing to compare them to.'

'I wish you'd travelled to Zone 5 with Samuel,' Maya said, poking a stick into the fire. 'That would have given you some perspective.'

Elise felt the air leave her lungs at Samuel's name and she struggled to hold the impassive look she had nearly mastered. She pushed the thoughts down quickly – they were discussing the wider world, not her relationships.

Maya jabbed the twig into the fire again, letting it burn this time. 'It's so important to see how the other Zones and settlements function – completely differently to ours, each on their own journey through what will soon be history.'

'Maybe I will one day,' Elise said. 'Once I've rebalanced this one.'

She knew she wanted change ... but in which direction? Would she even know how to judge the integrity of other settlements if she ever had the opportunity to visit them?

Maya glanced over at her. 'Come on, let's get some sleep. We're got another long walk again tomorrow. I'll fill you in on what we need to achieve then.'

*

Elise had never seen such rich, green countryside before – clearly the benefit of a climate that appeared to favour drizzle. The temperature was also warmer than she was used to. Morning dew moistened the bottom of her trousers as Maya led the way through thick, green grass grazed on by herds of cows, sheep, deer and goats. The animals barely registered the two intruders' presence, only turning to gaze briefly in their direction before returning to more important matters.

Mid-afternoon, Maya pulled out her screen and checked their co-ordinates.

'Nearly there,' she said. 'When we arrive, feel free to join in the discussions. I've got a feeling they'll respond better to you than me.'

Half an hour later, Elise peered into the distance. There was a brown line up ahead, but she couldn't decide what it was. As they neared this unusual sight, she realised that the brown line was a high wooden fence. To her right, a large buck spotted them and belted away in the opposite direction.

Whatever is beyond that fence can hunt.

This wall of wood looked so odd to Elise that she stopped to stare at it. Here, in the middle of some of the lushest country-side she had ever seen, was a jarring enclosure that made no attempt to blend into the surroundings or conceal its presence. It was so different from the camouflaged tree houses of Uracil and the gently sloping valley of her home in Thymine, she couldn't help but wonder at the design.

Behind the towering fence she could see a man peering at them from a raised platform. As they drew closer, he turned for a second and let out a shrill whistle. Maya put her arm in front of Elise, forcing her to a halt.

'We should wait for them to approach us,' Maya said. 'They can be a bit jumpy sometimes.'

Elise stared up at this elevated man. He didn't break eye contact with her, and she wondered if she should look away; what would be worse – looking overly aggressive or appearing weak? She didn't break eye contact – three years ago she would have made a different decision.

A few minutes later, they heard the sound of wooden planks being drawn back. One side of the large double doorway swung outwards and ten men approached Elise and Maya in a line, carrying an array of long-handled weapons. One had a spear, another a wooden post with metal spikes at the end. Elise reached for her sling; she could see Maya's approving look from the corner of her eye.

'We've come to trade,' Maya called out when the men were still fifty feet away.

A man with a long, shaggy beard stepped forwards and peered at Maya. 'You've been here before, haven't you? From Uracil. We don't need no Dermadew, thank you, *Midder*.'

Elise bristled at the term, realising why Maya had thought she should join in with the discussion. She stepped forwards. 'How about some antibiotics? I've got four courses in my bag.'

The man sized her up. 'What do you want in return?'

'We need to speak to David,' Maya shouted.

The shaggy-bearded man snorted. 'That ain't gonna 'appen.'

'Tell David we've got one of his. And he might want him back,' Maya called out.

The men looked at each other, then one with wild auburn hair turned and walked back to the settlement.

Maya fell silent and Elise was happy to follow her lead.

Twenty minutes later, he returned. 'He'll give you ten minutes. And we want all four lots of those antibio-whatsits.'

Elise looked at Maya, who nodded.

Maya held her head up high and walked towards the men as though she were ten feet tall. Strength radiated from her tiny frame and she met the eye of each man she had to pass to get to the gated enclosure. Elise copied her stance and made sure she displayed no sign of weakness. Stepping over the brim of the wooden doorway, she kept her features stilled as she surveyed what this fence aimed to protect from the outside world.

Wooden huts were dotted around in the mud, each one depressingly futile in its attempt to shield the occupants from the elements; planks were missing from the sides and straw roofs were sodden. A chicken extended its wings and squawked its way across their path. Maya ignored the bird and continued walking towards the largest of the wooden huts. A veranda snaked its way around the outside – this one at least looked to have been finished to a higher standard.

A couple of small children dressed in leather tunics stopped mid-game to stare at the newcomers as they passed. Elise smiled at them, but they did not respond. Her mouth dried as a woman dressed in a similar tunic scuttled back into her hut, calling for her children all the way. Once inside, the woman slammed the door shut. The timber frame shook with such force that, for a moment, Elise thought the whole structure was at risk of collapsing.

As Maya and Elise continued picking their way through the mud, Elise noticed a man standing in the far corner of the settlement, soaking a hide in a large barrel. When she met his gaze, he quickly looked down again. It wasn't just the women and children who were scared of outsiders. She tried not to convey any reaction to these sights. All the while, she could hear the snorts of laughter and chatter of the men walking behind.

Unhurried, Maya stepped onto the veranda of the largest hut and pushed aside the animal skin that hung in front of the doorway. Elise blinked as she entered the darkened room and it took a moment for her eyes to adjust. A long table filled the centre and at the head of it sat a man nearly the same height as Elise, even though he was sitting down. Positioned down the length of the aged table were a few other residents, mainly men. They all stopped speaking when Elise and Maya entered.

Maya made her way to the end of the table and took a seat. Elise pulled out the chair next to her and nodded to the few people who met her gaze.

'Thank you for agreeing to see us, David,' Maya said, addressing the man at the end of the table.

Elise stared up its length to the bear of a man. His face was obscured by one of the bushiest beards she had ever seen.

'You're back then?' David said, looking at Maya. His gaze switched to Elise. 'Haven't seen this one before.'

'This is Elise,' Maya said.

'They didn't do a very good job with your enhancements, did they?' David responded, picking some food out of his teeth with his fingernail. A few of the others snorted. David ignored them as he inspected his nail and flicked whatever he had collected to the ground. 'Did Uracil mess up your enhancements, or are you really clever or something?'

Elise didn't react; she knew she wasn't the prettiest or the tallest. She wasn't notable and never had been. She was used to these types of comments, and the insult slid away, unable to find its mark.

'I'm from Thymine. Born and bred,' Elise said. 'No enhancements.'

'Which part of Thymine?' a small man with a bald head asked.

'Outer Circle. North arc.'

'Do you know old Milly Thonken then?' the same man asked, smiling at Elise. 'I saw her two years back, before I made the final journey here. Not a tooth left in her head.'

Elise leant back in her seat before responding. 'I'm sorry to have to tell you this, but Milly died five years ago. She had pneumonia that wouldn't lift, and her family didn't have the Medistamps to treat it.'

The bald man gave Elise an appreciative nod. 'She's from Thymine alright.'

'We have to be sure of these things,' David said. 'We know you change your names to make yourselves anything you want to be. Your tattoos, too.' He leant back a bit farther, his gaze roaming around the room, appearing to be bored by their presence. 'So, what's it you came to tell me, then?'

'One of yours has made his way to Uracil. We wanted to make sure that you didn't want him back,' Maya said.

David leant forwards a fraction. 'If they're stupid enough to get so lost that they end up in your arse-reach of the woods, then we don't want them back. Who is it anyway?'

'He says he's called Lewis Thetter,' Maya responded.

Elise tried to look as if this weren't news to her as well. Lewis Thetter in Uracil?

'Never heard of him,' David responded.

The woman to David's right leant forwards and whispered something to him.

David let out a snort. 'Ah, that one. Got himself into trouble, he did. I'm told he got a bit too big for himself and had to be dealt with. You can keep him.'

Maya nodded. 'Before we leave, can I ask what he did?'

Suddenly, and with no warning, David stood and pushed back his seat. Elise tried not to flinch at the noise of the heavy chair tumbling to the floor. He was bigger than her dad and, now that she could see him more clearly, younger and stronger as well.

'Do I look like the half-sister you only get to see on special occasions? Do you want to come over here, stare into my blinkers, and braid my beard whilst I tell you all about it?'

'We just want to know if he's a danger to us, that's all. We'll leave in a minute,' Maya said.

Still standing, David placed his arms on the table. 'He can finish off the lot of you for all I care. You're not our kinsmen. You're not our friends. You tweak all your children in that northern ant farm of yours. And if you can't be happy with the way the stars make your children, then you've got no right to ask for any help from us.'

Maya stared up the table at him. 'We haven't come to discuss politics. We're only here to trade.'

After a few moments of silence, David made a great show of gesturing to the bald man, who scurried around the back of the table and righted his chair.

David sat down. 'What else you got on you besides the antibiotics?'

'I've also got some ether,' Maya said.

David grunted. 'Throw that in and we can talk a bit longer.'

Elise decided to take a big risk. 'I've got some painkillers on me, two packs. I'd also like to know if you've heard of someone called Holly. She joined your group about two years ago.'

David clenched his fists, rolling his head up to the ceiling. 'Gwentin, strip them of everything they've got. Then throw their meatless bones to the pigs.'

The bald man nodded and two large men emerged from the shadows of the hut.

Elise leant forwards and stared down the table. 'Uracil knows where we are. And if we don't return, they'll send every available agent here to find us.'

'That's a very big threat from a very small girl,' David said, still staring at the ceiling.

The men from the shadows peeled off and advanced down either side of the table. One of them was missing an ear and the other had a mottled burn mark all the way up his arm.

Elise could feel Maya tense next to her.

'I don't make threats,' Elise said. 'I just say the truth of the matter.'

The two men came closer. Elise watched their progress, running through escape options in her head.

She stared down the table. 'Antibiotics, ether and painkillers for two answers. And no messy fighting either. We'd kill two or three on our way out and then you'd have to deal with Uracil when we didn't return.'

'Please. We'd kill at least four,' Maya said, without looking at Elise.

The henchman closest to Elise snarled and made a lunge for her. Without blinking, Elise launched herself at him. He froze when her push knife pressed against his throat. Still seated, Maya smiled up at Elise and then down at David at the other end of the table.

David eyed them both. 'Give us the antibiotics, ether and painkillers and I'll answer both your questions.'

'Done,' Maya said.

Elise lowered her knife but did not sheathe it. Instead, she let it rest on the table, her hand gently playing with the hilt.

David reached for his cup and took a long gulp from it. The woman to his right whispered something to him while he drank. Elise thought he was smiling, but she couldn't be sure as his beard covered his lips from every direction.

'I'm told this Lewis was expelled from our organisation after he gave one of us up to the Potiors to save his own skin,' David said.

'I see,' said Maya.

'And what happened to Holly?' Elise asked, determined to get her question in.

David's cheeks puffed out farther – he was definitely smiling now. 'She's the one he sold out. A shame, really. I'm told she had real promise. She'll be dead by now.'

Elise clamped her mouth shut and nodded to Maya. Both women placed all their trades on the table and turned to leave.

'I'm told he's a snivelling sheensta,' David called out after them. 'Hope he don't turn on you too!'

The laughs from inside the cabin rang around Elise's head as she walked out into the rain.

'Who was Holly?' Maya asked, as she caught up with her outside Destin's gate.

Elise carried on at the same brisk pace, her head bent low. 'She was my best friend back in Thymine. She was like family, until she met Lewis and she changed overnight. Spent most of her time from then on purring at him. She wasn't a great friend at the end, but she didn't deserve that.'

'She could still be alive,' Maya said. 'Stars, everything David said could have been complete bull for all we know.'

'I know,' Elise said. 'But it wouldn't surprise me if it were true. Lewis was a complete ...' She threw her hands up. 'It just gets worse, the more I find out. Every time I think I'm dealing with it, something else comes along to knock me down.'

Maya pulled Elise's arm down and back until she was forced to stop. They were out of sight of Destin now. 'Yes, bad things keep happening, but there's plenty of good in this world and you know it,' Maya snapped.

'You really believe that? After everything you've seen?' Elise said, turning to her. 'Honestly, sometimes I think I might as well take my family and man one of the coves like Bertha. At least we'd be away from all this.'

'At least you have a family to run away with. Where would you go anyway?'

Elise shrugged angrily. 'There's other places in the world I could take them ...' She stared at Maya. She needed more information. 'How do you know when somewhere is a safe place to live? How do you know if it is functioning correctly and not just another cage?'

Maya eyed her and then sighed. 'Look at how they treat the physically weakest people. It'll tell you in a second whether you want to spend any real time there.' She cocked her head backwards. 'Take that place back there, so proud that they don't alter their children, but it's the largest, most aggressive ones who run the show. It's understandable that they want to live separately to the Medius, it's who happens to be leading them on this occasion that is the problem. There's no democracy or kindness there. It's just run by whoever can shout the loudest and scare everyone else the most.'

Elise thought back to the silent children and the woman who had run back into her hut. 'That just confirms what I was saying. Stars, I'm done with all of this. It's all too much.'

'Don't be so self-pitying,' Maya said scathingly.

'Why shouldn't I be?' Elise said, turning away from her. 'What would you know?'

'I know that if you don't find a way to see some joy in this world, you won't last much longer.'

'After everything I've been through? I don't know if that's possible.'

Maya took a step closer to Elise and lowered her voice. 'You're not the only one with a crappy tale to tell and you're certainly not the only one who was in a containment centre. I was taken to one too. Three years I lost to that place. And more as well. Same as you.'

Elise's head snapped up.

'And think about the Neanderthals,' Maya said, her voice rising. 'They might as well have lived all their lives in a containment centre. No family in there, no real friends.' Elise looked down at her shoes and Maya grabbed her shoulder, forcing her to look up. 'And every day they try. Every day they count the blessings the stars have bestowed on them ...'

Elise was knocked back by the truth in Maya's words. Kit and Twenty-Two had grown up with even less than her – not even a family to support and love them – yet she had never heard them once begrudge the unfairness of their situation.

It took her a moment before she could speak. 'I'm so sorry. I didn't know it had happened to you too.'

'I didn't want you to. It was over twenty years ago now. And not a day goes by that I don't get down on my knees and thank the stars for helping me get out of there.'

'How do you do it? How do you keep going? I don't know how to get rid of this darkness that follows me.'

Maya stepped away from Elise. 'How I face all those silent children, cowed men, caged animals and forgotten experiments? I remind myself that I can make a difference. One small thing, one day at a time. And I make the effort to find a little bit of joy whenever I can.'

Elise turned so Maya wouldn't see her tears. They walked in silence the rest of the way and Elise promised the stars that, whatever happened, she would find her way out of this darkness.

CHAPTER 11

Twenty-Two

The following weekend, Twenty-Two made the journey back to Jerome's settlement. She went alone as she wanted something that was just hers – an interest that she didn't have to share, and some time spent in solitude.

As she approached the cave mouth, Jerome was nowhere to be seen on the grass ledge. She was eager to see how the baby pine marten was faring, so she went in. The inside of the cave was dark, and she unfolded her screen to use its light to guide her. Near the entranceway were the remnants of a fire and lined up against the two cave walls were various cages and enclosures. She went over to inspect them and was surprised to see that one held tiny crickets, another a clew of worms.

'That's their food,' Jerome said from behind her.

Twenty-Two jumped and turned to stare at him.

'Have you come to help?' he asked, leaning down to pick up the container of crickets.

Twenty-Two nodded.

'Well, I need to shift most of these outside for the day, so they get a bit of sunlight. I take them in again at night now that the cold has set in.'

Twenty-Two picked up the container next to the crickets and followed Jerome back out to the patch of grass. They worked steadily for an hour, transporting containers from the inside of the cave to the light. As they went deeper into the cave, Twenty-Two began to get an idea of its size. The mouth gave the impression of just a small hollow in the cliff face, but in truth it spread out in all directions with antechambers stretching into the depths of the rock. The work soothed her. Back in Uracil her mind whirled around the confines of the base – interpreting, worrying, guessing, tracking, surmising . . . but never at rest. Here, it was quietened by the demands of physical work; there was no one to watch aside from Jerome – and he was equally focused on the task at hand – so there were no motives to guess at.

When the last of the containers had been moved, Twenty-Two looked around for the pine marten.

Jerome studied her. 'She's doing just fine. I can show her to you but you can't hold her again, or she'll get the taste for it. I want to release her in a few months' time if possible.'

He led Twenty-Two over to a small cage that had a piece of hollowed-out bark in the corner. He had a slight hobble and Twenty-Two wondered how old he was.

Poking out from underneath the end of the piece of bark was a furry tail. It twitched slightly and Twenty-Two longed to hold her new friend. She reached out to her.

Jerome grabbed Twenty-Two's hand. 'I said no touching!'

Twenty-Two snatched her hand back and retreated a step.

'I don't like people thinking they can come up here and pet the animals. They're not for that. It'd only be for your benefit, not theirs.'

Twenty-Two nodded.

'That's why I moved up here. They kept on trying to interfere, especially the children. They'd tug the tails of my little ones. It weren't right, but no one saw it as a problem. So, I did the only thing I could and moved away from them, as high up the mountain as I could, so little legs wouldn't follow.'

Twenty-Two longed to explain to Jerome that she wouldn't go against his wishes, but she knew that he couldn't understand her. Instead, she looked around for something else to do.

'You can bring some water up from the stream and fill their water bowls,' Jerome said, positioning himself between Twenty-Two and the pine marten.

Twenty-Two set off, determined to enjoy the quiet of a day spent by herself.

A week later, Twenty-Two dithered, holding her lunch plate in both hands. The voices around her were loud, multiple conversations happening at once, and drops of rain began to splash down on her head. It threatened to clear the seating area, so, pushing her feet forwards before she missed her chance, she took the twenty steps required and sat down at the table she had been resolutely avoiding. The three men sitting there stared up at her and one of them dropped his spoon.

He picked it up and jabbed it towards her while looking to one of the other men. 'Why has *it* come and sat *here*?'

Twenty-Two wasn't sure if he understood sign language, but she thought it better that she at least try to answer him. 'I wanted to speak with one of you,' she signed.

Two of the men looked at each other, confusion clear on their faces. The third man, Luca, followed the movement of her hands and lowered his head.

'Doesn't *it* know that we don't understand *it*?' the man with the spoon finally said.

The other guard, who also hadn't understood her, snorted and Twenty-Two glared at him.

'Pack it in,' Luca said to the man with the spoon. 'She ain't an *it*. And while we're at it, it wouldn't kill you to learn another language.'

'You're such a half-bake, Luca,' the man with the expressive spoon said. He turned to the other guard. 'Shall we go and find somewhere else to sit? Away from the killer.'

The other man nodded and they both loudly gathered up their plates and moved to another table. Luca and Twenty-Two had suddenly become invisible to them.

'Thanks for that,' Luca said, piercing three runner beans with his fork.

Twenty-Two wasn't sure what he was thanking her for, but she knew the polite response.

'You are welcome,' she signed as she tried to ignore the droplet of rain that ran down her nose.

Luca sighed. 'I wasn't really thanking you. I was being sarcastic. Why do you have to take everything so literally?'

Twenty-Two didn't think that she had got off to a very good start, so she decided to try and rectify the situation. 'I wanted to say that I am sorry.'

Luca looked up. 'Sorry for what? What have you done now?'

'Sorry that you miss Faye. I did not know how you felt about her.'

Luca stabbed at another couple of beans with more force than was necessary. 'Can't you ever have a normal conversation?

"Hi, Luca. I like your shirt. What are you thinking of doing tonight? Brrr ... it was cold yesterday!"'

Twenty-Two stared at him. 'I do like your shirt.'

Luca rubbed his forehead and muttered, 'Stars, what did I ever do to deserve this?' He shook his head and put his fork down. 'What can I do to make this conversation end? And preferably not repeat itself?'

Twenty-Two stared at him. 'She wasn't a good person. You must know that now?'

Luca pushed his plate away. 'Yes, I may have worked that one out by now. I might be slow on the uptake sometimes, but that doesn't mean I don't get there eventually.'

'So, why are you still angry with me?'

'Because that doesn't give you any right to go and do what you did. You can't just go around making decisions about whether people deserve to live or die.'

Twenty-Two studied Luca. 'I can understand why you might see it that way. And it won't happen again – I have agreed with Kit that I will speak with him first if a similar situation occurs.' The rain began to patter more loudly on the tables and a few people picked up their plates to take back to their tree houses. 'But are you sure that is why you are still angry with me?'

'Of course! I—' Luca slumped, and all his bluster sailed away. 'Ugh, I don't know. Perhaps I'm just angry at you because I've forgotten how not to be. Not all of us analyse everything from eighteen different angles. It's not a healthy way to live. Honestly, I'm just tired and a bit stuck in this new life of mine. It's not exactly what I imagined when I left Thymine.'

Twenty-Two tried to put herself in his position, and then she knew what was missing.

'What if I found you someone new to love? Would that help?'

Luca grinned and rubbed the back of his shaved head. 'Stars, that's the last thing I need. You as a matchmaker isn't going to work. I'll end up engaged to an angry badger.' He stared at Twenty-Two. 'But there is something you could do for me ...'

After a few weeks of working with Michael, Twenty-Two had come to the conclusion that it was very different to her time assisting Faye. Although she would never describe Michael as a friend, her initial fears that he would chastise or belittle her publicly to set an example to Uracil had never been realised. Instead, Michael spent his days absorbed in his work and barely noticed her presence, which suited Twenty-Two very well. She would rather have some quiet during her working day to counteract the stressful early mornings and evenings when she would expend all her energy and patience mixing with the other residents of Uracil. But the rewards for her efforts were blossoming – only this morning someone had apologised to her when they had accidentally trodden on her toe.

It had taken some effort, but Twenty-Two was close to persuading Michael to let her meet with Lewis and take down his version of events before his trial. She knew that Lewis had begun to learn sign language when he was preparing to be a Companion to Kit, so she hoped that he would at least be able to understand her questioning.

'As I said before,' Twenty-Two signed to Michael as he sat on the great oak platform 'I am ready to take on these extra responsibilities. Yes, I can remember what people like to drink and the arrangement of their cushions, but I'd like to do more. I want to use my mind in a different way ...'

Having laid out her reasons, she waited patiently for Michael to consider the matter.

He peered up at the tree canopy before responding to her request. 'And you promise that you won't decide on your own justice? You won't take matters into your own hands like you did before? Because if you do, there won't be another chance for you.'

Twenty-Two was able to answer his question with confidence. 'I promise I won't do anything to Lewis other than record his version of what happened in Thymine and then leave the cabin.'

Michael stared at her.

She wasn't sure that her statement had covered everything Michael had requested, so she quickly added, 'And I will leave him alive and unharmed.'

Michael let out his breath slowly between his teeth. 'Okay. But I'm trusting you, Twenty-Two. You say that you are honest, and I believe you. Don't make me regret that.'

Twenty-Two realised that this was her chance to ask the question that had been at the back of her mind for some time. 'But why are you trusting me? Why did you ask me to work for you, after knowing what I did to Faye? Ezra thinks I wouldn't be a ... likely choice for the position.'

Michael leant back in his chair. 'That's twofold really. Firstly, as I said before, I do believe in second chances, and I wanted to show Uracil – by example – that you shouldn't be treated as an outcast.' He rubbed the corners of his mouth.

'Secondly, I know I went into this job with the right motivations – I have no interest in power or the accumulation of status; I just wanted to help Uracil right itself after everything it's been through. But I also know that power is a corrupting force. Look at Faye. Have enough people line up patiently to speak with you every day and the authority to change their lives, and it can turn your head, make you believe that you're more special than the rest.'

Twenty-Two listened with care and studied Michael as he spoke. She didn't understand yet, but to her mind, his words were untainted by deception.

Michael smiled. 'In short, I only took this job because I never wanted it, but I also wanted an insurance policy ... to ensure that I wouldn't stray too far from myself. And that would be you.'

Twenty-Two stared at him in shock. 'You want me to do what I did to Faye?'

Michael slapped his knees. 'Stars, no! I like to think that you've learned enough to go about it the right way this time! Warn me if you think I'm heading in the wrong direction, and if that doesn't work, alert everyone to what is happening. Randomly killing people is certainly not how it should be done.' His face softened. 'But your ability to read the heart of people is an incredible gift, one from the stars themselves, and I'm glad to have you by my side.'

Twenty-Two felt a warmth spread through her. Michael's words meant more to her than she could ever convey; she knew it was the closest she would get to exoneration.

CHAPTER 12

* *

Genevieve

Following the conclave, Genevieve walked home as quickly as she could without drawing attention to herself. Her whole body screamed at her to run the entire way.

Another settlement has been discovered …

As she walked through the busy streets, she feared the weight of this newfound knowledge would reveal itself through her body language. *Which settlement is it?* She bent her head, and her left eyebrow arched ever so slightly. Resisting the urge to dip her head farther to hide her face, she picked up her pace. *How long ago did they find it?* Her hand reached to cup her mouth and she had to stop it midway. *What will the Potiors do?*

She blinked rapidly as the questions fired through her brain. She had to stop these thoughts – she was losing control.

It began to rain so lightly that it was almost indistinguishable from an early-winter mist. She had never been more grateful to feel fine drizzle dance across her skin. At the touch of a button, her umbrella popped open and she used it to partially shield her face. Five more minutes and then she would be home.

A crashing noise to her right made her jump. She pulled her umbrella down lower, as though it could protect her. Taking a deep breath, she stopped in the middle of the recycled rubber lane, her toes digging into the soles of her boots, trying to steady herself on the rust-coloured ground, before peering out from underneath the canopy of her umbrella. Her heartbeat slowed as she stared at the Sapien in front of her. He was bent over, picking up the goods that had fallen from his cart.

Genevieve didn't offer to help. Instead, she turned right down the forked lane. Glancing over her shoulder, she tried to establish whether anyone she knew could have seen her flinch at the noise of the cart. It was more than embarrassing; it was another sign of her weakening state. It was not like her to jump at loud noises. She had received years of training to push all her natural responses down and tuck them away with her secrets. She had to keep control.

To try and distract herself for the rest of the journey, she focused her eyes straight ahead and kept her features still, and reviewed the situation. The most obvious piece of information she was missing was *when* the Potiors had made their discovery. The Premier may have said that the Potiors were still deciding on their course of action, but that didn't ring true to Genevieve – the Potiors did not dither. It was also unlikely that they had known about the other base for more than a few months – the Potiors also did not delay.

Turning the corner into her lane, Genevieve had to stop abruptly to avoid bumping into two tall figures dressed entirely in black, one a man with grey hair and the other a woman in her forties with her hair scraped away from her face. Genevieve instantly knew what their clothing meant; no one else was allowed to wear an entire outfit of that colour. Without apologising, she tried to step around them.

Before she could take more than a single step, the man grabbed her shoulders. He peered closely at her, his gaze searching her features, no apology or permission required for this level of scrutiny, or his rough handling. The woman stood behind her colleague and ran her eyes over Genevieve.

Genevieve let her face relax and tried to block her thoughts; internally, she hummed to herself as she held the umbrella above them both. She knew he couldn't read her mind, which all of this was designed to suggest, but she was not foolish enough to underestimate their other capabilities. The Protection Department could read body language like no one else.

It felt like forever before the woman with the scraped-back hair spoke. 'Looking a little rushed there.'

Genevieve stared back at them impassively. 'I've just been at a conclave with the Premier. Check your screens and you will see its contents and my reasons for wanting to return to my home. It's level-seventeen clearance so we cannot discuss it in the street. I'm just a bit unsettled from this news.'

The woman pulled out her screen and took Genevieve's wrist roughly. There was no point in objecting. Like most residents of Adenine, she was detained around once a year for random checks. Genevieve was stopped less than most because of her level of self-control, but it still happened. This time was different, though – she had allowed a crack to appear for all to see. Pulling up Genevieve's sleeve, the woman scanned her tattoo and then tapped away at the screen before showing it to her colleague.

'Ah, yes. It is quite unsettling,' the grey-haired man said, after reading the contents of the screen. 'The Potiors will take care of it; you don't have to worry about that.'

Genevieve nodded, continuing to banish everything but mundane thoughts from her mind. In two minutes' time, she would be at home. She concentrated on what type of tea she would brew for herself. Perhaps peppermint ...

'You can go,' the grey-haired man said.

Genevieve nodded and, without looking back, crossed to her front door. She knew they would still be watching so she kept her pace slow, ignoring her mind's urging to get inside as quickly as possible. Resting her umbrella underneath the portico, she pulled out her key card, having readied it in her hand. Never had she been so thankful to be back home. As she held her hand against the reader, she was pleased to note that it wasn't shaking – she was back in control.

Kicking her heeled boots off in the hallway, she did not stop to take off her coat. Instead, she made her way straight to her bedroom. Passing Dina in the rear dining room, she gave her a curt nod and pretended not to hear the enquiry about her day.

Throwing her bag onto her bed, Genevieve shrugged off her coat and let it fall to the floor. She would pick it up later. Tugging at the zip at the back of her dress, she sighed loudly and made her way back through to the front of the house.

'Father, Father! Can you come and help me with this zip?'

With one strap hanging off her shoulder, she was clearly flustered at not being able to get the zip undone.

'Of course, my dear,' Mortimer said, placing his screen on the mirrored coffee table. 'Be there in one moment.'

Giving another tug at the back of her dress, she heard the rustle of Mortimer's salmon-pink silk jacket as he stood. Without waiting for him, she hurried back to her dressing room, her exasperation at his slow pace clear for anyone to see.

Standing in the mirrored room to the side of her dressing room, she waited while Mortimer caught up with her. Closing her eyes, she listened intently, straining to hear anything that shouldn't be present.

'There you are,' Mortimer said. 'Ah, I can see what the problem is. Wait a moment, I just need to get at it from the right angle.'

When Mortimer closed the door behind him, he was so near to her that she could smell his hair pomade.

He leant in even farther and whispered, 'Clear?'

'Clear,' she responded, double-checking the mirrors for any camera lenses reflecting multiple times in the mirrored room. There was an infinitude of Genevieves and Mortimers standing around them, the ones farther away shrinking in size as their reflections bounced backwards to mere dots.

Meeting one of his mirrored gazes, Genevieve continued speaking at the same low level. 'They've discovered another base.'

She watched Mortimer's reaction as he processed this, his usual joviality slipping from his features.

'Uracil?' Mortimer said in the quietest of tones.

'I can't be sure. They're saying it's populated with insurgents or refugees from another zone.'

She felt sorry for Mortimer; he only had seconds to process what she had known for hours.

'We have to work on the basis that it's Uracil for the moment,' he said quietly. 'Even if it isn't.'

Genevieve nodded and Mortimer spoke more loudly. 'Damn, it's got stuck in the cloth. I might have to cut it away.' He wasn't even looking at the zip.

'Whatever they've discovered,' Genevieve whispered, 'I think they're using it as an excuse for a quick invasion – round everyone up, no questions asked.'

'How long have we got?'

'I don't know; they didn't say when they discovered the base, or how they plan to deal with it.' Genevieve raised her voice. 'Try again, Father. I don't want to have to send this dress away for repairs.'

'From here, it would take them three weeks to get to Uracil if they know its exact location,' Mortimer responded. 'Possibly four if they only know roughly where it's situated.'

'We have to get a message out,' Genevieve said.

Mortimer nodded.

Genevieve took a deep breath, knowing that Mortimer would do anything to avoid what she was going to say next. 'This information is more important than our safety. We might need to break our cover.'

Mortimer blinked.

'For Uracil,' she said.

He took a moment before responding. 'For Uracil.'

CHAPTER 13

* *

Elise

'I am *not* wearing a wig,' Max said, folding his arms.

'Well, it's either that or you stay in camp,' Raynor replied. 'This mission's mine to lead, and I say you need to look less like you. Can't have a dead man walking around, or an unfamiliar Potior. If you want to enter Adenine, you need to look more like that Potior I saw a poster of last time I was in Adenine.'

Elise had arrived at the outskirts of Adenine the night before, following her journey with Maya. Max and Raynor had been bickering non-stop since then and she wondered if the argument had been going on for the entire three weeks she had been away.

'It's not even a man's wig!' Max said, shaking the long blonde locks.

'That doesn't matter to the Potiors,' Raynor said. 'Most of the men have hair down to their shoulders and beyond. It gives them that "flicks-hair-stare" that they use all the time.'

'I know the one,' Max said. 'They teach us that in school.'

'Do they really?' Septa asked, staring up at him.

'No, of course they don't!'

Raynor took the wig and shook it at him. 'Wig or camp? It's your choice.'

Max sighed. 'Wig ... but you can't laugh.'

Septa mimed sealing her mouth shut as Max placed the wig on his head and tucked his hair under the platinum-blonde locks.

Raynor looked up at him appraisingly. 'You look like a sassy giraffe.'

'*That's it!*' Max exploded, pulling the wig from his head.

Elise grinned. Since her time with Maya, she had rediscovered some of the energy that she had been missing, and she was trying her best to appreciate small joys, as Maya had advised. But she also felt focused on the change she could bring about, not what she had lost, and right now that meant getting the mission details finalised.

'Okay, that's enough,' she said, grabbing the wig from the ground. 'Max, grow up and put the wig on. Septa, don't laugh, or I'll glue it to your head. Raynor, what's the plan?'

Raynor gave an approving nod. 'Right. Me, Max and Septa are going to the museum. I need a Potior on this one to get us past the extra levels of security. The aim is to discover what's been hidden away in there for the past year and to find more information to confirm either Septa's Denisovan theory or Elise's new species theory. Elise, you're staying in camp. You're our safety net.'

Septa smirked.

Elise's features didn't alter, even though it stung that she had been chosen to remain. She wondered whether this was a subtle punishment for spending too long away from the group with Maya.

'Don't get too pleased with yourself, Septa,' Raynor said. 'I chose Elise to remain 'cause, apart from leggy Max here, she's our best runner.'

'When do you go in?' Elise asked.

'Tomorrow night.'

'Then, if you don't mind, I have something I need to do during the day tomorrow before you leave,' Elise said. 'Something I promised my dad I'd do next time I was here, and the perfect opportunity has just arrived.'

'That's fine,' Raynor said. 'But afterwards swing by Adenine's message collection point so we can deliver them to Uracil when we return. Someone's got to collect them so it might as well be you.'

Elise had only been to the docks three miles east of Adenine once before. To prepare, she had changed her clothing that morning and was dressed in worn trousers and a shirt that was missing a button. She had left her bag with all her provisions at the base camp and was only carrying a small satchel over her shoulder.

It was nearly 7 a.m. when she joined the queue of hundreds of men and women drafted in to offload the provisions shipped from Thymine, the production centre of Zone 3. Careful not to make eye contact with anyone, she kept her head down and stared at her worn shoes.

At 7 a.m. exactly, the foreman blew his whistle and unlocked the single door in the wire fence that laced its way around the docks. One by one, workers passed through the doorway, heading in the direction of the large sailboat that had anchored the evening before. Elise left her satchel inside the fenced area with the other workers' bags – the punishment for theft was severe and she didn't want to give the guards any reason to suspect her.

Still looking down, Elise followed the man in front of her onto the boat and picked up the first of many containers. She tried to ignore the members of the Protection Department who were overseeing the proceedings, but she was always aware of their presence out of the corner of her eye. She carried the box back off the boat and walked the two hundred metres to the start of the mechanical winch lines trailing their way up to Adenine. These retractable lines would hoist the goods the rest of the way. She rested for a moment before returning to the boat for the next load. While she worked, she thought about the man in Lab 412 and wondered whether Maya had arrived in Cytosine yet. Elise hoped that she had managed to find out more about him.

Three hours later, the foreman blew his whistle again for the fifteen-minute break. Elise's body was aching and she longed to rest, but she knew she only had limited time. She had spotted the woman she needed earlier in the day, but she'd looked the other way when they had passed each other.

When she went to fill her water container at the treated pump, the woman came up behind her. Elise moved over to make room for her. The woman stretched for a moment to straighten her back; the click of a bone in her shoulder could be heard slotting back into its rightful place. She quickly knotted her long brown hair onto the top of her head and, at that moment, Elise was able to slip the handwritten note into her pocket without anyone seeing.

Walking back to the docks, Elise drank deeply from the bottle. To keep her cover, she'd have to finish the shift; she couldn't risk leaving early. She could only hope that the woman would be able to pass her message to their operative in the Data Office. Perhaps then her dad could finally find out what had happened to his brother and sister over twenty years ago.

CHAPTER 14

Twenty-Two

As she approached the cabins where she'd been incarcerated for eighteen months, Twenty-Two felt ready. She'd spent several days preparing for this meeting with Lewis – she'd researched the Commidorants, spoken with everyone she could think of who knew about the events in Thymine and even learned a little about Uracil's legal system. She could do this.

The guard standing outside Lewis's cabin looked her up and down when she arrived. 'Are you here for a visit?'

She was slightly out of breath and tried to still her nerves. The guard was older than most she'd met, and Twenty-Two could see that he had started the slow descent into his middle years. His belt didn't quite sit square on his waist and it was looped under what she suspected was the beginnings of a stubborn belly.

At the sound of the guard's voice, the occupant of another cabin, on the opposite side of the pathway, started banging on the walls.

'Let me out, I say! It is an *injustice*.'

The guard barely glanced at the cabin. 'Shut up, Thiago! You say that every day and we still don't care!'

Twenty-Two held out her screen to the guard and waited patiently while he read the official notice from Michael that confirmed why she was there.

The guard read slowly and then shrugged. 'If Michael wants you in there, then that's what he'll get.'

Twenty-Two glanced over to the cabin with the shouting man. He was still hammering on the walls.

'Don't worry, that's not the cabin you're going into. That's Thiago, the old Head of Intelligence. No one's coming to hear his side of the story – not after what he did. He was the one that was working with Faye—' The guard stopped himself. 'Oh, well, I suppose you'll know all about that ...'

He turned to the cabin behind him and unlocked the door. 'Now, mind yourself with Lewis. I haven't had a squeak out of him but that don't mean he won't turn on you. If he does, then get out as fast as you can, or bang three times on the wall and I'll come in and get you.'

Twenty-Two nodded, happy to get away from the hammering Thiago and the awkwardness of the guard. She idly wondered what would happen if she could only manage to bang on the wall twice rather than the required three times.

She pushed open the door and waited a moment before stepping inside. Lewis was curled up on his side on the bed, the cover pulled over his head. Twenty-Two moved to the window and opened the curtains so some light could penetrate the room.

Lewis let out a groan. 'Have you brought more painkillers?'

He was still turned from her and she didn't want to answer him vocally, so she waited until he shuffled round and peered at her. His face was still bruised but the swelling had gone down.

'You're a Neanderthal.'

'Yes. You are a Sapien who does not want to live with the Medius.'

She signed slowly, hoping he knew enough to understand.

Lewis followed the movement of her hands and sat up. Still sitting on the bed, he shuffled towards the wall and leant back. He pulled the blanket around him, even though it wasn't that cold.

'I'm sorry, I don't understand. My sign language wasn't the best even two years ago. Perhaps you could write it out on your screen?'

Twenty-Two typed out the line 'Is it correct that you are a Sapien who doesn't want to live with the Medius?'

She held the screen up for him to read, but not close enough that he could snatch it from her.

'That's what I was,' he said. 'I don't know what I am now, apart from a prisoner.'

Twenty-Two sat down on a chair angled towards the opposite corner of the room and typed out her next message. 'I have come to take your statement from you, as your sentencing is in a week.'

Lewis nodded. She noticed his eyes were drawn to the door and she wondered if he was considering making a dash for it.

'There's a guard stationed right outside,' she typed. 'He's wearing those glowing gloves as well. I don't think you would make it very far.'

Lewis gave a half-smile. 'You're very bright, aren't you? I always thought the Neanderthals would be. I never thought it was right to lock you up like that.'

'Shall we start with you getting the job at the museum in Thymine?' Twenty-Two wrote.

Lewis ran through the events and reported them much as she had suspected he would. He did not deviate from the version she had heard from Georgina and Luca. He admitted all and regretted everything. He had been young, drawn in by the Commidorants' hyperbole about freedom for the Sapiens; but he now understood that it should be freedom for all. When asked, he put his change of heart down to a mellowing that had come with experience; but Twenty-Two suspected that it was more down to a clash of ideology.

Through it all, Twenty-Two recorded his statement through a device on her screen and acted as the unbiased observer she had promised to be, but she also watched him and considered the authenticity of his account from her own perspective. He was awash with self-pity, but she believed the truth of his regret.

'And what happened after you left the museum in Thymine?'

Here Lewis faltered. '... I went to the small camp the Commidorants set up a few years ago ... it's where people go when they can't stay in the bases. I spent a couple of years there, helping out, hoping to prove myself so I could be sent over to live in Destin.'

Lewis leant over and took a sip of water. Twenty-Two waited for him to continue.

'After a few months, I started to realise we had some pretty different ideas about what living separately from the Medius and Potiors meant. I thought once we had our own lands, we'd make something of ourselves; build universities, proper schools and hospitals. But most of them were happy to swill around in the mud with the pigs. They thought my ideas meant that I admired the Medius; they thought I should be happy with what the Sapiens already had.'

Lewis paused. 'I tried to change their minds, but they thought it was a joke. That I was a joke. They started sending me on more and more dangerous missions. That's when another comrade and I were captured by the Protection Department. I managed to talk my way out of it. She didn't. I returned to camp without her and they blamed me for leaving her behind. They said I should have killed her rather than leave her alive in the hands of the Protection Department. After giving me a beating that nearly finished me off, they upped sticks that night and moved camps. They took part of my ear with them.'

'What happened to the comrade?'

Lewis's eyes flashed. 'That's not important. I've told you everything about Georgina and Thymine and the Commidorants. That has nothing to do with any of this.'

'So, you are unwilling to answer any questions about what happened with the Protection Department?'

'It has nothing to do with it.'

Twenty-Two nodded. She had everything she needed.

That evening, Twenty-Two made her way to Luca's cabin. He let her in without speaking and gestured for her to sit down. She tried to breathe through her mouth – there was a decided aroma of cabbage and unwashed bed sheets. In the corner of the room a few canvases leant against the wall. Bright colours were smeared across their surfaces but they did not represent anything that Twenty-Two could recognise. Despite this, she was drawn to their vibrancy.

'Ignore those. They're nothing,' Luca signed, not quite meeting her eye. 'I've been trying to learn to paint this last year, but it hasn't been going well.'

'Why?' Twenty-Two signed.

When he frowned at her, she quickly continued, 'I mean why only in the last year? They are very good.'

'I got my genome sequenced by the people in Uracil who deal with genetic engineering. I wanted to work out what my parents had chosen for me. What had gone so wrong that they decided I wasn't worth it.'

'And what did it show?'

Luca rubbed the back of his neck. 'Turns out they can't tell me what didn't take, probably being tall or something obvious like that. But they said I had quite a few markers for heightened creativity. Perhaps that was one of my parents' selections.'

Twenty-Two scrunched her eyes. 'I like that idea. It's good that they had such a rounded view of what would benefit their child.'

Luca nodded and then glanced around the cabin. 'Sorry about the mess – haven't had much time to tidy the place up recently.'

Realising that he no longer wanted to discuss his parents, Twenty-Two sat down on the floor, as far away from the unmade bed as possible. 'If you want a girlfriend, I think you will need to clean your cabin.'

Luca snorted. 'You sound just like Seventeen.'

Twenty-Two scrunched her eyes. 'Do you miss her?'

'Seventeen? Every day. She would have loved being out here in Uracil. By now, she would have befriended half the residents and probably changed her name to Star-Sister or some other twaddle. She could be achingly honest, but she loved people. Loved their company.'

Twenty-Two watched as Luca seemed to disappear for a moment. He stared at the cabin wall.

'She should be here with us. With Bay,' he finally signed. The truth of the statement seemed to bring him back to the present. 'Why haven't you changed your name? Like Kit did? I always wanted to ask you that.'

Twenty-Two thought about it for a moment. It was the first time she had been asked about her name and she felt it needed some consideration. 'Because I have always been Twenty-Two and I don't really see the point in changing it.'

'But it's the name you were given by the Potiors. And it's not really a name; it's just a number. Just the Potiors showing again how little they care.' Luca looked up at Twenty-Two. 'I'm sorry ... I didn't mean to upset you.'

Twenty-Two rubbed her eye; she had never thought about it that way. 'It is strange growing up thinking that you are cared for by someone, but then realising you never were. I am sure at least that Dara loved me, in her own way. They may have given me a number, but she made it a name. Anyway, I like it. Much better than the number eighteen.'

Luca gave a half-smile. 'I wish I'd had a chance to meet Dara, she sounds like someone I might have got on with.'

Twenty-Two scrunched her eyes at Luca. 'Are we friends again?'

Luca snorted. 'We were nev—' He stopped and rubbed the back of his head. 'Let me try again. Yes, we are friends.'

Twenty-Two hugged her knees to her chest. 'This has been a very good day.'

'I'm glad you think so,' Luca signed as he stood up to make his bed. 'What happened with Lewis, then?'

'I think he's telling the truth about what happened – he's here because he was expelled from the group. I also think he regrets what he did to Georgina.'

'Well, that makes me feel a bit better. At least he's not here to spy on us. I still think he's an idiot, and that he should be expelled.'

'I pushed him, as you asked me to. About what happened when he left Thymine. He refused to tell me everything.'

'Good,' Luca signed, before straightening a pillow. 'That should show the Tri-Council he's being uncooperative, hiding things. Might add a year or so to his sentence.'

Twenty-Two considered this for a moment. 'I think he should be expelled too. What he did to Georgina was very wrong and I cannot see any benefit to him remaining in Uracil.'

Luca snorted. 'I think Seventeen would have liked you a lot.'

Two weeks passed for Twenty-Two in a whirl of work and early-morning training. On the last day of each week, she visited Jerome and enjoyed the quiet while caring for the animals. She had realised that she needed this time to reflect upon the week and prepare for the coming one. She also liked having something that hardly anyone in Uracil knew about. The key for her to be able to live alongside all these people was not to give them everything; what she held back from them was hers and hers alone.

She did not sleep well the night before Lewis's sentencing hearing. In the morning she hurried to the central clearing. When she arrived, the Tri-Council were already seated on the three tree stumps in the centre, and quite a crowd had gathered. She took her place on the sawdust-covered ground.

As was the case with her own hearing, nearly two years ago, everyone who wanted to speak had been given a chance to do so.

Georgina was the first to give evidence. In a clear manner, with no trace of the emotion she had displayed when she had first seen Lewis, she briefly told the court about her relationship with him, and what had happened in Thymine, before being asked to explain the effect his actions had on her.

Lewis's advocate, a tall woman with a sharp nose, listened to her carefully. 'And what if I were to tell you that he has changed. That he has seen the wrong of his ways. Surely everyone should be granted the opportunity for redemption?'

She looked around at the crowd for a reaction and some were nodding their heads.

Georgina spoke directly to the Tri-Council. 'There are some people in this world who are incapable of empathy, love or kindness. They are rare, but they exist, and they were wired that way from birth. Compassion will not change them. Everything I know about Lewis tells me he is one of those people. No lengthy sentence will reform him and for the safety of Uracil, he should be cast out, and his memories of this base removed.'

A few people clapped and were immediately halted by the look Raul threw at them.

Twenty-Two stared over at Lewis whose head was bent. She had heard of people who were missing their essential human traits – a disproportionate number of the Pre-Pandemic books she had read had been fixated on them – but she didn't know if Lewis was one of them. She trusted Georgina, but she'd felt the truth of his remorse.

When it came to Lewis's advocate presenting her own evidence, only Lewis had been called up. No one else was prepared to speak on his behalf.

'And what would you say you have learnt over the past few weeks?' she asked, her hands clasped behind her back.

Lewis raised his chin, his fading bruises drawing murmurs from the crowd. 'That there is another way to live outside the bases that doesn't require the separation of the species.' Lewis looked around at the crowds. 'I always knew that there was something deeply wrong with the way we are taught to live in the other four bases. I knew there was a problem, but I was wrong about the solution. Perhaps if I had found Uracil earlier ...'

'And if this were your last day of possessing your memories of Uracil, what would you want to tell its residents and leaders?'

'That I am sorry.' He stared directly at Georgina. 'If I had the power to reverse time I would. But I don't. So all I can do is prepare for atonement.' He turned his head to the Tri-Council. 'Please give me a chance to show my worth and reform, to become a useful member of Uracil and redeem myself. The memories I have of Uracil and the right way to live are part of me now. Please don't take them.'

Twenty-Two's gaze was drawn to an older woman in the crowd who was dabbing her eye with a hanky; sitting right next to her was another woman who was glaring at Lewis as if he had done those things to her rather than Georgina. Twenty-Two could not guess at the Tri-Council's ruling and looked to them eagerly as they whispered amongst themselves.

Flynn stood up. 'We have decided that we need longer for our deliberations and will require the evening to make our decision. Our judgment will be announced at ten a.m. tomorrow.'

Twenty-Two sighed inwardly, along with a few of the crowd who were more forthright in letting their frustration be heard. They would have to be patient.

A day later, Raul tapped his walking stick on the ground as he summarised the evidence and thoughts of the Tri-Council.

'It is, therefore, the decision of the Tri-Council that you serve a minimum of three years in captivity,' he concluded. 'The sentence is longer than we would normally hand down, as your given testimony proves that you have not been forthcoming about all the events that followed your time in Thymine. Reform cannot take place without recognition and acceptance. During your time of incarceration you will be monitored and we will try to rehabilitate you. If we see a decline in your behaviour, then we will reassess our decision.'

Lewis nodded before dropping his head but Twenty-Two caught a glimpse of joy beneath the surface. He did not look up again as he was led back to the cabin that was to be his home for the next three years. Georgina turned and left the platform, pulling away from Twenty-Two when she tried to comfort her.

After packing everything away for the evening, Twenty-Two approached Michael and handed him some water. He took the glass from her and then, seeming to remember his manners, thanked her.

'Why did you believe Lewis over Georgina?' Twenty-Two signed, knowing she would only have his attention for a few moments.

Michael stared at her wearily before responding. 'It's not about believing one person over the other; it's about listening to them both and deciding what is best in the long run.'

'Lewis is of no use to Uracil.'

Michael stood up and took his cushion over to the pile by the main seating area. 'Has anyone ever told you that you look at life in a very black-and-white way?'

Twenty-Two thought about this. She had come across the phrase before and knew its meaning. 'Perhaps I look at life that way because I can usually see people's true meaning. There is only room for grey if you are not sure of someone's intentions.'

'I don't think that grey just covers the truth behind someone's words. It also makes allowances for the capacity for change, not knowing what a person has been through and what drove them to act in the way that they did.'

'Maybe. But we all have a history. We cannot rely on it to make excuses for us.'

Michael leant back. 'The Tri-Council didn't take that view in your case.'

Twenty-Two picked up the empty plate beside him. She didn't like how this conversation was proceeding.

'Everyone deserves a second chance,' Michael continued.

'Are you sure that *everyone* does?' Twenty-Two signed with one hand.

'You were given a second chance.'

'Yes, but—'

'One rule for you and another for everyone else?'

Twenty-Two didn't really see the problem with this as she was certain that she was honest and always acted with integrity. But it was difficult to explain this to someone else – they would never know her thoughts and reasoning as intimately as she did.

'Why did I only receive eighteen months when Lewis was sentenced to three years?'

'Because you are you, and Lewis is Lewis. If Lewis had killed Faye in the same manner, we would have wiped his memories and expelled him. But your reasons for acting as you did were very different to Lewis's reasons. Frankly, he should have known better. You were just starting out in life.'

Twenty-Two didn't think that Lewis was that much older than her. She had lived for nearly fifteen years when she had made her decision. She would be deemed an adult in any of the other bases. Why did everyone believe that her life had only begun when they had first met her? It bordered on arrogance.

'I wanted to thank you, by the way,' Michael continued. 'For speaking with Lewis and taking down his account with little fuss. You helped us decide on the correct sentence.'

Twenty-Two nodded, and in a rare conciliatory moment, she forgave him for thinking that she was only two years old.

CHAPTER 15

Genevieve

Genevieve continued for the next few days as if everything were normal, just as Uracil had trained her to. Collect information, pass it on. Don't get caught, don't break cover.

Unless Uracil is under direct threat.

She had thought of little else since her meeting with the Premier. Was Uracil under direct threat? Was it even Uracil that had been discovered? Could it be one of the other settlements on the islands? Somewhere she didn't know about? How had the Potiors found out about it? The questions pounded in her brain, and were left unanswered. She knew there were other operatives in Adenine aside from Mortimer and herself, but she didn't know who they were or any details of their assignments. This was for everyone's safety. No risk of bringing down the entire base's network if you don't know who your co-conspirators are. Only Mortimer was in her safekeeping, and she in his.

Collect information, pass it on. Don't get caught, don't break cover. The familiar mantra was all she'd had to hold on to. She was so deeply embedded in her role that she sometimes forgot she had been anyone else – lived any other life. She felt ashamed when she caught herself genuinely enjoying one of the dinners she held. Even though most of her Medius acquaintances had been completely indoctrinated by the false histories they had been raised with, some of them were still good company – witty and alive. Among them she saw the occasional spark of independence; a flicker of indignation that the person struggled to conceal. They were the people she had to try the hardest with – to be most wary of. She could not afford for them to recognise the same glimmer of rebellion in her. It was why she'd sent Elijah away from her at the dinner party all those weeks ago.

Her role had started as a simple one, but the waters had muddied the longer she had spent wallowing in them. Through her work for the Potiors she was responsible, in a way, for helping them retain control. Her carefully constructed messages were sent to every household screen, and a fraction of hope was snuffed out with each one. Compliance was fostered, independence suffocated. Of course, the Tri-Council were fully aware of her work. In fact, they had encouraged her to ascend through the ranks: the higher she went, the more restricted information she had access to. At night, Genevieve often lay in bed by herself and wondered if that information was worth it. Did the good outweigh the bad? Sometimes, 'For Uracil' could not be distinguished from 'Three First'.

She only hoped that if her role was ever laid bare before all, she would be judged fairly. By refusing to relinquish her undercover role after the required seven years, she had sacrificed her chance at a normal life. She'd willingly given that up for her belief in a better future. She turned away from that stream of thought. After all, it was not only her own life she had sacrificed for her cause …

For now, all she could do was one final act to help Uracil. It had been for this reason, on the fourth day after the conclave, that she'd slipped out of the house once more, and taken the unprecedented risk of visiting the message drop-off point. She rarely sent messages outside of Uracil, and then only in the most controlled of situations. An unprecedented risk for unprecedented circumstances.

The pathways had swelled with people trying to return to their homes after work, and she'd immersed herself in the crowds, for once not using her height and status to push ahead and get to her destination as quickly as possible. Instead, she'd drifted alongside them through the Medius district, not drawing a second glance and avoiding any actions that would place her in anyone's memories.

A screech of alarm from another resident had caught her attention. She'd glanced over to the bridge on the pathway across from her to see a man had missed his footing and was dangling over the side. Several Sapiens had stopped to help pull him back, the urgency in their approach suggesting that they were saving him from whirling rapids, rather than the early summer puddle below.

The things they have been taught to believe ...

'Ow!' Genevieve exclaimed, her head whipping round to the person who had stood on her toe.

A short woman stared up at her. 'I'm very sorry,' the woman stuttered. 'I was looking over there. It was my fault, I'm sure.'

'It was,' Genevieve said sternly. 'Mind yourself in the future.'

The woman nodded and scuttled around her. Shaken, Genevieve had continued to the wooden arched bridge up ahead that linked the Sapien and Medius districts to the east side of the base. In that moment she'd hated herself for the role she played. She knew she was just as much at fault for bumping into that woman, but she could never apologise to a Sapien in public. That sort of thing would stick in someone's memory.

She'd stopped when she reached the gentle arch of the bridge. Pulling out her screen, she'd responded to a blithe message from Mortimer before dropping the screen and cursing. She'd leant down to pick it up with her right hand, and tucked a rolled-up note into a small hole on the west-facing post of the timber bridge with her left.

After standing and finishing her message, she'd closed the screen and carried on over the bridge, her footsteps echoing off the wood alongside all the others. When she'd descended onto the soft rubber pathway that would lead her into the Sapien districts, she'd stopped again and rolled her eyes at a new message from Mortimer, telling her that she should hurry back soon from her evening walk as it was looking like rain. He had timed the sending of the planned messages to perfection – he never let her down.

As she'd crossed back over the same bridge to return home, she'd almost tripped over a scruffily dressed Sapien woman with short brown hair who was bent down, tying her shoelace – a worker at the recycling centre or docks by the looks of her worn trousers. The Sapien's hand had flicked over to the hole in the wooden post and Genevieve noticed that her thumb was oddly bent. Casting her gaze ahead, Genevieve gave her a wide berth; it was never a good idea for an undercover agent to linger in the proximity of Uracil's Infiltration unit.

CHAPTER 16

Elise

Elise noticed the tall woman with the perfectly smooth skin as soon as she approached the bridge to pick up the messages for Uracil. Another high-end Medius surveying her world in a long coat that probably cost more than a Sapien earned in a month. She scowled at the thought. But when the woman dropped her screen by the edge of the bridge, a suspicion began to form. Could she be an agent for Uracil? If so, Elise was impressed – she hadn't considered that an agent might reach so high up the food chain.

When Elise reached the bridge she bent to tie her shoelace and as she did so, the tall Medius woman nearly bumped into her. Elise did not react and instead balled herself up smaller to prevent any sort of conflict if her suspicions were wrong. Knowing she had spent a touch too long tying her lace, Elise quickly pulled three notes from the knot of wood before balling them in her hand. Glancing upwards, all Elise could see of the woman was a swish of her long coat as she disappeared into the crowds. She probably would never know if they were on the same side ... Lowering her head, Elise joined the crowds once more before circling back to base camp.

Raynor lifted her head on her return. 'How did your day at the docks go?'

'Fine,' Elise responded, slinging her satchel to the floor. She hadn't told them the reason for her journey, but she'd had to let them know where she would be. 'Are you all ready for tonight?'

Raynor glanced over at Max's slumbering figure sprawled out under one of the trees.

'They prepare in their own ways,' she said, shrugging.

'Where's Septa?'

'She's gone to practise with her throwing knives.' Raynor pointed to the south of the camp.

'Oh,' Elise said, suddenly remembering. 'I picked up the messages from Adenine.'

She handed them over and then walked across to one of the wider trees and began changing back into her normal travelling clothes, before returning to sit by Raynor.

'Pfff . . .' Raynor snorted while reading the second note. 'No chance of that happening . . .'

Elise pulled out her sling – it was beginning to unravel at the end and she was keen to make it last for as long as possible; the treated leather for the pouch that held the stones required a level of work she did not have time for. She had recently made a trade for some throwing knives, but they were more deadly and she was reluctant to begin practising with them. She didn't think she was ready to use something that could so easily kill.

Raynor sat bolt upright. Elise glanced over; all the colour had drained from Raynor's face.

The older woman scrambled to her feet. 'Max! Get over here now! I'm going to find Septa; I know where she practises.'

Max sat up and was by their side in three seconds. Raynor pushed the note into his hand and he began to read it as Raynor sprinted out of the clearing.

Elise stood up and watched her retreating figure. 'What's happened? What does the message say?'

Max's mouth opened and closed a few times before he could speak. 'The Potiors know about another base. But the operative cannot be certain it is Uracil.'

Elise froze; the air left her lungs and she struggled to take a breath. What if it was Uracil? Her brother was there, her parents, all her friends ...

'We have to go; we have to get there and warn them,' Elise said, pulling her bag out from under the bush where she had hidden it. 'I'm leaving right now; I'll see you all back at Uracil.'

Max raised his head. 'Wait. We have to make this decision together. We *have* to wait for the others.'

Elise stared at him. 'You want to delay telling Uracil? We have to warn them!'

'Of course. But we can't go running off without telling Raynor and Septa what we are doing.'

'I'm leaving.'

Max grabbed her arm. 'Wait just ten minutes and they'll be here. We work better together.' He paused and let go of her arm. 'For Uracil.'

Elise took a deep breath. 'For Uracil ...' she mumbled.

The next ten minutes were the longest of Elise's life. She paced in circles around her backpack, trying to rationalise the news. The Potiors finding out about another base didn't mean the worst had already happened. It could be somewhere else.

She'd only just found out about Destin – it could be their fate that was about to be changed. From what she had seen, their security was lax and their membership disloyal, so it would make more sense if they'd been discovered. And if it *was* Uracil, perhaps the Potiors were aware of its existence but didn't know where it was. They could even know its location and have no immediate plans to go there. There was still hope. She clung to this as she strained to hear the others approach.

A few minutes later, Septa ran into the clearing, followed by Raynor, who was dripping with sweat and shaking. She sank on to the ground and lay back on the forest floor, her legs and arms splayed out as far from her body as they could manage.

'We need to leave immediately,' Elise said. 'We have to warn them.'

'A…greed,' Raynor said, still gasping for mouthfuls of air.

'We'll have to leave you behind, Raynor,' Elise said, too worried about her family to try and soften the blow.

'No,' Max said. 'We have to stick together. We're a unit.'

Elise raised her head to meet his gaze, nearly two feet above where her own ended. 'You want to delay us again?'

'Max does seem a little hesitant to get going,' Septa said, stooping over to pick up her bag. 'Leopards can't change their—'

'What you saying?' Raynor said, still lying on the ground. 'That Max is intentionally trying to delay us telling Uracil?'

'Well, he hasn't left yet, has he?' Elise said quietly.

'You watch yourself. Both of you,' Raynor said, sitting up and jabbing her finger at Septa and then Elise. 'That man's saved my life multiple times and I won't hear anything against him. It's not his fault he was born a Potior. Just as it's not

Septa's fault that she was abandoned by her parents because her Medius traits didn't take. Or Elise's fault that she was born in the arse-end of Thymine, where everyone thinks lobbing sticks at a bowl makes for a fun night's entertainment. We all have the option to change.'

'Raynor, shush!' Septa exclaimed. 'I'd had too much to drink the night I told you that. It's private.'

Raynor eyed Septa. 'Well, Max can't hide where he came from, so it's only fair that he knows about both of you.'

Septa kicked at some leaves which flew up in the air before gently drifting back down again. 'If we hadn't been looking out for the other bases, none of this would have happened. We should never have stopped focusing on Uracil.'

'It has nothing to do with that,' Elise said.

'You're just saying that because you've got your head halfway up Maya's—'

'Watch where you're going bringing Maya into this,' Max said. 'She gave me a chance when no one else w—'

'There's a reason no one else would give you a chance,' Septa interjected, her voice rising to match Max's.

Elise took a step back and watched the three of them gesture furiously at each other, their voices growing louder by the minute. This was madness. She took out her sling, placed a rock in the holder and circled it above her head. When she released the stone, the loud crack boomed across the forest and the birds could be heard taking flight in every direction. Everyone fell silent.

'Everybody just shut up. We have to leave now,' she said, as calmly as she could manage. 'We all have people there we love. Let's go.'

*

Max was practically carrying Raynor by the end of the second week of their journey back to Uracil. They had taken the risk of walking in the evening during the full and crescent moon as well as during the lighter hours. They only stopped when they needed to eat and sleep each night. But, as the days ticked by, the moon retreated to just a sliver in the night sky and they were forced to stop earlier each evening. The days were shortening as winter set in and they found themselves with more darkened hours than light.

As Elise packed her belongings one early morning, she calculated that they were about a five-day walk from Uracil. Shrugging her backpack on, she tried to wait patiently as the others gathered up their belongings. *It might not even be Uracil. The Potiors might have found out about another settlement. Please let it have been Destin.*

Elise stopped herself as she thought of the small children she had seen there.

Septa shoved her bowl and cup into her bag and then looked around at the others. 'Are we ready?'

An uneasy truce had settled among the group, made easier by the physical exertion required of them each day. They were each absorbed in their own thoughts.

'I think so,' Elise responded, looking up at the sky.

There was an ominous-looking cloud forming from the east. If a thunderstorm was on its way, they would have to stop and take shelter. They couldn't risk getting soaked and becoming ill, delaying their arrival even further.

'I'm set,' Raynor said, bending to pick up her bag. She made a low groaning noise as she straightened.

'I'll take that,' Max said, reaching for her bag.

Holding the bag away from him, Raynor gave a half-smile. 'Sometimes, I wish you'd known me when I was younger, Max. Quick as a fox, I was. And strong as an ox.'

'You're still as stubborn as one,' Max said, pulling the bag from her hands and slinging it over his shoulder.

Elise led the way and set the pace for the day. For the entire journey she had been searching for tracks that could have been caused by an advancing army, but nothing looked out of place. The countryside was untainted by mass human movement and she was beginning to allow herself an inkling of hope. Perhaps they would make it in time. Perhaps it had all been a misunderstanding.

The group had been walking in silence for two hours when Elise's attention was drawn by a distant humming. She looked around but couldn't see anything untoward. The noise seemed to be coming from behind them and she wondered if it was the impending storm. She caught Max's eye and he shrugged.

'I heard it a couple of minutes ago,' he said. 'I don't know what it is either.'

The noise grew louder, and the four of them stopped and looked around. Nothing.

Elise felt uneasy; she didn't like not having full grasp of a situation. Spotting a small copse to the right, she started to walk towards it. 'We should take cover.'

Raynor nodded and the group headed towards the bunched trees. The heavy clouds were closer now. As they walked, Elise pulled out a light raincoat from her backpack.

The humming grew even louder, impossible to ignore. Elise's heart began to thump in her chest. She glanced at the others for reassurance, but their faces reflected her confusion.

In silent agreement, they began to run. They were too exposed.

Max reached the trees first. When he turned to face them, his expression changed from confusion to terror. He shouted to them, but his words were lost beneath the droning noise from above. His gaze was locked onto the sky. Elise put her head down and ran faster.

She skidded to a halt next to Max and spun around, desperate to know what he was staring at. The noise was deafening now, and she followed his gaze up to the sky. Flipping open the lid of the camera box with one hand, she gestured for it to record what was happening above.

She had never seen anything like it. An enormous creature with a pointed nose was passing through the sky; it appeared to be bigger than even the boat she had helped take deliveries from. Two more were flying above it, much higher up. Though they were travelling at considerable speed, their dark-grey wings did not flap. Instead, they headed with purpose in one direction, never craning their necks to see below them or to the sides.

'What in the name of the stars are *those*?' Septa panted as she slid to a stop next to Max.

Elise looked for Raynor and realised she was still fifty feet away. 'Raynor, run!' she shouted.

But her words were lost in the noise. It grew even louder and Elise had to cover her ears with her hands. Her mouth twisted in a scream. Still forty feet out, Raynor stumbled and tripped, landing heavily on the ground.

Before Elise could react, Max broke cover and ran to her. He scooped her up and threw her over his shoulder. In one seamless movement, he spun and began to run back towards Elise. As he ran, tiny explosions sparked around his feet, shooting clumps of earth into the air. Elise tried to make sense of it but couldn't. It looked a little like heavy rain falling onto the surface of a lake, but what could do that to earth?

With a soundless scream, Max jerked and fell, launching Raynor towards them. Elise leapt out of the way and Raynor spun in the air, tucking herself into a ball before landing on her side. She groaned but managed to roll onto her back, staring up at the sky.

Without thinking, Elise scrambled out to Max and began dragging him towards the trees.

'*Septa, help me!*' she screamed.

But Septa was frozen, staring upwards as the winged shapes passed overhead.

Elise looked down at Max. Blood was pouring from his leg, but he was still conscious.

'You have to stand,' she said.

Gritting his teeth, he nodded as she bent to support him. Pulling himself to his feet, he dragged his leg the last few steps into the safety of the trees before collapsing onto the ground.

Elise knelt next to him and tried to ignore the noise from above. Blood was spreading rapidly from Max's thigh, staining the cloth of his trousers, but she didn't think his artery had been sliced; he would be unconscious by now if it had.

'I need to cut your trousers open,' she said.

He nodded, his face now ash-white.

Using one of her push knives, she nicked his trouser leg and ripped until the wound was exposed. Cutting away another section of cloth, she used it to try and stem the blood.

Max screamed.

Elise flinched and pulled her hands away.

'There's something in there,' he said, eyes wide.

He suddenly looked very young and Elise saw a vulnerability in him that she had never been allowed to witness before.

Taking out her medical kit, she glanced over at Raynor and Septa. Raynor had rolled onto her side and Septa was still staring up at the sky, her face slack.

Maya had taught her basic field medicine but Elise had never needed to use it before. Sterilising the tweezers, she pulled on the plastic gloves she always carried in her medical kit.

She looked back to Max. 'Try not to scream; we don't know if there's more of them.'

Max nodded grimly and Raynor rolled over to him and offered her hand. 'Don't break my bones if you can help it, Maxi-Boy.'

He took her hand and looked away.

Elise took a breath and then pulled apart the laceration. Max growled and her stomach rolled but she couldn't afford to become squeamish. Peering into the cut, she couldn't see anything – there was too much blood – so she tentatively stuck her little finger into the opening and felt around. Max's growl got higher in pitch as she pushed her finger farther in. There. Something hard. Pulling out her finger, she stretched the cut and inserted the tweezers.

Max screamed and Raynor clamped her hand over his mouth.

Elise felt the tweezers catch muscle as she pushed them deeper into the cut. When she managed to locate the alien object, she pulled at it, ignoring Max's cries. It slowly slid upwards and blood pooled out after it. Applying pressure to Max's wound with one hand, she inspected what she had pulled out, placing it on her knee.

'It's metal,' she said. 'A small, metal … ball, I suppose.'

Raynor held her hand out for it and rolled it around her palm.

Max pushed down on the wedge of cloth stemming the wound and Elise stood and went over to Septa.

She placed her hand on Septa's arm. 'We need your help.'

As if coming around from a dream, Septa blinked at Elise and her eyes began to slowly focus. 'What was that?'

'Some sort of giant bird,' Elise said. 'I don't know; it didn't move like any animal I've seen before. Come and help me stitch Max up.'

Septa nodded and grabbed her own medical kit from her backpack.

'It … bit me?' Max said as he stared up at the sky.

The noise had receded, its cause now mere specks on the distant horizon.

Septa's hand shook as she took out the needle from her medical kit.

Max looked at her. 'I think Elise had better stitch me up.'

Septa nodded and took a step back as Elise bent down next to Max.

'Were they animals the Potiors made?' Septa asked, staring up at the sky again. 'Like the ones in Cytosine?'

'The Potiors didn't make those,' Raynor said. 'We have the Sapiens to thank for them.'

Elise stopped trying to thread the needle and stared at Raynor.

'Don't none of you know your Pre-Pandemic history? Didn't you listen in your classes?' Raynor said as she rolled the metal ball in her other hand. 'They weren't birds.'

'Then what were they?' Elise asked, as she threaded the needle to stitch Max's wound.

Raynor stood up. 'Airplanes. And they're heading to Uracil.'

CHAPTER 17

. . . .

Twenty-Two

Twenty-Two woke with some excitement at the prospect of another Saturday spent training. Kit had taken an interest in her new regime and joined her in the northern glade most weekends so they could spar with each other. Ezra was still trying to learn to shoot stones from the sling but, if Twenty-Two was honest with herself, he didn't seem to be making much progress. Nathan was very patient with Ezra, but she would've expected that he could at least get the stone within three feet of where he was aiming for by now.

When Kit arrived at the edge of the forest that morning, they began to practise together. Aiden watched from the side, making suggestions and occasionally stopping them to correct their stances. They were both careful to make sure their blows did not connect, but the odd one still slipped through.

They first went through a succession of practised moves until Aiden indicated to them that they should begin to improvise. Kit punched lower this time, towards her abdomen. Twenty-Two moved her arm in front of her to protect herself, but she wasn't quick enough and winced as his fist glanced off her forearm. Kit took a step away and apologised, before suggesting that they stop for a moment and rest.

Twenty-Two consoled herself that Kit had to be careful to avoid her blows just as much as she had to avoid his. She was not quite as powerfully built as Kit, but she was far stronger than most Sapiens and Medius. Aiden had been showing them how to knock a person out with one blow to the head – the trick was to carry the weight of your body behind it. Twenty-Two was certain that she had the strength to do this, but she knew she would probably never have the chance to practise. It was a bit too much to ask Kit if he would let her knock him out.

While they rested, Twenty-Two asked Kit about Raul and his need for a walking stick. The fact that he had changed so much while she was serving her sentence had been bothering her.

'I thought the Medius ones did not age,' she signed.

'The Medius ones age, just as the Potiors do,' Kit responded. 'They may look youthful on the surface, but inside they are still ageing. Some of them have genetic enhancements to delay the process, but that is very rare. All Potiors have them, but it costs so many tickets that only the very wealthy Medius can afford it.'

'Did Raul have those enhancements?'

'I do not know. But I know he does not have access to the healthcare the other Medius do, or Dermadew. A year after you last saw him, he had a fall and broke his hip. After that, he seemed to deteriorate overnight.'

'They both appear so much older,' Twenty-Two signed, as she watched Nathan duck to avoid a stray stone from Ezra's sling.

'It was a blow to them both, what happened with Faye,' Kit signed. 'And the fact that they missed the changes in her, that they handed so much power to her without further thought – they could not forgive—'

Kit dropped his hands and stared into the woods. Twenty-Two read his body language – something was wrong. She turned to see what he was looking at, but nothing seemed out of place.

Then a low rumble of voices began to push through the woods towards them. It reminded her of the first time she had entered Uracil, when she could hear people approaching to stare at her but couldn't yet see them.

She tried to remain calm. She reminded herself that she hadn't made any choices recently that Uracil would object to, so it was highly unlikely that the voices were coming for her.

I have done nothing wrong.

Aiden stood and turned towards the woods. He gestured for Nathan to stand next to him.

The voices increased in volume and cries began to float out from Uracil. It sounded like a small group of people were moving towards them. Twenty-Two looked to Kit to ask what was going on, but he was staring up at the sky.

A thin young man was the first to appear, his feet almost slipping beneath him in his haste. The five of them stared as he hurtled in their direction. Twenty-Two didn't know whether to run to help him or to prepare to defend herself.

'They're coming!' he cried out, still racing across the clearing.

'Who? Who's coming?' Aiden shouted. He stepped towards the man, who pelted past them, gasping, 'In the sky! Just get away! Get away from Uracil!'

Twenty-Two took a few steps towards Uracil. In a moment, she felt Kit by her side.

'No, take Nathan and run,' Aiden signed with one hand, before grabbing her arm. 'Take him far from here and look after him until I get back to you. I have to go back for Sofi.'

'No! I'm coming with you to find Mum,' Nathan signed, pulling himself up and meeting his dad's eye.

'You bloody well aren't,' Aiden signed. The voices were getting closer now. 'She'd kill the both of us if anything happened to you. Go with Kit, Ezra and Twenty-Two. Meet me at the tree we sat under when we went for that walk a couple of weeks ago. That should be far enough.'

Nathan looked like he was going to object but conceded when he saw the resolution on his dad's face. 'You'll find her and come straight back?'

'Promise. And listen to what these three tell you to do. You may be tall, but you're not grown yet,' Aiden signed.

He clasped Nathan's shoulder before turning and sprinting back towards Uracil.

Twenty-Two felt sick. What about her other friends still in Uracil? Turning, she looked to Ezra, who was bent over double.

'Just breathe, just breathe,' Ezra mumbled to himself.

She laid her hand on his back, and he glanced up at her.

'Come with me to the tree and wait with Nathan,' she signed. 'You can look after him, can't you?'

Ezra nodded; his face was paler than she'd ever seen it before.

'Then Kit and I will come back for the others,' Twenty-Two signed.

She turned to Kit, who was staring up at the sky again. She knew he would not leave his friends behind either.

More people had broken from the treeline and were streaming past them. The noise was getting louder and the chaos around her was beginning to feel overwhelming. Panic was etched across the faces of the people leaving Uracil, but they did not stop to explain what was happening. Some were running, clasping small children to them. Others were propping up older residents. There were no guards. No officials.

Nathan was still staring at the point where his dad had entered the forest when Kit grabbed hold of his hand.

'We have to go,' he signed with one hand.

The four of them turned and began to run towards the edge of the island. Holding Ezra's hand and pulling him along beside her, Twenty-Two thanked the stars that they were at this end of the island – up ahead was the submerged walkway to the mainland. She concentrated on her breathing as she ran, trying to push down the panic.

It will be fine, this is just a misunderstanding. There will be a reasonable explanation.

They had only been running for a few minutes when she glanced behind her. She thought she could hear a low humming noise approaching in the sky.

Turning away from it, she carried on, tugging at Ezra's hand as she pelted towards the walkway hidden beneath the lake. Kit was slightly ahead of her, holding on to Nathan so they didn't become separated.

The droning noise was clearer now. Fear of the unknown clawed at Twenty-Two. When her bare feet met the sand by the edge of the lake, she ran around an older woman. Pulling Ezra roughly onto the walkway, she took a second to balance herself.

A sob caught in her throat, then she walked as quickly as she dared across the lake. She couldn't run on the surface of the bridge – it was too slippery, and the water was icy cold beneath, the lake resolutely ignoring the changing of the seasons.

Twenty-Two gasped as a huge flock of birds passed overhead, flying away from the noise. Their panicked calls echoed across the water and she knew then that her instincts had been right – something was seriously wrong. She trusted the reaction of the animals implicitly.

They were halfway across the walkway when Nathan stumbled. Kit grabbed hold of him with both hands and stopped him from falling. Nathan looked back at Twenty-Two for just a moment and she could see the tears streaming from his eyes.

They carried on pushing ahead, water splashing up their legs, eyes straight ahead.

Almost there. Fifty more steps at most.

Sweat poured down her face from the exertion of keeping both herself and Ezra upright. The person behind Twenty-Two had caught up with them, and, unable to pass her on the narrow walkway, was jabbing her in the back, urging her to hurry up. The jabbing grew more forceful and Twenty-Two turned to glare at him.

As she did, her eyes flicked up to the sky. What she saw defied belief. Something enormous was flying towards Uracil. Something far too big to have been made by the stars.

An explosion rang out.

Startled by the overwhelming noise, Twenty-Two flinched and her leg slipped off the side of the walkway. With nothing to hold on to, she plummeted under the surface of the lake, pulling Ezra with her.

CHAPTER 18

Genevieve

The house was quiet apart from the hourly chimes of the hall-way clock. Unable to discuss their fears for Uracil, Genevieve and Mortimer had lapsed into silence more often than not, unwilling to arouse suspicion in the servants. They had devoted both their lives to building their cover, integrating themselves into the complex social network that was the upper echelons of the Medius who called Adenine their home. Consequently, they could not cast it off without considering every alternative first.

Years ago, when they had left Uracil, an elaborate backstory had been created, memorised and never deviated from. Mortimer, a social climber from Cytosine, had secured a transfer to the Shipping Department and had decided to make Adenine his home, bringing his only daughter with him. They had begun in the lower ranks of Medius society, so heavily populated that two new members were barely registered by their peers. How could the gossips keep tabs on thousands? Genevieve had her own carefully crafted story of a daughter who had taken refuge away from the world in the home of her father after having been abandoned by her partner. What had happened after had *not* been planned, but it had strengthened the sadness of her position; the unexpected intertwining of truth with fiction.

Of course, Mortimer was not really her father and, despite how deep their stories went, he had never felt like one to her. He was, however, her best friend, and she his. He was the one person in her life who she could reveal her true self to, even if only for brief moments. It was essential to both their wellbeings that there be one other person who knew where the lies ended and the truth began. A Companion of sorts, in this filtered mesh of a life.

When Genevieve glanced over at Mortimer sitting by the fire that evening, she could see worry had set in and would remain with him for the rest of the day. He had been smiling at her while bemoaning the lack of petunias in the Emporium, but she could tell that his thoughts were elsewhere. He'd pulled out the locket he had recently begun wearing underneath his shirt and began idly twisting it. Genevieve heard the tiniest of rattles inside it as he pulled the locket around. She raised an eyebrow towards him in enquiry.

He blinked. 'An insurance policy, my dear.'

Genevieve was about to reply when Dina opened the door, carrying a tray laden with sandwiches, delicate cakes and freshly brewed ginger and honey tea.

'Excuse me for interrupting, but I thought you might need something to keep you going until dinner,' Dina said, bringing the tray over to the squat coffee table that sat between them.

Mortimer leant forwards to clear the table for her as he eyed the spread. 'What a good idea! Just what I needed on an afternoon as drab as this one. The first days of winter are certainly upon us once again.'

Genevieve watched Mortimer as his eyes eagerly followed the tray. Not for the first time, she wondered how he would fare if he returned to life in Uracil. He'd become so accustomed to the comforts of their present lives, she could not imagine him returning to a tree house, or sitting at a communal table, eating what was presented to him, without choice or selection. Perhaps he was too old for compromise or change. Genevieve knew that she would be in a similar position in the years to come.

Dina placed the tray on the coffee table and laid starched napkins on each of their laps. Without asking, she handed out plates and used tongs to transfer a selection of sandwiches to the white porcelain. She nodded at the appreciative noises Mortimer was making and turned to the fire to add three more logs to it. They caught quickly and heat pushed its way into the room. Genevieve felt herself snuggle farther down into the soft hold of her armchair. Her lids felt heavy and she closed her eyes for a moment.

When the door closed and they were alone once again, Genevieve sat bolt upright and placed her finger against her lips. Mortimer gave a nod as Genevieve pushed herself up from her chair and moved silently to the door, depositing her plate on the table. There were no sounds coming from the corridor. She waited five minutes before opening the door, just wide enough so she could slip out.

She walked quietly to the end of the house, checking each room was empty before entering it. When she reached her bedroom, she paused outside for a moment. Pushing open the door, she was surprised to see that it too was empty. Her eyes darted to her dressing room; the door was slightly ajar. Genevieve crossed to it in four steps, her tread as light as she could make it. She pushed at the dressing room door and watched as Dina pulled out another drawer, feeling the top and sides of it with her palm.

Genevieve had Dina's other arm up and behind her back before she could turn around.

'I cannot think of any reasonable explanation,' Genevieve said, her mouth pressed against Dina's ear. 'But if you want to try to give one, please do.'

Dina craned her neck, trying to meet Genevieve's eyes, but she was prevented by the angle of the hold; it clearly hurt her too much. 'Let go of me. You've no right!'

'I have every right while you're in my house. I should call the Protection Department and have you expelled from the base. Snooping around a Medius's bedroom is a very serious offence. Is it secrets you crave? Want to know what the Potiors have planned? Are the Reparations you live under not clear enough for you?'

Dina tried to crane her head around again, but Genevieve's grip was too strong for her, and she sagged slightly against the dresser. 'I wasn't doing anything wrong. I was just organising the drawers for you.'

Genevieve hesitated. The door opened again, and Mortimer entered the dressing room, softly closing the door behind him.

'Well, well. What do we have here?'

'She had her hand in my drawers, so to speak.'

'And what does she have to say for herself about the matter?'

Genevieve smiled. '"Let go of me. I wasn't doing anything wrong . . ." The usual.'

She loosened her grip and allowed Dina to turn and face them.

Dina pulled her sleeve down and stood as tall as she could, which, at just over five feet, was not very impressive compared to the statuesque figures of Genevieve and Mortimer. Even though Mortimer's spine had begun to curve with age, he was still over a foot taller than her.

'Please. I'll leave today,' Dina said, her eyes darting between the two of them.

'Not until you tell us what you were up to, my dear,' Mortimer said, folding his hands in front of him.

'My life's not worth it. I ain't saying nothing.'

Genevieve had Dina back against the dressing table in an instant, her arm pressed even higher up behind her back. She could feel the bone resisting but Genevieve knew she had the strength to break it if she wished. For a moment, she tested its snapping point, absorbed in the frailty of the human body. Everything broke, under the right force.

'*Ahh—*'

Dina's cry was cut off as Genevieve placed her other hand over Dina's mouth. She loosened her grip on Dina's arm. 'We'll ask again. What were you looking for in my room?'

Dina made a muffled cry.

'If you tell us, we won't report you. We just want to know for ourselves.'

Dina quietened and Genevieve began to lose her patience. She pushed up on the arm. 'Who do you work for? Is it another Medius family?'

Dina shook her head. The arm went higher, and Genevieve studied the droplets of sweat forming along Dina's hairline.

'You're not one of those misguided Sapiens, are you? The ones that believe they should live separately to the Medius? Did you hope to find something here you could bargain with and secure your own lands?'

Genevieve moved her hand away from Dina's mouth so she could answer.

Dina dropped her head, her breath now coming in small pants. 'Them? *Never.*'

Genevieve's stomach dropped. Her grip tightened before she asked the next question. 'Were you placed here by the Potiors?'

Dina began to cry, tears streaming down her face. 'They told me I had to come and watch you. Now that you're Assistant Director. And after what happened, back in Thymine.'

Genevieve let go of Dina and pulled her roughly around so they were facing each other.

'Please, please, don't tell them that you caught me,' Dina babbled. 'I need the extra tickets.' She sobbed and buckled to the ground. Genevieve let her fall. 'Stars knows what they'll do to my family if they realise I've failed.'

Mortimer looked down at the crumpled figure on the ground. Genevieve stared at him, wondering what he was thinking; she would've given anything to be able to speak openly for once.

'Well, you better get back to it,' Mortimer said, after what felt like several minutes. 'We wouldn't want to upset the equilibrium. If the Potiors feel that we should be watched, then we need to be watched.'

Dina jerked her head upwards. 'And you won't tell them?'

Genevieve glanced over at Mortimer before speaking. 'Who are we to question the Potiors' decisions?'

She held out her hand to help the woman up. Dina reluctantly grasped Genevieve's hand with her good arm, cradling the other one against her.

'I'll go and start on dinner then,' Dina said, her eyes darting between the two of them.

'If you would,' Mortimer said. 'Could you make one of those crab soufflés that you do so well? I've been thinking about them all week.'

'Yes, I can do that.'

'Yes ... what?' Mortimer said, eyeing her.

Dina paused. 'Yes ... sir. I can do that.'

'Splendid! My stomach is rumbling with anticipation just thinking about it.'

Mortimer gave an appreciative pat to his belly, which was straining against the buttons of his waistcoat. He then moved aside to let Dina pass. Still only using one arm, she opened the door and closed it behind her. She didn't look round as she left.

Mortimer glanced over at Genevieve. No words were needed. The Potiors were spying on them. They could never speak openly to one another again.

CHAPTER 19

Elise

Elise felt her legs go from under her as she stared over what remained of Uracil. They were too late.

They had barely stopped for the five days since encountering the airplanes. Each of them had pushed through the pain of constant walking and near-sleepless nights. They had known that they were days behind, but had carried on in the hope that their worst fears would not be realised.

Elise had run ahead when they'd reached the final crest, desperate to see that hope fulfilled. Now she wished she'd held back, given herself a few more moments of ignorance. It was a few minutes before the others caught up with her.

As they stared down at the scene below, Septa let out a sob and sat down heavily on the grass. Without thinking, Elise leant over and put her arm around her. Septa shrugged off the embrace.

A dozen or so open craters consumed the forest that had once sheltered Uracil. Scattered between each of the gaping holes were the few scorched trees that had managed to survive the blasts. Their root systems were tangled in the mess of blackened earth and charred remnants of what had once been alive

A. E. WARREN

and part of the world. Rather than giving Elise hope that nature would eventually prevail, they only accentuated the depth of the destruction around her.

Not even the lake had escaped unscathed. Loose rafts of timber, which together had once provided homes to thousands, bobbed on its surface, nudging up against the everyday items of life floating next to them. Elise could only guess at what the lake kept hidden beneath its depths.

The silence was the only thing that surfaced in Elise's mind. All the animals had fled from what remained of Uracil and none of their familiar calls or songs filled the air. They had turned away from the destruction and chaos sent by man.

'Shall we go down?' Max said eventually. 'See if anyone ... ?'

There was little hope that anyone who had been injured would have survived the cold nights without shelter and warmth, but Elise's desire for action overruled logical thought. She had to do something, *anything*, or she would just break. And with Uracil gone, how would she ever fix herself again?

'Let's go to the walkway, see if we can get to the island,' she said.

As she spoke, Elise felt as if she were floating above herself. She could hear the words coming from her mouth, see what was below her, but she was disconnected from it all.

Slowly, the four of them stood and, in single file, walked down the steep hill to the edge of the lake.

Close to the walkway, they had to change direction to traverse the edge of a crater blocking their path. Elise felt her eyes drawn to the depression even though she knew she should avert her gaze. She doubted the charred remains – the first confirmation of death – would ever fade from her memory. Still, she stared at the crater, her mind unable to process what had happened.

Closer to the trees, lying on his front, was the body of a man. One arm was stretched out in front, his hand dug into the sand – he must have been trying to crawl to safety. Elise walked over to him in a trance and knelt down next to him. She turned his face towards her and paused. Milo. She thought of the sixteen-year-old she had taken on his first mission and who, in his innocence, had dressed like a member of the Protection Department. He'd looked older, but really, he'd been a boy, and had deserved the time to learn and grow. Reaching out to him with the tips of her fingers, she pulled his eyelids down and said a silent prayer to the stars.

'The walkway's gone,' Raynor called out, standing at the lip of where it should have been. 'Damaged in the blast.'

'We'll have to find another way across,' Max responded.

'I can't swim,' Elise said, standing, her voice higher than she remembered it.

'Neither can I,' Raynor said. 'I'll have to stay here.'

'I can ... but not very well,' Septa added, turning away from the remnants of the crater.

'I can swim,' Max said. 'I'll go over, take a look around the island ... see if there are any survivors.'

He clasped his hands as he spoke, but Elise could see they were shaking.

She stared up at him. 'Leave your bag here; only take the essentials. I'll start a fire so you can dry off when you get back. Don't take any risks.'

Max looked down at her and dropped his bag by her feet. 'What are you going to do whilst I'm gone?'

'We're going to bury them,' Elise said, nodding towards the crater.

Max's eyes widened.

'The Neanderthals were burying and honouring their dead forty thousand years ago,' Elise said. 'I'd like to try and be as civilised as they were.'

Max nodded and pulled his jumper off. 'I'll be quick. Get that fire going in an hour so I have a point to swim to. If I'm not back in three hours ... well ...'

'We'll come and get you,' Elise said.

Two and a half hours later, Elise and Raynor had moved Milo's body, and all those from the crater, and placed them underneath a large pine tree. They had no digging equipment so the best they could do was to cover them in leaves and rocks to try and protect them from any scavengers that might return. Elise had asked Septa if she would help, but she had just shaken her head and begun to build a fire, her hands trembling. Elise had left her to it; she knew they each had different coping strategies.

Elise was no stranger to the dead. As a known healer, her mum had regularly attended deathbeds to provide pain relief for the dying and comfort to the family, and Elise had often accompanied her. She had therefore witnessed the last hours of many of Thymine's sick.

Elise hadn't recognised any more of the people they had buried, but Raynor had known two; the rest of the remains were too charred to identify. When they had finished, Raynor had sat cross-legged next to the mounds of leaves and rocks, and spoken quietly to the dead.

Leaving Raynor to her grief, Elise circled the shoreline, searching for any sign of Max. At the sound of splashing water, she lifted her head. It was beginning to get dark and the cold was really setting in, so she walked over to her backpack and pulled out her sleeping blanket. For a moment, she stared at the hands holding the blanket and wondered if they would ever feel like her own again.

As Max waded out from the water, he tucked his hands underneath his arms. He was shaking so much that, even with his hands clamped down, his torso was still shuddering. Elise ran over to him and wrapped her blanket tightly around his shoulders. Taking his arm, she guided him back to the trees where Septa had set up their camp and lit the fire. She'd also tried to fashion a tent out of the bits of material that had washed up on the shore.

'Sit here for a minute,' Elise said, 'and then change into your dry clothes.'

Max nodded.

'Did you find anyone?' Elise asked after a moment.

Max shook his head and then stood up to change.

When he was dressed, he hung Elise's sodden blanket next to the fire and pulled out his own dry sleeping blanket. He wrapped it around his shoulders and stared into the flames.

'I found around a hundred people, but none of them were alive. Theo was ... Theo was one of them ...'

Max hung his head and Elise wrapped her arms around him. They stayed there for a while as Max cried silently, tears dripping onto the sand below.

Eventually he raised his head. 'Where's Septa?'

Elise leant back. 'She went off an hour ago, said she wanted to spend the night by herself. She promised she would be back in the morning.'

Raynor came over and sat down next to them. 'Who did you see, Max?'

'Theo.' Raynor leant over and patted his hand. 'Raul and someone ... who I think was Flynn. There were lots of guards; I think they must have stayed behind to evacuate people.' Max stared up at the sky and rubbed his eyes. 'I also saw Jessica, from the school.' He blinked. 'There were a ... a few children with her.'

'Oh, stars ...' Raynor mumbled, burying her face in her hands.

Max turned to Elise and she knew straight away.

She leant away from him, trying to shield herself from what was coming. 'Who was it?'

The question tumbled out even though she didn't want to hear the answer.

'It was your dad. I'm so sorry.'

'Nathan? My mum?'

'I didn't see either of them. I don't know what that means ...'

Max held open one side of his blanket as tears streamed silently down Raynor's face. Elise curled herself around him and let her own tears come.

Elise woke from a restless sleep to the sound of Septa shouting.

'Those *bastards*,' Septa screamed as she kicked at her backpack.

'What's going on?' Elise asked. She untangled herself from her bed roll and got to her feet. Raynor and Max were both staring at Septa.

'Max told Septa that he found Raul's body,' Raynor said quietly, as she watched Septa tear up a fern from its roots and fling it across the small clearing. 'He was the closest person she had to a mentor; kept an eye out for her when she first arrived in Uracil.'

'Look at what they've done!' Septa said, a sob escaping from her as she stared towards what remained of Uracil. She turned around and surveyed the damage she had caused to their base camp in the space of a few minutes. 'Look at what they've done to our home.'

She crumpled to the ground.

Elise paused for a moment before moving to her side. She tentatively laid her hand on Septa's shoulder, half expecting her to shrug it off again. Septa let it remain.

Max came over to them, his face pale. He leant down next to Septa. 'I'm so sorry you lost Raul. Theo's gone too, and Elise lost her dad as well. I didn't know how to tell you …'

At the mention of her dad, Elise felt a pain so sharp that it took her breath away. He was gone. And what of her other family, her friends? Any number of them could have died and she wouldn't know. She might never know what had happened to them …

Septa slowly raised her head, her bloodshot eyes fixed on Max. 'Did you know about this? Did you know they had air-planes and bombs?'

Max lurched backwards as if he had been struck. 'No, of course I didn't. I would have told Uracil if I did.'

Septa scrambled towards him, not letting him out of her sight. Max was twice as big as her, but at that moment she looked as if she would tear him to pieces with her bare hands. 'So you're telling me that you lived all those years as a Potior, learning all their Potior ways and *not once* did they mention the Pre-Pandemic weapons they'd kept?'

'That's enough, Septa,' Raynor said, moving towards her. 'Why don't you sit yourself down again?'

Septa ignored Raynor's request.

'I didn't know,' Max spluttered. 'I wasn't told much more than a schoolchild.'

'So you never happened to come across a *giant airplane*?' Septa spat. 'In all the time you lived with them, had access to their world and their plans, you didn't see anything that made you just a teensy bit suspicious?'

Septa pointed her sharp chin up towards Max, hate burning in her eyes, searching for a direction, a target.

Elise stared at Max. His gaze flicked between the three women, looking for an ally.

She was too crushed by her own losses to be his champion.

It was Raynor who answered Max's silent pleadings. 'Max was only a pup when they thought he'd died. It takes a long time to work your way up the Potior ranks.'

Max looked at each of them in turn. 'I promise I didn't know they'd kept those airplanes. I believed, like everyone else, that they'd turned their backs on all Pre-Pandemic weapons. I didn't know.'

'None of us knew they had them,' Raynor said. 'And we need to stop this right now. Max isn't at fault for what has happened here.' She put her hands on her broad hips. 'Have none of you wondered where everyone is? Max only saw around a hundred people over there. There's probably about twenty scattered around the lake, double that probably in the lake. But where are the rest of them? Where is Michael and all the countless others who we should have found?'

'You don't think that the bombs would have ... evaporated them somehow?' Elise said, hardly believing the questions she was having to ask about her own family and friends.

Raynor sucked the air in between her teeth as she considered this. 'Even if everyone was bunched up exactly where the craters are, there weren't enough hits to get even a quarter of Uracil's population.'

A small glimmer of hope, the first Elise had felt in nearly two days, began to unfurl in her chest.

'No, not possible,' Raynor continued. 'They must be somewhere else.'

'They must have escaped, then,' Max exclaimed, his voice rising.

'Hold your cart, Maxi-Boy,' Raynor said.

'I didn't listen that much in school,' Septa said. 'Could the airplanes do anything besides drop bombs?'

Elise looked up at the scrap of sky she could see through the tree branches. She half expected another airplane to fly overhead. 'They could also transport people, like the sailboats do.'

'So, either a large number of people managed to escape the bombs,' Septa said, ticking the points off on her fingers, 'then get far away enough from here not to be picked up by the Protection Department, and then lasted outside for five days with no supplies at the beginning of winter. Or they've been captured.' Septa paused. 'Not great odds for survival either way ...'

Elise wasn't really listening to Septa. She knew the odds weren't in their favour, but there was still a chance. A chance that the rest of her family and friends were still alive.

She turned to the other three. 'What else do you think the Potiors have kept from Pre-Pandemic times?'

Max frowned. 'If they've secretly kept bombs and airplanes, then we can presume that they've kept a whole host of other things.'

Elise spent the next two days detached from herself. Whenever her grief for her dad threatened to paralyse her, she sent a plea up to the stars to watch over those that she may not have lost, and then busied herself with another task.

They had spent the second morning building two rafts from the planks of wood scattered along the shoreline. In silence, they had made the journey across the lake to what remained of Uracil.

For as long as she could remember, Elise had witnessed the death of someone she knew at least once a year: a young friend at school, a neighbour, her own grandparents. With medical help mostly unaffordable, a long life as a Sapien was a gift rather than expected.

What Elise saw when she stepped off the raft and onto the island was different – it was the mass extinction of life. Not just human life, but animal as well. As Max led them around the island, Elise had known the only way that she could cope with what was required from her now was to shut down all her thoughts and feelings, to allow herself to drift upwards and watch from afar.

They had done their best to honour and preserve the dignity of the dead. Raynor had found a spade and a small axe that had survived the blasts. Elise, Raynor and Max had taken it in turns to dig shallow graves. Raynor then spent hours saying words over the final resting places of the dead, rocking and keening until she was spent. Septa had simply stared blankly at the dead before mumbling about looking for medical supplies, the most precious of Uracil's resources.

While Elise dug a shallow hole for two people who had clung to each other in their last moments, she thought of Raul's saying: 'If an act is not witnessed, it may as well have never occurred.' Dropping her shovel, she pulled out the small camera from her bag. With a flick of her wrist she sent it high up into the air, way above what remained of the trees, so it could record from above the damage to Uracil. She then brought it back down again and directed it to circle the island and document each person who had lost their life. Between the four of them, they could name most of those who had died, but a few of them they recognised but couldn't recall their names. Elise hoped that recording the dead would one day enable them all to be identified, and provide some peace to their family and friends.

That evening, the wind picked up and they were forced to remain on the island instead of returning to their previous camp; they couldn't risk being capsized when most of them couldn't swim. Without the need for discussion, Elise led the group to the southern tip of the island, as far from Uracil as possible. On the way, she stopped and stared at a brightly coloured square on the ground in front of her; the first glimpse of colour she'd seen in the otherwise bleak landscape. Pulling it out from underneath a piece of timber, she realised it was one of the crochet squares that had decorated some of the tree houses. Unable to let it drop to the ground, she folded it up and slipped it into her pocket, a reminder of what Uracil had once been.

Without saying a word, she continued to drag the tarpaulin they would use to shelter from the wind. Once it was strung between two tree branches, Elise lit a large fire. They would keep it burning until the sun rose as it was a moonless night that required the soft glow of a fire to ward away their memories of the dead.

As she watched herself from above, Elise wondered why she had ever believed that her family and friends would be safe. Why would she be the exception? Just because she was the central character in her own life did not mean that she would be shielded from the same overwhelming and unjust loss that was the only thing this world seemed able to guarantee. Life did not work that way. She had buried her father today, as well as Raul, Flynn and countless others. All good people who didn't deserve to die. She had found Lewis's body as well, buried beneath the remains of the hut where he had spent his last few days of incarceration. Even he did not deserve to die in that way. None of them would have woken up that morning and known that it would be their last; instead, their minds would have been occupied with the mundane matters of life. All over the world, at any given point in time, people were trying to protect those that they loved while leading quiet lives, and they would fail.

Elise thought of the bedtime stories that her mum had told her when she was a child. They would snuggle under her blankets and dim the lights, back when Elise's innocent hopes for the future had burned bright. She'd listen as her mum wove tales of kind, honest people who, after some trials, would succeed in what mattered most to them. Those tales of good prevailing over evil had cloaked a small child from the realities of her world but had done little to prepare her for them.

The sound of distant thunder snapped Elise back to the present and threatened to pull her back down to her body. The thought terrified her and, without bothering to eat, she curled up with her blanket and willed sleep to take her for the night.

The next day the weary group finished burying the dead, before taking the rafts back over to the mainland. As they drifted towards the shoreline, Elise turned to stare at Uracil. It would likely never be home to a human settlement again now that the Potiors were aware of its location. Cautiously, the wildlife would return, and after around ten years, nature would finish reclaiming what was rightfully hers. In thirty years' time, the island would recover from its fifty years of habitation and the thirty minutes that it had taken to destroy it.

As they clambered off the rafts, Elise found herself checking the sky again. She wondered whether this new impulse would ever fade.

'Where do we go now?' she said, more to herself than in expectation of an answer.

Her voice was croaky from lack of use over the last two days. They had spent their entire time of mourning in silence.

'I've been thinking about that,' Raynor said, clearing her throat when her voice came out lower than expected. 'I think—'

Elise held up a hand. Her attention had been caught by movement on the distant hill to her left. She stared and eventually it resolved into a person, waving in their direction.

'There, look over there!' she said, tugging at Raynor's sleeve.

Max and Septa turned towards where she was pointing.

'I'm going to run up to them,' Elise said, shrugging off her bag. 'They might need our help or even be able to tell us what's happened here.'

'I don't know, Elise,' Raynor said. 'We have no idea who it is.'

'I agree,' Max said. 'It could be the Protection Department; they might have sent a few people back.'

'So what if it is?' Elise said. 'There's only one of them. I could use someone to blame.'

Max gave a half-smile. 'I thought you blamed me?'

Elise thought about it. 'Honestly, no. Until recently, I carried around this guilt about being a Sapien because of what they had done before the Pandemic. But more recently, life has taught me that you have to look at the individual's actions, not the collective. I have to look at you that way as well.'

'That is the nicest thing you've said to me all week,' Max responded. He looked up at the figure. 'Come on, we'll go together.'

They dropped their bags at Septa's and Raynor's feet, before setting off at a quick pace that Elise knew she would be able to sustain for the distance required. She could sense that Max had let her decide on their speed and was happy to take the lead.

As they got closer, the waving became more frantic. Elise focused on the figure and tried to prepare herself to either immediately help this person or leap into a fight. She was thankful that she wasn't alone; she hadn't slept well for days and her brain was fogged with grief.

As they neared the figure, Elise could make out more details. They were short and dressed in grey clothing and were therefore unlikely to be a member of the Protection Department. She picked up her pace and Max increased his speed with ease. She needed to help someone, do something useful to push away the thoughts of what she had lost and who she still had to lose.

She let out a sob when she recognised the person, but then bit her lip to try to keep everything contained. One of her friends had survived. They were unharmed and alive. Without slowing her pace, she threw herself into his arms.

'Stars, am I glad to see you. I thought I was the only one left,' Luca said, as he stumbled backwards under the force of Elise's embrace.

They held each other close and hugged for so long that Elise lost track of time.

'We should get back to the others,' Max said, after a few minutes.

'Max, this is Luca,' Elise said, spinning him around to face Max.

She felt giddy. If Luca had made it, perhaps there was hope for others. Maybe her brother …

Luca looked Max up and down. 'So, Uracil was destroyed and nearly everyone is dead, and you tell me that the Potior survives? Sounds like a fix to me.'

'Leave it, Luca,' Elise said. 'Max had nothing to do with the attack. He's proven himself time and again. He saved Raynor's life when we were trying to get to Uracil. He's spent the last two days over on the island with us burying and mourning the dead. He's not a Potior.'

Max looked down at Luca. 'I'm glad that you survived.'

Luca paused for a moment. 'Thank you. I probably didn't deserve it, but for some reason the stars decided to leave me here a bit longer.'

'What happened here?' Elise asked, desperate for any answers her friend might be able to provide. 'Have you seen anyone else? My brother or mum?'

Luca rubbed the back of his head. 'I don't know, Elise. I'd fallen out of favour with the other guards thanks to Twenty-Two and I was sent on patrol outside of Uracil last week.'

Elise stepped back. He almost sounded angry with her. He never normally used her first name.

'Sorry, I wasn't here so I don't know about anyone,' Luca continued. 'On the first day on patrol, I heard some noise and I thought it was thunder as the sky was dark that day, but I had to go all the way to Three Stone Drift, which takes days, so I carried on. When I came back, it was like this.' He gestured to what was below. 'I decided to camp farther away to be safe and have been coming back every day since then. I thought I saw a fire on the island last night but I couldn't get across; the walkway's gone and I can't swim.'

Elise could see Septa and Raynor below them. They both waved, Septa jumping up into the air as she did so.

'Come on, we'd better get back to them,' Elise said. 'They'll be wondering what's going on.'

The three of them trudged back down the hill.

'So, you think some people may have survived?' Luca asked.

'We're hoping that most of them did; there's not enough bodies,' Max said. 'They might have been captured by the Potiors.'

'We might not have lost everyone, then,' Luca said quietly.

'We found my dad over there,' Elise said.

'Well, that's great!' Luca exclaimed. 'Where—?'

He stopped mid-sentence when he caught the look Max shot him.

Luca put his arm around Elise. 'I'm so sorry, Thanton. He was a giant of a man ... was always nice to me—'

'Don't,' Elise said, shrugging off Luca's arm. 'Don't do that. I can't yet. Talk about something else.'

They fell into an uncomfortable silence, but Elise didn't care. Social ease was not something that concerned her when she had lost her dad. She reminded herself that she was lucky to have had her dad for the years she had been given; Luca had never known his parents. Kit and Twenty-Two had never even *had* parents. Remembering her conversation with Maya, she repeated to herself that she was still one of the lucky ones. She thanked the stars out loud, and Max and Luca exchanged a look but didn't say anything.

Elise turned her gaze up to the darkening sky. Yes, she was one of the lucky ones.

CHAPTER 20

· ·

Twenty-Two

One week earlier

Twenty-Two plummeted under the surface of the lake, pulling Ezra with her. She had tried to let go of his hand, but he held on tight, following her beneath the black surface.

I can't swim. I can't swim. Ican'tswim

Panic flooded through her as this thought repeated itself and she sank farther and farther down. Her chest began to feel tight and next to her Ezra began to flail in desperation.

A moment later, her feet touched the bottom. Using all her strength, she bent her legs and pushed herself back towards the surface. Instinctively, she kicked to try and propel herself upwards, pulling Ezra with her.

When her face broke the surface of the water, she gasped in as much air as she could take. A second later, Ezra, mouth clamped shut, bobbed up next to her. They stared at each other for a moment as they desperately tried to gulp in as much air as possible before they sank again. She tilted her head back and gulped at the cold air one last time, trying to get every last bit into her already-burning lungs.

A hand grabbed her arm, yanking her upwards.

Pain shot through her at the roughness of the hold, but she felt only relief. Banging her knee on the side of the walkway, she spluttered and gasped as she rolled out of the water. Face to the sky, she watched as Kit turned to help Nathan pull Ezra out of the water. Other residents of Uracil scrabbled to pass her, barely giving her a second glance.

When the shock of what had happened began to recede slightly, she realised that she was too vulnerable lying down on the walkway; one of the people hurtling past could easily knock her back into the water again. She scrambled to her feet, her knee and shoulder protesting at the movement.

'We have to keep going,' she signed when Ezra was back on his feet and spitting water over the side.

Taking his hand, water dripping from her hair onto her already-soaked tunic, she pulled him towards the shore as quickly as she could. Kit and Nathan followed close behind. She could feel Ezra shivering, and realised she was doing the same – they had to get dry.

They were only twenty feet away when another explosion rocked the air behind her.

The surface of the lake shook and she leapt off the walkway into the now-waist-height water. Pulling her legs up high, she tried to run towards safety. An impossibly loud droning noise came from above and she instinctively turned her head towards it. Way up, nearly touching the clouds, a giant object was circling the hills above them. She had no name for it, but knew that it must be responsible for the destruction raining down on them. Like a bird, it swooped and turned in the sky, making its way back to the lake.

Nearly out of the water, Twenty-Two tugged at Ezra's hand, frantically pulling him as she pelted towards the trees – they would protect them.

When she reached the pines, she breathed deeply, and for a moment their scent placed her back in her pod. Turning at the sound of the others catching up, she signed at them to keep moving, but Kit wasn't there.

She took a step forwards, her eyes scanning for him. People were stumbling off the walkway. Some were rooted to the spot staring up at the sky; others were flinging children over their shoulders and racing towards the trees. She searched their faces, but none of them were Kit.

And then she saw him, still by the walkway. He was bending down, helping an elderly Sapien man get back to his feet. Kit glanced up at her and their gazes met for just a moment before a teenage girl sprinted in front of Twenty-Two's eyeline.

The third explosion was deafening.

Twenty-Two couldn't believe that the world could produce such volume. It was the closest one yet and she covered her ears and screwed her eyes closed, wishing she could be back in her pod, listening to birdsong while Dara chattered about how they would fill their afternoon.

When the last vibrations faded away, Twenty-Two opened her eyes. The only movement was the dust settling onto the newly arranged scene. People were lying, motionless, in a variety of poses on the ground. All of them fanned away from a giant hole in the earth, right where Kit had been.

Twenty-Two struggled to process what she was seeing; where Kit had been, there was now just a hole.

92THE FOURTH SPECIES

She blinked again, as if this would give Kit the chance to reappear. She quickly signed to Ezra and Nathan that they should stay under the trees and ran over to the blackened hole. Kit was not there; there was no sign of him. A crippling tightness formed in her chest.

Twenty-Two knelt down next to the old man Kit had been helping to ask him if he had seen where her friend had gone. She shook his shoulder and his head lolled around. She had never seen a dead person up close before, but she knew that this man had passed over to the stars – he was empty of their light.

Unable to look at him any longer, she turned towards the shoreline. Her focus settled on a body in the water, their head below the surface. Recognising Kit's ponytail, she sprang up and struggled over to him, feet slipping in the sand. Pulling his face from the water, she rolled him over. He was still, his eyes closed.

Staring up to the sky, she ignored the giants circling above and stretched all her thoughts upwards, past the dust and over the clouds. She called for her ancestors. Her body began to hum with the effort of willing something with every fibre of her being. She would promise them anything if they would return Kit to her. She had never asked for anything in this way before. She had always been happy to follow the path the stars thought best. But not this time. Kit belonged here, with her.

Kit coughed and turned his head. With a rush, Twenty-Two felt herself pulled back to earth. She stared at his face, willing him to move again. Water spluttered out of his mouth and he rolled onto his side and retched. Twenty-Two sent silent thanks to her ancestors and the stars, knowing that she was in their debt. She just hoped one day she could repay them.

223

When Kit's breathing began to settle, she looped her arm under him, pulled his body over her shoulder, and began to stand. She thanked the stars again, this time for making her a Neanderthal; she would never have been able to lift him off his feet if she had been born Sapien. Kit, only half conscious, barely moved as she made her way slowly to the trees, each step carrying the threat of her legs buckling beneath her.

When she reached the others, she slowly knelt with Kit still over her shoulder. Ezra and Nathan's eyes were wide as she gently laid Kit onto the ground.

Kit opened his eyes. 'Leave me here. I need to rest.'

Twenty-Two glanced up at the sky. The unnatural thing circled around; it was getting lower. She didn't know what it was, but she knew she didn't want to face it when it landed.

'No, you have to come with us. I'll help you.' She turned to Ezra and Nathan. 'You two run to the rocky outcrop up there. Hide behind it when you get to it. We'll be right behind you.'

She felt more comfortable with them up ahead. She glanced behind her and could see one of the unknown *things* had landed on a long strip of grass close to the lake. People were screaming and fleeing to the cover of the trees.

Twenty-Two turned away from Uracil and looped Kit's arm around her shoulders again. She felt the muscles in her barrel chest take the strain as she lifted him so he was standing. Planting her feet firmly on the ground, she acknowledged her strength. She'd been made for this. She could make it.

Every few metres she set herself a new target to reach, Ezra and Nathan always up ahead, her and Kit following. She focused on the present, not allowing her thoughts to send her into a panic about everyone else she loved. She had to help the ones with her first.

After a while, Kit was able to walk with less support. There was a distant succession of further explosions and she glanced back down at Uracil. It was unrecognisable; broken and torn. The three giants she had seen in the sky were now resting around the shoreline. She peered at the dots of people around them and wondered why they would get so close.

When they stopped again, Uracil was out of sight. Kit was now walking with only minimal support and she felt far away enough to stop for a moment to check on him.

'Where are we going?' he signed.

'I do not know. Away from that,' she said, gesturing at what lay behind them.

'We need to get dry or we will not survive the cold of the night.'

Kit's hands shook so much as he signed that she struggled to understand him at first.

'You know how to make a fire, don't you?' Twenty-Two asked.

'Yes, but we have nothing with us to make one.'

Twenty-Two looked around at the four of them, all shivering from the cold and shock. Even if it had been the height of summer, she knew they would have difficulty surviving out here without basic supplies.

She thought for a minute. 'I know somewhere we can go.'

'I told you, no visitors,' Jerome said when Twenty-Two approached him on the grassy outcrop. 'Get back with you. You can't just bring people up here like it's some sort of day out.'

Twenty-Two gestured for Ezra to come around and join her; she needed an interpreter.

Jerome stared at them all. 'Why would you bathe at this time of year?'

'Uracil has been destroyed,' Twenty-Two signed to Jerome with Ezra speaking the words for her.

Jerome swayed slightly. 'Oh ... I don't ...' He stared around him and started rocking on the balls of his feet. 'But where will I get medical supplies for the animals?'

'I do not know, but we can try to help you with that,' Twenty-Two signed. 'But first we will need to stay here for a bit.'

Jerome's hand fluttered as he turned abruptly and hobbled back into the cave mouth. From inside the darkness, there was the sound of boxes shifting. Kit stared at Twenty-Two and she could guess what he was thinking, but they had agreed halfway up the mountain path that she would take the lead as she was the only one who had met Jerome before.

'I've stockpiled a bit. I probably have about four months' worth of supplies, but you'll need to bring more,' Jerome called from inside, before emerging from the cave. 'I don't want to risk getting close to running out. I've got the animals to think of.' He stopped in the cave mouth. 'I said no children. He can't stay. It's not possible!'

Twenty-Two followed his gaze. It was not Nathan he was looking at, but Ezra.

'I'm not a child,' Ezra said. 'I'm just short. And why are you worrying on about me when we just told you that Uracil has been flattened, probably along with everyone who lived there?'

Tears formed in Ezra's eyes and he angrily wiped them away with the back of his hand.

Jerome studied him. 'How old are you?'

'I'm sixteen and eight months and I've been this height since I was twelve. No more growing for me.'

'And you won't go touching my animals, will you?'

'I'm not some sort of animal obsessive! I can resist furry coats!'

Twenty-Two was watching Nathan, who, at the mention of Uracil, had moved behind Kit. She wanted to put her arm around him and pull him close but didn't want to draw attention to his age; his height was the only thing protecting him from Jerome's attention.

She could only guess at what Nathan was feeling. She didn't know where her friends were either, whether they had survived. Her heart ached as she thought of Bay and Twenty-Seven.

'We would be grateful if you would build a fire,' she signed to Jerome. 'Nathan here has family back in Uracil.'

Jerome looked around him, as if for support. 'Well, I've got family right here; they need me too. They've got no one else to look after them.'

'We'll help you look after them if you let us stay for a bit. And we won't touch anything unless you ask us to.'

Twenty-Two glanced at Ezra, who had been translating for her the whole time. His voice was flat and his eyes unfocused.

Jerome sucked in his breath between his teeth. 'And you'll get me more supplies?'

Twenty-Two tried to keep the frustration from her features as she stepped closer to Nathan. 'Yes, we'll help you get supplies. But unless we warm up soon, we'll all get ill.'

Jerome thought about it for a moment.

'We could just stay here, whether he agrees to it or not,' Kit signed to Twenty-Two.

'I know,' Twenty-Two responded with one hand, careful that Ezra wouldn't see what she was saying and accidentally translate it to Jerome. 'But let's try it this way first.'

However difficult Jerome was, she admired how much he cared for his animals. If at all possible, she wanted to avoid taking what she needed by force.

'You can stay for bit, but when I ask you to leave, you have to go,' Jerome finally said. 'And you have to get me those medical supplies.'

Twenty-Two didn't bother to scrunch her eyes; he wouldn't understand the gesture anyway. 'Thank you. Now, let's make a fire and warm up.'

An hour later, Twenty-Two had changed into a pair of Jerome's trousers and a jumper. She hadn't worn trousers since the night she had escaped Cytosine and it felt funny to have cloth all around her legs. She ate quickly and looked around at Kit.

'I'm going back out to search,' she signed. 'I need to find Bay, Twenty-Seven and Georgina.'

Kit nodded. 'I am coming with you.'

'Me too. I want to look for my mum and dad. I said I would meet Dad by that old tree,' Nathan signed.

Twenty-Two scrabbled around for a reason to make him stay; he was safer here than anywhere else and she had made a promise to his father. To her relief, Ezra stepped in.

'We'd better stay here together,' he signed. 'Make sure Jerome doesn't change his mind. And he might think I need a babysitter ...'

Ezra tried to smile at his own joke, but there was such sadness behind his eyes that Twenty-Two felt the need to rub her own.

'Alright, but will you look for my mum and dad too? Please go to the tree I promised to meet him at,' Nathan signed, leaning forwards.

'Of course,' Kit signed. 'Do not tell the old man, but we are going to bring back anyone we can. Especially the children.'

Nathan glanced over at Jerome, who was fussing over a small hedgehog, dropping splashes of liquid into its tiny mouth. 'How are we going to find Elise?'

'I do not know,' Kit said. 'It is going to be difficult to reach anyone now, but we will think about that when we get back.'

Twenty-Two looked at the silent Ezra, who was staring blankly at the wall of the cave. 'You will look after Nathan?'

Ezra's eyes focused and he nodded.

She turned to Nathan so Ezra wouldn't see the movement of her hands. 'And you will look after Ezra?'

'Yes. I will,' he signed, shooting a look of distaste at Jerome's back.

After Nathan had carefully explained the location of the towering Sitka spruce he and his father had agreed to meet at, Ezra turned to Twenty-Two. 'You're coming back, aren't you?'

'I promise,' Twenty-Two signed. 'We won't be separated like we were back at the museum.'

Ezra continued to stare at her, eyes wide, and she knew it called for more.

'I swear on Jupiter and all the planets above.'
Satisfied, Ezra let her go.

They had three hours before it would get dark. Hurrying together, Twenty-Two and Kit made their way back to Uracil. The temperature had dropped, and Twenty-Two's heart sank as she thought of anyone having to try and survive the night in this weather. After ten minutes, Kit had fallen back so she slowed her pace. He was clearly still weakened from the events earlier in the day.

As they curled down the twisting paths, Twenty-Two scanned the mountainside for any signs of the residents of Uracil. She could hear her panting breath, loud in the silence of the countryside that surrounded them.

From afar, they located the giant conifer tree Nathan had told them about, but as they drew closer it was clear that no one was sheltering next to its wide trunk. They turned from it and continued their search, not wanting to discuss what this might mean.

When the first hour had passed, Kit began to call out even though he struggled to link the syllables, his voice low and guttural.

'Bay! Geor ... gi ... na! Twen ... ty ... Se ... ven!' he called, desperation in his voice. Panic circled Twenty-Two and she joined in with him, letting her own calls bounce around the mountainside.

An hour later, they were getting desperate; without screens or torches, they wouldn't be able to see anything once the sun had gone down. They would already have to walk part of the way back to the cave in the dark.

As they passed a large dip in the grassland, in between their shouts, Twenty-Two's attention was caught by a small mewing noise. She stopped for a moment and listened.

The mewing noise came again. A small child. She scrambled up the side of the mound expecting to see Bay's familiar bobbing hair.

Instead she saw the body of an unfamiliar woman. Crawling over her curled-up form and pulling at her hair was a baby girl, no older than two years. Her heart in her mouth, Twenty-Two half fell down the side of the bank. The girl turned to face Twenty-Two and began to cry more shrilly, tears squeezing out from the corners of her eyes.

Even in her panic, Twenty-Two realised that she was scaring the girl, so she tried to slow down. She held out her hand for the girl to see and scrunched her eyes, hoping she would understand the friendly gesture. Kit slid down the bank behind her, and at the sound, the child howled even more loudly, the tears falling down her plump cheeks. Twenty-Two dithered, wanting to comfort the girl but also realising that their presence was the cause of her distress.

Kit knelt by the woman and put his hand close to her mouth. 'She is still breathing. You take the girl. I'll carry the mother.'

Twenty-Two looked behind her. The sun was low in the sky. 'What about Bay and Twenty-Seven?'

Kit paused for a moment. They both stared at the little girl, who was now screaming, her voice catching in her throat and making her cough. Her eyes flicked between the two strangers as her cries grew shriller.

'There's nothing more we can do for them tonight,' Kit signed. 'We do not even know where they are. But we can help these two. If we leave them, they will die.'

For a moment, Twenty-Two didn't care. Bay and Twenty-Seven were more important to her. She pushed it away as she drew on her humanity.

All lives are precious.

'I will carry the woman. You take the girl,' Twenty-Two signed. 'You are still weakened from earlier.'

Ignoring the girl's protests, Kit scooped her up in his arms, leaning away from the tiny hands that clawed at his chest. Twenty-Two positioned herself so the girl could see that she was lifting up the woman and bringing her with them, hoping that this would calm her. Sobbing, the baby's eyes never left the older woman. The girl jammed a fist into her mouth and sucked on it as Twenty-Two and Kit started the long climb back to Jerome's cave.

All the way, Twenty-Two thought of Bay and Twenty-Seven, wondering where they were, trying not to think about the worst alternatives. Her heart keened for them, the youngest and most precious of her kind.

Three hours later, they turned the last corner of the pathway, the darkness and strain of carrying the woman having slowed Twenty-Two's pace. Exhausted, the baby had fallen asleep on Kit's chest and he cradled her close.

'You're back, you're back!'

Twenty-Two recognised that voice and her eyes darted to the cave. Joy burst through her chest as Georgina ran over to her, shouting all the way, Bay and Twenty-Seven close behind.

'We were so worried,' Twenty-Two signed, trying not to drop the woman as both Bay and Twenty-Seven hugged her legs.

'We'd been out walking all day,' Georgina gabbled. 'And when we got back ... this was the only place I could think of to come ... Stars, what happened to her?'

'We found them about halfway back to Uracil,' Twenty-Two signed, after gently laying the woman down inside the opening to the cave. The woman had started to come round and had been groaning quietly for the last half-hour of their trek.

Without another word, Georgina went and checked on the two newcomers, much to Twenty-Two's relief. Now that her hands were free, she went straight to Bay and Twenty-Seven and knelt next to them, holding them both until Bay began to squirm.

Georgina examined the woman and, with some gentle coaxing, found out that her name was Milly. She had escaped Uracil with her young niece, Annabelle, and then everything had just gone black. Georgina thought it most likely that she had tripped and fallen, knocking her head in the process. Following a careful examination, Georgina confirmed that she seemed to have a mild concussion, but no further damage from the fall.

Annabelle, clearly distraught from the day's events, took a few hours to settle, but was now happily sitting on Twenty-Two's lap, accepting the cooled soup that Nathan spooned into her mouth. Twenty-Two had been pleased to find out that Jerome had gone to his sleeping area in one of the antechambers before they had returned. She couldn't face his questions and indignation tonight.

'What happened to her parents, Milly?' Georgina asked.

Milly stared at Annabelle and shook her head. 'I don't know what happened to her dad. Her mum, my sister ...'

Milly let out a sob and Georgina put her arm around her.

'Why don't you both try and get some sleep? I've set up some blankets on the right side of the cave. Take Annabelle with you, but call if you need me.'

Milly nodded before making her way farther into the cave.

'I'll check on them both in an hour,' Georgina signed, pulling the now-sleeping Bay closer to her.

Twenty-Seven had already curled up on a blanket between her and Ezra and was fast asleep.

'You'd better tell me what you know,' Georgina signed to Twenty-Two and Kit.

They filled her in on the limited information they had.

'Have you seen Tilla?' Georgina asked, her hands shaking.

'We have not seen anyone who isn't here,' Kit signed.

Georgina nodded and her eyes welled up. She glanced at Nathan and quickly blinked the tears away. 'I'm sure we will have some more news tomorrow, Nathan. I'm sorry we couldn't find your father.'

Nathan had been staring at his shoes, but he raised his head to follow the movement of her hands. 'I want to go and find them.'

Georgina looked over at Kit.

'We will go out again tomorrow, first thing, at dawn,' Twenty-Two signed. 'And we will go out every day until we find everyone who can come back with us.'

She had made a promise to the stars, and in return they had delivered Kit, Bay, Twenty-Seven and Georgina to her. She had a debt to repay.

CHAPTER 21

Genevieve

Stomach churning and eyes feeling like grit, Genevieve made her way to Adenine's Museum of Evolution to deliver her completed project to Constalian. She had spent three months pondering the best approach to convince the Sapiens that this would be beneficial to both them and their children. Never had her work disgusted her so much. She was sick of selling her ideas to the Potiors in pursuit of ideals that she would never believe in. 'Delusory' would be the word she would use to describe herself, and she was tired of it. This was not the reason she had left Uracil and her child behind.

For the past three weeks, Genevieve and Mortimer had tried to continue with their roles, but without knowing what had happened to Uracil, or the ability to discuss their worries with one another, a sense of isolation had set in.

Genevieve had tried to fuss over Mortimer in small ways that wouldn't raise the suspicions of their household. She had found his favourite petunias at the Emporium and ordered the servants to cook all his preferred meals. She had held regular dinner parties, as he had always enjoyed the company of their social circle alongside a glass of good wine. But all of this had passed

A. E. WARREN

without acknowledgement from him or any sign that it was helping; he seemed to barely register her presence and spent his free evenings brooding in front of the fire. Unable to speak openly, Genevieve had sat opposite him and silently watched as he pulled farther away from her. She would give anything to know what he was thinking.

As for Genevieve herself, she barely slept. She had longed to pace up and down her bedroom in the early hours but knew that the sounds of restless movements would raise the suspicions of the servants. It was a risk that she couldn't take when Dina was stationed in her household and no doubt reporting anything and everything back to the Potiors. Instead, in the quiet of the night, Genevieve lay in her bed and stared up at the ceiling, trying to guess what was happening outside Adenine. She had loved ones back in Uracil and the thought of anything happening to them kept her awake until the birds began to sing.

She kept her chin lifted as she walked along the pathways towards the museum. The surface of her façade was still solid, but she knew that inside it was beginning to crumble. Only that morning after pulling herself out of bed, she had started her exercises but given up on them after the first set. What was the point when Uracil was in danger and she could do nothing about it?

Before she'd left that morning, Mortimer had refused to go into work. When he told her that he wasn't feeling well, she could see the strain behind his eyes. She knew he was trying to tell her something, but she couldn't work out what. Holding his arm, she had helped him back to bed and ordered some tea, before instructing the servants to leave him to sleep and prepare some partridge for his dinner. She didn't know whether she would make it back in time for the evening meal.

As she approached the Museum of Evolution, she slowed her pace. She was early, as always, and there was no need to appear flustered. Pushing through the main doors, she let the calls of the animals wash over her and for once found a moment of peace in this setting. Perhaps there was more to the museum than she had ever allowed herself to notice.

After sweeping through the back corridors to Constalian's room, Genevieve hesitated for just a moment before knocking. The door was pulled open, and after a few pleasantries, Genevieve handed over her screen.

'These should work,' Constalian said, as she stared at the screen.

They were sitting in the same office as before. It was cold and Genevieve snuggled her chin farther down into her knitted scarf as she studied Constalian's reaction, her own features blank and wiped clean of thought. Genevieve knew it wasn't her best work, but she had been unable to focus on it these last few weeks. Staring at Constalian's face, pinched in concentration, she wondered if Constalian was one of the Potiors who received reports from her household. Maybe Constalian had ordered that Dina ... no, surely not. It didn't make sense for her to be the one who had arranged for them to be watched. Constalian was a woman of science, not politics. Genevieve wouldn't let herself swing into paranoia; it wouldn't help, not when there was still hope.

'I think they'll see the benefit to Zone 3,' Constalian continued, her eyes scanning the various releases that she had been presented with. 'I also like the suggestion of "Homo vitalis".' She stopped for a moment. 'Yes, that could work.' She cast her gaze towards Genevieve. 'Did you know that there was a suggestion they should be called Homo guanine? Absurd. Hmm ... yes, definitely lead with the fulfilment angle. Very good ...'

Genevieve leant forwards. A wave of sadness encased her and everything suddenly felt futile. What had she done? Why had she continued with this work when she knew that Uracil might no longer exist?

'Is there something wrong?' Constalian asked, her tone softening, approaching something close to concern.

'No. Apologies. I just felt a moment of dizziness,' Genevieve said, trying to regain control of her thoughts. 'I've been working late, and haven't been sleeping very well.'

'Well, I have just the thing to cheer you up,' Constalian said, slapping both of her knees. 'Would you like to meet him?'

'Him?' Genevieve said.

'The prototype for the new species.'

No, I would not.

'Yes, that would be the ... perfect end to this project.'

Ten minutes later, Constalian led Genevieve along a corridor into an area of the museum that she had never visited before. There were doors to the left and right, but Constalian headed for the one at the end of the corridor.

Genevieve drew her coat closer around her as she waited for Constalian to pull back the steel bars on the door, glad for something to do with her hands. Her scarf was still wrapped loosely around her neck and she took a deep breath of her lavender perfume. A wave of calm washed over her and she took strength in the feeling.

'There is a viewing deck upstairs,' Constalian said as she held her card up to the reader. 'The other doors lead to two of the other projects we are working on.'

Genevieve nodded. She didn't dare imagine what else the Potiors had been brewing behind the other two doors. She would probably find out in a few years' time when she would be asked to prepare a release on their content.

For the first time, it struck her that she might not be working for Adenine in the future. Where would she be? Back in Uracil if it was still in existence? Or would she be starting a new role in another base?

Constalian pushed open the door and led the way inside.

'Ben!' she called out. 'I've brought someone to meet you!'

Constalian turned to Genevieve. 'We decided on one-syllable names to differentiate the new species.'

'Inspired!' Genevieve replied, as she followed Constalian inside the pod, her eyes wide.

Genevieve hadn't known what to expect of the pod, but she certainly hadn't anticipated something akin to paradise. 'Tranquil' would be the word she would use to describe the large garden. Its glass ceiling was high enough to accommodate a few trees in the centre of the pod, and a hammock was strung between two trunks. Nestled in between the trees was a fountain; Genevieve wondered at the sparrows that were taking their morning bath in its chiming waters. Facing the fountain was a bench with a rug hanging over one end. Flowerbeds circled the gravel path that edged the trees and faded into the long-grassed meadow that took up the rest of the pod.

Small rubber pathways spiralled away from the fountain, one to a sleeping area, another to the opposite corner where a few simple wooden tables were set out. One had chairs around it; another was higher, with a few items scattered upon its surface. It was beside this that Ben was standing.

'Come over, Ben, and meet Genevieve,' Constalian called out.

Genevieve swallowed as he turned towards them, responding to Constalian's request.

He looked no different from a Sapien; he was on the stronger side perhaps, but was still short and stocky. His brown hair was cut close to his head and he was pale, despite the glass roof above. Genevieve guessed that he probably only saw two hours of direct sunlight on a clear day. He was wearing a simple green tunic over trousers and his feet were bare.

Ben raised his hand and walked over to the two women. His expression gave no hint of what he was feeling.

'Does he have a Companion?' Genevieve asked, as she stared at the man approaching them, trying to guess his thoughts.

'No, of course not,' Genevieve said. 'He is not a Neanderthal. The Neanderthals were for conservation purposes only; this is something quite different. We have developed a few of his kind and, from a young age, socialised them with each other. In the last year we have transferred all of Guanine's stock over here. We needed to ensure they would work in teams. The environment they grow up in is just as important as the genetic selections. Without the correct outside influences the engineering has much less chance of working.'

'Hello,' Ben said, when he joined them. 'I am Ben. It's nice to meet you.'

Constalian nodded approvingly.

Genevieve felt sick.

'It is nice to meet you too, Ben,' she said eventually, looking down at him. He was over a foot shorter than her. She had a thousand questions for him but didn't think that Constalian would permit her to ask even one.

'What were you doing?' Constalian asked.

Before he answered, her attention was diverted to the viewing deck above them and Genevieve followed her gaze. Directly above was a woman tapping at her screen.

'I was practising with the rivets,' Ben said. 'John brought them with him last time he was here.'

'Excellent,' Constalian said. 'Well, best get back to it, then.'

Ben nodded and turned for the path that led to the table he'd been working at.

Genevieve stepped forwards, her hand outstretched but not daring to make contact in case she scared him. 'I ... I hope—'

She stopped. Constalian was staring at her, a frown forming on her face.

Genevieve quickly recovered. 'It was a privilege to meet you, Ben. I hope your work goes well.'

Ben stared at her for a moment before a brief smile crossed his lips.

Genevieve smiled back at him. And in that one smile she tried to convey everything that she was feeling. She wasn't sure whether she had retained the ability to convey human emotion through just a look. She'd tightly controlled every emotion for so many years that she didn't know if she could even classify herself as human any more. She merely operated, selecting a particular pose or gesture from her catalogue of tricks. Even when she had heard that her only daughter had died … She pushed the thought away, as she always did.

Gazing around the pod, an idea formed and she let out a small sigh. 'It is paradise itself. I wonder if you would consider recording Ben working here. That would really show the Sapiens what you are trying to achieve.'

Constalian looked around her, seemingly with new eyes. 'Do you think so? Well, I'll give it some thought …'

Turning, Genevieve followed Constalian out of the pod. As she pulled the door closed behind her, she glanced over at Ben again. He had his back to her as he leant over the table. She tried to sear that image into her mind. She wanted to close her eyes every night and see him and what had been done to their world, the consequences of the role she had played.

Constalian pushed the bars across the steel door. 'Is there something wrong? You don't seem quite yourself.'

'I've … ah … I've just been so worried about what I heard at the meeting with the Premier.' Genevieve stumbled, unsure which path her voice was leading her down. Panicked at hearing the words tumble out, she tried to think of how to rescue her blunder. 'About them descending upon us, taking what we have. We haven't heard any more about it.'

'I wouldn't worry about that; it's been dealt with. They are no longer a threat.'

Genevieve nodded, bile rising in her throat. 'That is a relief … it had me awake at night.'

Constalian leant forwards and said, 'You don't seem very relieved. Perhaps select another response from your repertoire.'

Genevieve's stomach dropped and her vision blurred. All she could do was nod.

'You had better be getting back,' Constalian said, stepping aside to let Genevieve pass. 'I do hope your father recovers from his illness.'

'Thank you,' Genevieve mumbled as she started down the corridor.

Stumbling out of the doors of the museum, she felt the cold air hit her but it did little to calm the panic that had set in. She hadn't mentioned Mortimer's illness to Constalian.

The biting wind heightened her realisation that this was the beginning of the end.

She stumbled around to the side of the museum and leant against the icy brickwork. If the settlement had been Uracil, it was gone.

Genevieve tapped at Mortimer's door but there was no answer. Pushing it open, she stood in the doorway. There was a shape under the covers of his enormous bed, but it was so still. Too still. She pushed the door closed behind her and took a few hesitant steps towards the bed. Her hands shaking, she sat down next to him and nudged his shoulder to wake him. He stirred slightly and she breathed a sigh of relief.

All the way home, she had been deliberating whether to tell Mortimer what Constalian had said. He deserved to know, and she knew that he would find out eventually – he was not so immersed in their façade that he wouldn't question why they hadn't received any further messages from Uracil – but he was so fragile. She gathered her nerve and prodded him again, harder this time.

'What is it?' Mortimer asked, only opening one eye. He leant over and flicked on the light. Taking one look at Genevieve, he sat up. 'How bad?'

'They've destroyed a settlement. And I think it might be Uracil,' Genevieve said quietly, not bothering with any of the precautions that had been second nature up until now. What was the point? It would all be over soon.

'I'm so very sorry,' Mortimer said, pulling her into his embrace.

He stroked her hair as if she were really his child and she let the tears come, silently and with little fuss.

Genevieve pulled away from him and wiped her eyes. 'You should go to one of the coves, travel to one of the other Zones. Maybe Zone 4. You might like it there.'

Mortimer studied her before shaking his head.

She took both his hands in hers. 'I only have a day or so at the most before I am arrested. I made a mistake today ... I'm so sorry to have jeopardised your life here ...'

'I'm not leaving you,' Mortimer said. 'We'll have these final days of freedom together.'

Genevieve wiped her face with the back of her hand. She had lost everything. Only Mortimer was left.

'Please don't do this,' she said, her voice firm with resolve. 'We need someone alive who knows what happened here. For all we know, we could be the only two left. They'll be tracking my every move now. But there's hope for you ... if you leave tonight.'

'Tonight?' Mortimer spluttered. 'But ... I ...'

'Please. Do this for me. Don't make this even harder than it has to be.'

Mortimer looked to the door. 'But tonight? Surely we have more time.'

'As much as I wish we did, we do not. I'll help you pack. You can slip out in the early hours when the servants are asleep, head to the south-east cove.'

Mortimer paused before nodding. 'But what about you? Why don't you come with me? We could both leave.'

'If I leave, they'll only follow. This way, at least one of us will escape.'

'I don't want you to just give up!'

Genevieve patted his hand. 'I'm not giving up. I'm just doing the right thing, the brave thing, for once.'

Tears streamed silently down Mortimer's face. 'But if they take you, you'll be tortured for information and then thrown in a containment centre, if you're lucky ...'

'I know, but it's better than us both facing the same fate.'

They spent the rest of the day quietly packing a bag for Mortimer. Every item had to be considered; he was limited in what he could carry and, several times, Genevieve had to gently suggest that he would have to leave behind more than he cared to.

'But it was handmade for me, fits me perfectly. And I've worn it on every single one of my birthdays,' Mortimer lamented when Genevieve unfolded the magnolia waistcoat he intended on packing.

'I know it's important to you,' she said. 'But there is no room for sentimentalism. Practical items only. That means your warmest clothes and sturdiest boots. Any other item must only be included if it will help you survive.'

Mortimer pushed the waistcoat away from him. 'Yes, you're quite right, of course. Practicalities only,' he sighed. 'Stars, I don't think I am built for the outside any more ...'

'You used to be quite the outdoorsman, before we came here,' Genevieve said, balling up a pair of woollen socks. 'You were a great fisherman if I recall correctly.'

Mortimer smiled. 'That I was. It was a different life, though, wasn't it? Sometimes I cannot recognise the person I have become.' He slapped his knees. 'I have become quite the pampered pooch in my twilight years, have I not?'

Genevieve just smiled at him. 'I have so missed talking to you these last few weeks.'

'I too,' Mortimer said. He took her hand. 'And Genevieve – I am sure he will be alright. He is strong and clever, just like his mother.' Genevieve felt a tear form and tried to will it away as Mortimer continued. 'As soon as I can, I shall begin to make some enquiries, see if I can locate him—'

The door opened and they both jumped up. Without pausing, Genevieve lifted her wrist to her mouth and flipped open the latch on her bracelet. Mortimer had done the same. None of the servants would enter without knocking first.

But she paused before she swallowed the small pill. She'd grown up in Uracil, so it would wipe an entire lifetime of experiences, leaving her a mere babe in arms. Could she really erase all those memories? Who would remember her children for her?

Before she could decide, a strong hand circled her wrist, pulling her arm away from her mouth and restraining her. 'None of that now,' the man dressed entirely in black said, his three colleagues standing behind him. 'We want you alive and your mind fully intact.'

Genevieve tried to struggle but he was too strong. She crumpled. How could she have hesitated? A whole life spent in service of Uracil to fail at the last hurdle. She should have wiped her mind clean.

'No more words for us,' she said, turning to Mortimer, but he hadn't hesitated in the way she had, and his pill was already taking effect. He reached for her but tripped, hitting his head on the side of the bed, and landing heavily on the floor. He stared up at her and confusion crossed his features. For the first time, Mortimer looked all of his years, his hair dishevelled and eyes wide. A trickle of blood ran down his temple. Genevieve struggled and flailed to reach him but two of the Protection Department were holding her now.

'You didn't have to let him fall,' the man who was holding Genevieve said to his colleague.

His colleague shrugged. 'I didn't have to catch him either. Stupid old man.'

'Yes, but we need him compos mentis. And he might not be that way if you let him bash his head on everything between here and the Department for Justice. Did you see him take a pill?' The man smiled to himself. 'He looks like he would be a talker in the right circumstances.'

Genevieve stamped her foot down on the guard's foot. He winced and let go of her right arm. With her free hand, she swung around to knock the other guard who was holding her left arm, catching him square on the jaw, and he fell backwards. Her strength surged as she leapt away from the third guard.

Genevieve whipped around to Mortimer to help him back to his feet but he was frothing at the mouth and his eyes were rolling back up into his head.

She bent down and took his hand. 'What have you done?'

Laid against Mortimer's double-breasted waistcoat was the open locket. What had he taken? She glanced down at his wrist; the container holding his memory-blocking pill was still closed.

She scrambled to her feet but before she could straighten, fifty thousand volts of electricity dropped her to the floor.

The guard who had administered it loomed over her, holding his jaw. A blur of red danced across her vision, and with her cheek pressed against the wooden floor she watched Mortimer take his last breath.

CHAPTER 22

Elise

They couldn't continue to delay leaving the lake where Uracil had once been. Winter had crept up on them and the first snowfall threatened to arrive any day. Elise knew that if they didn't find permanent shelter soon, they would not survive to see spring. In previous years, they had tended to return to Uracil for the month of snow, but with this no longer an option, Luca had spent the past two days building a structure similar to the one he had made for Seventeen back in Thymine's Museum of Evolution. His work was impressive, but they all knew it would not withstand the depths of winter. Regardless, for now, it had kept them dry and sheltered from the wind at night.

The rest of the group had spent the time working as scavengers, searching and sorting through what remained of Uracil. They had packed their bags with any medical supplies they had found, and other useful items they could carry. The rest they had buried in metal boxes that had survived the blasts. The group was hopeful that they would be able to return to them in a few months' time, once they had found a more permanent place to camp.

'We need to finalise where we are going,' Max said, as he stared up at the sky.

The moonless night provided an incredible display of stars. A whole galaxy was visible, a spectacle that Elise had only witnessed a few times in her life.

'I know a place near Adenine,' Raynor said. 'I've stayed there the last two winters. But it's a three-week walk; I doubt we'll get there before the snows set in.'

'The only place I know,' Elise said, 'is the cove at the southwest shoreline. It's too far away, but we should go there once winter passes. And the other coves as well. We need to regroup. There must be other agents left; not everyone was in Uracil.'

'I know somewhere,' Septa said, still staring up at the night sky. 'It's only a three-day walk north from here. It's where I hid out after—'

Silence descended upon the group.

All kept their gazes on the sky apart from Luca. 'After what?' Septa squirmed.

'After she tried to bump off Elise,' Max said.

'Oh, so you're the one ...' Luca said. 'Didn't spend much time back in Uracil after that, did you?'

'I was working,' Septa responded, eyes firmly on the ground.

'Sure you were,' Luca said, eyeing her over the fire. 'I hear Maya got the better of you, saved Elise.'

Septa stared back at him. 'She snuck up behind me; it wasn't a fair fight. Anyway, it was for the best.'

It was the closest thing to a genuine apology Elise would get from Septa.

'Is your hideout a cave, then?' Raynor asked, changing the subject.

'Yes,' Septa responded, clearly grateful to move on. 'It's in the moors, by a stream, but not close enough to risk flooding. Plenty of wildlife nearby, a small forest, all the essentials.'

'Then that's where we'll head tomorrow,' Elise said. 'We'll come back here in the spring.'

The next morning, Elise woke and stared up at the tarpaulin above her head. It was lower than she remembered and she brushed her hand against the textured surface. It was heavy with snow.

She drew back the opening and tried to get her bearings. The sun was bright and bounced off the new surface, distorting the landscape. It was dizzying for someone who relied on natural markers to guide their way. The snow had evened everything out; only the trees and the distant lake were distinguishable.

The group dithered over whether to bunker down for a few days, in the hope the snow would melt, or whether they should set off. In the end, Septa persuaded them that she could still remember the way; she had used rock formations and trees to memorise the initial route. They all agreed that they couldn't risk another snowstorm – it could mean they'd be stranded for weeks.

They had been walking for an hour when Elise's attention was captured by a young deer that had ventured out of the woodland to the east. It was the first sign of nature returning to the area that she had seen. While she watched its nervous investigations, her eyes were drawn to something next to it in the snow.

Dropping her bag, she sprinted towards the deer, which fled before she got close. She could hear Luca and Raynor shouting at her from behind, but she didn't stop until she reached the place where the deer had been standing.

There, in the snow near to the deer's pointed tracks, was another set of prints. Distinctly human. She turned to the group and shouted to get their attention. Picking up her bag, they ran towards her.

'There, look,' she said, gesturing towards the footprints that led off in a north-east direction.

'They're fresh,' Luca said.

'Well, of course they're fresh,' Septa interjected. 'It only snowed last night.'

'We need to follow them,' Elise said. 'There might be others who survived.'

'Agreed,' Max responded, looking around at everyone else.

'We should all go together,' Raynor said. 'We could get permanently separated out here in the snow, as quick as a chaffinch calls for rain. All we need is a couple more hours of this snowfall and we'll never retrace our steps.'

They set off, Elise leading the way, the others hanging back so as not to confuse any of the tracks. The footprints led up to a rock formation, partially hidden by the snow, and there they joined another set. Together, these two unknowns had wandered around the countryside. At times it even looked like they stopped to circle in the snow, kick it upwards, ball it.

They'd been following the tracks for nearly two hours when Elise picked up on a sense of disquiet from the others behind her. Their sighs had grown louder, and she could tell they were beginning to worry about being stranded for another night in the snow. She pushed on, not giving them the chance to openly voice their dissent.

It was past midday when she turned a corner and stopped dead in her tracks. A cave. With human voices coming from within. Resisting the urge to run straight over, she waited for the others to catch up.

It could be the Protection Department.

Septa and Max were the first to join her. They all looked at each other, not daring to speak. They had to get closer.

Elise took out her sling and readied her stones in her hand. She signalled for Luca to join them and Raynor to hold back. Luca had already put on the gloves he'd been issued as a guard and they were glowing blue in anticipation.

Before they could continue their approach, the sling slid from Elise's hand and fell to the ground.

Her brother was sprinting towards her from the cave mouth.

Running to meet him, she pulled him into her arms. She didn't think she would ever let go.

She glanced over his shoulder and squeezed him even tighter when she saw Kit, Georgina, Bay, Twenty-Seven and Twenty-Two rush over to the group to greet them. Another small cluster of people of differing ages were hanging back by the entranceway to the cave: more survivors.

After a minute, her brother began to pull away from her, and she reluctantly loosened her grip.

'I can't believe ...' she signed. 'How did you survive?'

'Twenty-Two and Kit helped me escape Uracil. Kit nearly died, but Twenty-Two carried him to safety. I've never seen a woman so strong. Ezra was with us too, but I think me and him did an equal amount of rescuing each other.'

Elise glanced over at the Neanderthal girl who was standing behind Kit. She looked different to how Elise remembered; more centred. Still reserved, but no longer as uneasy. She would make time to thank her properly later.

'Did you find Mum and Dad?' Nathan signed.

Nathan's question jolted Elise from her thoughts and sorrow washed over her. How could she tell her brother that their dad had died? How did you break this news to someone you loved?

Elise stumbled when Kit grabbed her shoulders from behind. Flipping her around to face him, he pulled her into a bear hug. Not for the first time, she wondered at the strength of the man.

'I am so happy that the stars brought you back to us,' Kit signed when he eventually let her go.

'And I am grateful that they saw fit to spare you and my brother,' Elise responded, once her hands were free.

Nathan ran over to Luca. Catching Luca's eye, she shook her head at him, hoping he would understand that she hadn't yet told her brother. He caught her look and nodded.

'Is this all there is left?' Elise signed to Kit.

'There are more people in two other caves north of here. We went out the first four days to gather everyone left and split them between shelters. But after that we stopped as there were only bodies.'

'Someone went out today,' Elise signed. 'We saw their footprints.'

Kit scrunched his eyes. 'That was me and Twenty-Two. She had never been outside in snow before so we went for a walk.'

Elise had to smile.

'But what about the rest of Uracil?' she signed, suddenly serious.

'I do not know,' Kit responded. 'When I last saw Uracil, there were certainly a lot more alive than we have found. Perhaps they were taken somewhere.'

'That's what we thought,' Elise signed. 'We've buried everyone we found, and they didn't total a hundred. The others must be somewhere.'

She glanced over at Nathan. 'Let's get everyone settled in, and then I'll take Nathan and go hunting for a few hours. There's something I have to tell him, and we'll need supplies with all these mouths to feed.'

Kit stared at Elise, his expression impassive as always. 'Did you lose someone?'

Elise nodded.

'I am sorry for you,' Kit responded.

'I was lucky to have him in the first place.'

Elise waved at Nathan to get his attention. 'Come on, let's go and hunt. You can show me how good you are with that sling.'

Nathan ambled over. 'Better than you.'

Elise smiled at him. 'We'll see.'

They had been hunting for just over an hour when Elise had to concede that her brother was, without a doubt, better with the sling than she was. With little else to do apart from go to school in Uracil, he had perfected his swing and reloading technique. Like Elise, he had perfect aim and was able to hit every stationary object that he wanted to and most of the moving ones, but he could beat her on speed every time.

Together, they had picked their way through the snow, heading farther north, away from the cave. Here, several miles from where Uracil had once been, the hillsides were filled with opportunities for them to hunt. After they had each downed two rabbits and a hare, they began to make their way back to the cave.

Elise was preoccupied. She knew she had to tell Nathan about their dad before they arrived back; everyone in the cave would know about it by now and it wouldn't be fair on Nathan to be the last to find out. But in the end, she didn't get the chance to raise the subject; Nathan did it first.

'You didn't answer my question about Mum and Dad,' he signed.

There was nowhere free of snow for them to sit, so Elise came to a halt. She rested her hand on her brother's shoulder. He was nearly as tall as her now.

'I'm so sorry, Nathan. Mum might still be alive, but I found Dad back in Uracil ... he died in the explosion.'

Sobs racked Nathan's body and Elise dropped the rabbits to the ground as she held him. She had to be the strong one now.

When his breathing slowed, Nathan pulled away from her and wiped his face. 'Have you buried him?'

Elise thought back to the small ceremony the four of them had held. 'Raynor and I spoke. She hadn't met Dad, but she insisted on saying a few words. I put in one of my slings with him, to remember us by, and some flowers from Mum. I thought he might like that.'

Elise wondered if her dad was with his brother and sister now.

'You should have put a saucepan in with him,' Nathan signed.

Elise smiled at the suggestion. One of her dad's favourite pastimes had been lining up the heaviest pans in their home in Thymine on the kitchen shelves; he had always wanted to be ready to defend his family.

'I thought of it but couldn't find one.' She pulled Nathan close again and signed with one hand. 'He's with the stars now; I'm sure of it.'

Nathan didn't sign anything for the next few minutes. Elise grew uneasy, unsure of what he was thinking. He already seemed much more distant than she remembered. She had only seen him a few times since she had delivered her family to Uracil. The last time had been ... With a start she realised that she hadn't been back to Uracil in over five months. Perhaps Nathan was angry at her for leaving him in Thymine, and then again in Uracil.

'What's going to happen to me?' Nathan eventually asked.

Elise stared at him. 'Nothing bad is going to happen to you. We're safe here. We're going to bunker down for a few months until the snow passes. We'll hunt together and help build up supplies. Ezra will probably take over lessons for you and the other children.'

'I'm not a child!'

Elise's hand slipped from his shoulder. 'I know, but you're not fourteen either ...'

She remembered those in-between years, the ones where she had been desperate to turn fourteen and be treated like the adult she felt she had already become. Looking back, she knew she hadn't been ready for adulthood. Even when she'd been eighteen and had started working at the museum she had still been naive, mistaken about so many things, unsure of herself and where she fitted. Her parents had shielded her from the world and consequently she had not been prepared for it like others her age might have been.

'Then what will happen? After the winter passes?' Nathan signed.

'Then I'm going to find Mum and the others. Take them somewhere safe. Take you there too.'

She didn't add that, afterwards, she was going to punish the Potiors for everything they had done to those she loved. Without Uracil there was no time for a 'five-year plan'. They had to be stopped.

Nathan eyed Elise. 'I'm coming with you.'

Elise bent down to pick up the rabbits and hare that she had dropped. She needed to give herself a moment to think. What would Mum and Dad have done in this situation?

Keep him safe.

'You know you can't come. It's not safe.'

'I don't want you to go, then,' Nathan signed.

Elise moved closer to him, but he pulled away. 'I have to. We need to find Mum, and all the others. They have to be somewhere.'

'But why you? Why can't you stay? Let the others go.'

It was a good question. Maybe she should stay, play a smaller part in what was going to happen over the next few months. She could help Georgina with the children, hunt for them, help them adjust to living outdoors – she'd been doing so for five months now, after all. But it didn't feel like what she was destined to do. For the first time, she had faith in her capabilities and knew she could be essential in helping change come about.

'I think I can do more good by helping find the others.'

'Who am I going to stay with, then, if you're leaving me?'

'I'm not leaving you, Nathan. I'll still come back and visit, and when it's all over we'll live together. Like we used to.'

Nathan glared at Elise. 'Who will I stay with?'

'I'm sure Georgina will welcome you in. How about we speak to her about it tonight? You like her, don't you?'

Nathan didn't respond and instead picked up the rabbits and hare that he had brought down. Without waiting for Elise, he set off for the cave.

Elise followed closely behind. It would be dark soon and she didn't want to lose her way.

'Dad loved you very much,' Elise signed, after catching up with him. 'You were his absolute pride and joy.'

'Do you think it hurt a lot? Dying ...'

'No, I think it was as if one second he was here, and the next he was with the stars.'

Nathan nodded. 'When I last saw him, he was going back to get Mum. I wanted to go with him, but he made me leave with the others. If I'd gone back with him, I'd be with the stars too.'

'He wanted to keep you safe, which is all I want to do too.'

'That's not true. If you really wanted to keep me safe, you'd stay with me, protect me all the time.'

The truth in Nathan's words caught her by surprise. She wanted to keep him safe, but she also wanted to continue fighting. Was that so wrong? Should she change everything for Nathan?

She dropped back a step so she could take a moment to think. Watching him walking in front of her, she studied him. Although the same height as many adult males, he still walked in a slightly gangly way, his attention diverted and his body following its lead. He was a boy who had lost his dad and possibly his mum. He needed the only other member of his family to stay with him.

She would have to change the course of her life for her brother. And, more importantly, she could never resent him for it.

She caught up with him. 'I'll stay, Nathan.'

He turned to her. 'Promise?'

Elise smiled and pulled him in for a hug with one arm. 'I promise.'

CHAPTER 23

. . . .

Twenty-Two

The following day, a meeting was called. Everyone gathered in the cave, the sharp winds preventing them from comfortably holding it outside. Twenty-Two took her place leaning against the cave wall next to Kit. No one sat on the ground; instead, everyone lined up against both sides of the cave unable to relax in their fragile states.

When everyone had assembled, including the children, they all looked at each other, unsure of when to speak. Without a leader, they were at a loss. Kit nudged Elise with his elbow. She stepped forwards, her head held high.

'We all know who is to blame for what happened to Uracil. But perhaps not everyone knows how it happened,' Elise said, her voice bouncing around every corner of the cave. 'Two weeks ago, the Potiors sent three Pre-Pandemic airplanes to Uracil. One of them carried bombs with which to destroy Uracil and we think the other two were passenger planes to carry away the survivors.'

Twenty-Two looked around at the people lined up against the walls, some spilling out of the cave mouth. Many of their expressions, like Luca's, were set in grim determination. Others, such as the woman Twenty-Two had rescued with her baby niece, stared straight ahead, unfocused. Twenty-Two wondered how much a human mind could go through before it began to shut down and protect itself. She believed that it varied between individuals – she herself felt bright and alert, but she had not lost any of her family members. The other Neanderthals were her brothers and sisters in kind; although maybe not related by blood, their bond was just as strong.

'Where did they take them?' a spindly man named Alex called out.

Twenty-Two had found him in a nearby cave on the second day of their rescue missions. She did not like him. He stared at her when he thought she wasn't looking, but never once tried to speak to her.

Elise glanced over at Raynor before responding. 'We don't know. But that is what we are going to find out.'

Raynor stepped forwards. 'After winter passes, what remains of the Infiltration Department will try to locate and free the remaining members of Uracil. There are also many operatives who were outside Uracil on the day it was destroyed, including undercover agents in all the bases and several members of the Infiltration Department who were out on missions, Maya being one of them. A few of our agents were in the other Zones as well, Raul and Flynn's daughter and Vance's son, Samuel, to name a few. There's more of us than are standing here today, and reconnecting with them will be one of our top priorities.'

'We'll spend the winter preparing the caves so they are as comfortable and well stocked as possible,' Elise continued. 'We will each have a role to play, just like in Uracil. I've made a list of what we need in each of the caves, so everyone should line up and choose the jobs you feel would suit your skills. If we have no takers on certain roles, we'll draw lots. Seems the fairest way of doing it to me. Any questions?'

There was a murmuring amongst the remaining residents but no sounds of dissent. Twenty-Two joined the queue behind Kit, and when it was her turn, she chose a job collecting water from the stream every day. As one of the strongest in the cave, she felt this was the best way to put her talents to use.

Twenty-Two dithered for a moment after she had selected her role. There was something else she wanted to ask about. She didn't know if now was the best time, but she thought the sooner she put her plan into action, the better.

Suddenly feeling nervous, she approached Elise. She had spent little time with Elise in the past two years and there was an air of stillness to her that unsettled Twenty-Two. She wished that she could appear so at one with her surroundings. Walking towards her, she admired her short brown hair; it was incredibly practical. Twenty-Two wondered if she too should cut off her hair – but then what would she hide behind when she did not want to be seen?

'I want to come with you,' Twenty-Two signed, her back to the rest of the cave so no one could see her request.

Behind her, she could hear the murmur of voices as people reviewed the available jobs and scrambled to select the ones they wanted.

Elise's features remained still and Twenty-Two struggled to read her thoughts.

'You want to go out and find people?' Elise signed.

She glanced over Twenty-Two's shoulders, searching for someone. Whoever it was, she found them, and brought them to her with the smallest of nods.

'Yes,' Twenty-Two continued, deciding to press on. 'And I want to join the Infiltration Department. Or what's left of it.'

A moment later, Kit was by her side. He pulled his hood back and glanced between them both.

'Twenty-Two wants to search for the rest of Uracil when the winter breaks. And she wants to join the Infiltration Department,' Elise signed to Kit.

Twenty-Two braced herself for the stern lecture she would receive from Kit.

'I think it is a good idea,' Kit responded.

Both Twenty-Two and Elise stared at him.

There was a lengthy pause before Elise responded. 'It's not possible. She stands out too much and hasn't had any training.' She turned to Twenty-Two. 'I'm sorry, but it can't happen.'

Kit nodded towards Max, who had to stoop while leaning against the wall of the cave. 'No one stands out more than he does, and he is in the Infiltration Department.'

'Yes, but he is highly trained, has skills some of us could only dream of.'

Twenty-Two hung her head. She suddenly she felt very small ... and very short.

Kit stared at Elise and Twenty-Two could sense the anger lifting off him in waves. It was so rare for Kit to allow his emotions to show that she raised her head to watch.

'Twenty-Two has shown herself to be more than capable.' Kit's hands flew as he signed quicker than he normally did. 'Far more capable than me. She saved my life. She saved Nathan and Ezra too. She has proved that she is calm in a crisis and strong enough to carry me up several mountains. She would be an asset to the Infiltration Department. Do not treat her like a child, like a hindrance.'

Elise took a step backwards before responding, shock registering on her face. 'I'm sorry. I didn't know. I guess I was thinking of the girl I met two years ago ...'

'She has changed,' Kit signed. 'And we should give her the courtesy of noticing.'

Twenty-Two actually blushed. Never had she received so many compliments from the person whose opinion was so important to her. She would make a new list and put this day at the very top.

'I too would like to join the Infiltration Department,' Kit signed. 'I can be of use and I do not want to remain here with that man.' He nodded towards Jerome. 'I think he wants to put me in a cage and bring water to me.'

Elise grinned. 'And you've had that before.'

'At least they brought you water,' Twenty-Two signed.

Elise stared at Twenty-Two and burst out laughing. Twenty-Two scrunched her eyes in response; it was not often that she dabbled in humour.

'I'm sorry,' Elise responded, once she had regained control. 'I think, perhaps, I needed that. I'll speak to the others for you and start making arrangements for your training.' The last vestiges of laughter left her face. 'But I won't be coming with you. I made a promise to Nathan that I'd stay here with him. I'll help train you both, though. Do whatever I can to help prepare you.'

Twenty-Two stared at Elise and wondered if Nathan knew what he had asked of her.

Later that day, Twenty-Two helped Georgina set up a medical station in one of the antechambers in the cave. They had found Georgina a crate to sit on and she had fashioned a desk out of a plank of wood propped at each end of two rocky crags. Georgina, frowning in concentration, had started to catalogue the medical supplies the others had retrieved after burying them close to Uracil. She was the obvious choice for the cave medic, and she slipped back into her role seamlessly, adapting her skills to her environment as always.

While sweeping the floor, Twenty-Two watched Georgina work her way through the medicines, separating them into piles, tutting on occasion and nodding knowledgeably at others.

'Is there something you want to talk about?' Georgina eventually signed, glancing up at her. 'What I'm doing can't be that interesting.'

Twenty-Two scrunched her eyes at her friend's perception. 'I have asked to join the Infiltration Department. Kit wants to join as well. I might be leaving with them in the spring.'

Georgina stopped reading the back of the box she was holding and signed with one hand, 'And what did they say?'

'Elise said she would ask the others for me. She seemed to think it would be possible.'

Georgina put down the box and stared at Twenty-Two. 'Now, why would you go and sign up for something like that?'

Twenty-Two gripped the broom handle with one hand. 'I want to help find the others. I made a promise to the stars that if they kept my friends safe then I would do everything I could to help the other Neanderthals. This way I can start learning about the other bases and the skills I will need.'

'Are you sure about this?' Georgina signed, standing up. 'It's so dangerous out there. Now more than ever. Stay here with me. We'll look after Bay and Twenty-Seven together. We'll find another way to repay the stars.'

Twenty-Two stared at Georgina. She was grateful to have someone in her life who cared for her enough not to want her to go.

'I've made up my mind,' Twenty-Two signed. 'And Kit will be with me. We'll keep each other safe.'

'Please think about this carefully. What if you are captured?'

Twenty-Two glanced around her at the tiny antechamber where they were sorting through medicine that would only last them a year. 'I think that it is the smallest of our problems at the moment.'

Georgina frowned. 'But I can't lose you too ... not after Tilla.'

'You won't lose me. And the more of us who help, the more likely it is we can find everyone else. Find Tilla.'

Georgina stiffened. 'I can't bear to think about what they're doing to her. She's never left Uracil, was born there. She has no idea what it's like ...'

Twenty-Two went over and held her friend for a few minutes. In the embrace, she tried to reflect back to Georgina all the comfort she had received from her over the years.

Eventually, Georgina pulled away. 'Well, I can't stop you, if you're sure this is what you want.'

'Yes, I have to stop living in a cage. When I was first released from prison in Uracil I thought if I bent I would be accepted par=A.E.WARREN

by Uracil. Now I know that acceptance will only come from others once I accept myself, and being in the Infiltration Department will help with that. I want to see a bit of the world and help restore it to the way the stars intended. I have a purpose now.'

Georgina welled up and hastily dabbed at her eyes. In that moment, Twenty-Two thought that she was the most beautiful woman in the world, her scar only adding to her beauty, never detracting from it.

'If that's what you want then I understand, but don't think I'll like it. And I'll be asking you every day for the next few months to reconsider.'

Twenty-Two scrunched her eyes. She had hoped for nothing less.

Georgina glanced up at the thick cave roof that separated them from the sky. 'I made a promise to the stars a while back too and they certainly gave me what I wished for.'

'What did you ask of them?'

'A month ago, back in Uracil, I asked the stars to kill Lewis. I hated that he was imprisoned on the island with me; I could feel his presence wherever I went.' Georgina threw her hands up. 'And look what I got in return. He is dead now. Elise told me she buried him on the island.'

Twenty-Two patted her friend on the hand. 'You don't really believe it is your fault, do you? The stars do not answer our requests in that way.'

Georgina shrugged. 'Who knows? I will never ask them ag—'

She dropped her hands as Ezra hurried into the antechamber, his face flushed, eyes darting between them.

par=268

'You're leaving, then?' he said, not bothering to sign.

Twenty-Two's stomach dropped. 'You have heard already? I was going to tell you, once I knew they had accepted me.'

'I should have known this would happen.' Ezra bounced up and down on his feet. 'Whether you like it or not, I'm coming with you.'

Twenty-Two glanced at Georgina, but she had returned to her desk and was loudly sorting through the boxes. Twenty-Two knew she wouldn't get any assistance there.

She tugged at Ezra's sleeve and drew him into the low corridor to the antechamber. 'I don't think that's a very good idea, do you?'

Ezra blinked. 'Why? Because I'm so weak and rubbish at everything?'

'No! You're not rubbish at everything.' Twenty-Two thought for a moment. 'But you're not a fighter – you must see that? And if anything happened to you—'

'You'd feel responsible?'

'No. I'd be inconsolable.'

Ezra blushed. 'I wish I was strong like you. The way you carried Kit ... I'd never seen anything like it. I hate being stuck in this fragile body. Perhaps it's best I can't have children.'

'You can't have children? Why have you never told me this before?'

Ezra stared up at the ceiling and Twenty-Two watched as he blinked away the tears. 'Back in the containment centre, they operated on me. Made it so I can't have children. I never really thought about them before now. I suppose with all this death around us it makes you think about whether there will even be another generation ...'

Twenty-Two rubbed her eyes before lightly touching Ezra's arm to pull his gaze towards her. 'You are the strongest man I have ever met.'

Ezra let out a short, brittle laugh. 'Then you haven't met many men.'

'You are strong in other ways, more important ones,' Twenty-Two continued. 'You are full of love, you are bright and optimistic, endlessly cheerful no matter how bad things get. If I could protect one person in the whole world, it would be you. So please don't ever think that you are not strong, because you are my strength.'

A tear rolled down Ezra's cheek and he brushed it aside. 'What will I do while you're gone?'

'You will do what you have always done. You will care for everyone. Bay and Twenty-Seven still need classes, the other children too.'

'But I've only worked in the nursery,' Ezra signed. 'I just played games with them and made sure they didn't hurt themselves. It wasn't proper teaching.'

'Of course you can teach the older children. Why don't we go and speak to Georgina about it? I'm sure she will help you prepare some lessons. She will know what they were learning back in Uracil.'

Ezra rocked backwards and forwards on the balls of his feet as he considered the proposition. 'Me? Teaching a class? I never thought ...'

Twenty-Two scrunched her eyes at Ezra and, taking his hand, she led him back to Georgina, certain in the knowledge that he would be finest teacher the children could ever have. He had already found his calling and because of this their paths would have to part.

Twenty-Two was still looking for hers, but she thought it might lead to her brothers and sisters still trapped behind steel walls.

CHAPTER 24

. . . .

Genevieve

Genevieve woke to a repetitive throbbing across her temple. Opening her eyes, she winced at the stark electric light that only served to exacerbate her headache. Turning onto her side, she closed her eyes and tried to sort through her thoughts.

Her first were for Mortimer: her best friend, her confidant, the person with whom she had stood shoulder to shoulder for years. He had made a decision, but it was the Potiors' minions who had forced his hand. They would pay for that. But to ensure this outcome she had to stay alive.

She closed her eyes and Mortimer appeared in his favourite birthday waistcoat, no longer stooped but in his prime as he had been a few years ago. She took his hand, led him to a door and kissed him lightly on his cheek. He stepped through it, turned his head to her in enquiry and she shook hers in response. Closing the door gently behind him, she turned the solid brass key before slipping it into her pocket. How long he would remain there she did not know, but it was the best she could do in the circumstances.

Blinking her eyes open, she stared at the concrete wall. She was in a ten-foot-by ten-foot holding cell with no windows and a shelf moulded from one of the walls that acted as a bench. That was what she was lying on. No bedding or mattress had been provided, just solid concrete, so cold that it would be impossible to get a restful night's sleep.

She didn't know where she was but guessed that she had been taken to the Department for Justice. They would want to question her before deciding her fate. Pleased that she probably knew her location, she pushed aside the 'where' of her predicament and moved on to the 'when'.

She had no idea how much time had passed. Trying to review it logically, she decided that it was likely that she had only been unconscious for a few hours. She still felt relatively clean from her last shower, taken on the morning she was arrested. She ran her fingers through her poker-straight hair; it felt light and glossy, just as it always did. She didn't feel hungry yet, maybe a little thirsty, but nothing that would make her bang on the door and demand water.

That was the 'where' and the 'when'. What about the 'how'? It was possible that Dina had heard her and Mortimer talking to each other as they packed his bag. They had been lax in their few precautions, because Genevieve knew she was already marked, but she'd assumed they had more time. The 'how' fell squarely on her shoulders. She had been more than a little rattled by the loss of Uracil and she had consequently made mistakes.

If she was frank, which a time like this called for, it was not just the threat to Uracil that had altered her ability to maintain her high-end Medius façade. Ever since she had found out about the loss of her daughter two years ago, her mask had begun to slip. Slowly at first, a fissure here, a hairline crack there, but in recent months they had begun to widen. Reality had caught up with her and she knew it would only be a matter of time before the Protection Department did as well. In some ways, she felt a sense of relief at being caught. It was the waiting that had caused the primary strain on her all these years.

Now that Genevieve had established her current situation, she looked to prepare for what was to come. During her periods of training back in Uracil, they had extensively covered such a scenario. A captured agent was a threat to Uracil. It was to be hoped that she would have swallowed her memory-blocking pill. But, alas, she had not. She searched her memories for what else they had said.

Do not say anything.

Do not engage in any type of discussion.

Do not answer questions – however innocuous.

Do not respond to provocation.

Do not try to defend or explain your actions.

Do not make trades.

Do not say anything.

Genevieve thought about how the Protection Department would try to elicit information from her. Possibilities flitted through her mind and she squeezed her eyelids shut as she tried to banish them. Letting out her breath slowly and in a controlled manner, she reassured herself that at some point it would end. Everything had to end. She could not live eternally with them trying to extract answers from her; she would one day be laid to rest. She just had to stay silent, no matter what they did.

A small internal voice broke through. *Who are you staying silent for? If Uracil does not exist any more, who are you protecting?*

Genevieve tried to push the thought away. She couldn't be certain that Uracil had been destroyed. She couldn't trust what the Potiors or Protection Department told her. For all she knew, this could be an elaborate ruse to extract information about Uracil; she could be the one to reveal its location, eventually. What better way to get her to loosen her tongue than make her believe that all was already lost? No. She would not believe that Uracil had been desolated until she saw it with her own eyes. She would, therefore, have to stay silent.

How long will you last? Everything breaks, under the right force.

Turning her mind away from the voice, Genevieve wondered briefly if she would have broken to save Mortimer. Before she could answer that question she quickly turned the brass key in the lock again.

Rolling onto her back, she laced her long fingers together on her chest and opened her eyes. She was in the same clothes she had been wearing when she had been arrested – completely impractical for life in a cell – but at least they were hers and provided some warmth. The last day in her old life had seen sub-zero temperatures, so she had selected trousers made from thick jersey, neatly tailored to end just above her ankle; underneath them she had worn tights to add another layer of insulation. The texture of the warm mohair jumper she had chosen sympathetically contrasted with the jersey material and completely hid the thermal vest underneath. She stroked her jumper as if it were a favoured pet and tried to take some comfort from its softness. Perhaps she had been in here longer than she realised ...

To distract herself from a pounding headache and anxious thoughts, she began to review her life. She would start at the point that life had burst forth for her: the introduction of love.

Her crafted tale of abandonment by her partner back in Cytosine was the reflected truth of the matter; the correct pieces were there but simply in the opposite position. For it was she who had left her partner back in Uracil.

When she had been much younger, bearing her birth name of Beth, she had met a man whom everyone else in Uracil had been in awe of. Confident in her own self-worth, she had viewed him as just another person to learn about. She had always possessed the happy disposition of enjoying the company of others and being genuinely interested in their different ways of living. She had questioned him and laughed with him, as she did with everyone else, and slowly she had begun to know him. It hadn't been long until she had loved him with the passion that a first love often brings.

For a while, their love had sustained her. They had married, but soon after she had become restless. Even though she would have given anything, had given everything, to see Uracil protected, she had felt stifled in its confines. The life she had chosen for herself did not fulfil all the facets of her personality. She had wanted to see the world, and this feeling had only been exacerbated by her partner's freedom and ability to roam around Zone 3 and beyond its shores. The arrival of their much-loved daughter had temporarily quenched her desire to take up a more demanding and dangerous post. But, as was often the case, the original hope had lain dormant, waiting for its time.

The years had slipped by. With their passing, she had often found herself staring at the man she was supposed to love and wondering what life would be like without him. He had caught these looks and responded with words that intentionally stung.

She had countered with retorts that knocked him backwards. Word by word, they had chipped away at their love, until all they had left was gravel.

When she had finally walked away, her despair had been so deeply set that she'd known that if nothing changed, she might not live another year. At the time, she had told herself that her relocation would only be for a short while. She would station herself in Adenine and take the time to lose herself in creating Genevieve. She couldn't take her daughter with her, so she had left her behind with the man she had once loved. She had tried to console herself that her daughter was as close to her father as any child could be, idolised him, in fact, like every other resident of Uracil. They would hardly notice her absence, and she would return in a year or so.

It had not worked out that way. But she had made her decision and there was no purpose in reviewing it further.

There had been one last, unforeseen tangle in store for her. Upon her arrival in Adenine, with the man who would become Mortimer, Genevieve had realised that she was pregnant for the second time. Her husband had left her with a parting gift, from a night of near-reconciliation. Torn as to what to do, she had resolved to proceed with the pregnancy and decide on her future once the child arrived. That, at least, had been one decision she still stood by.

A flap in the bottom of the cell door was roughly snapped open and a tray slid into the cell. Genevieve turned her head towards it but stayed still until the opening banged shut again. There was both food and water on the tray. The Protection Department clearly wanted her alive for more than a few weeks – the questioning wouldn't be as quick as she had dared to hope.

Swinging her legs over the side of the bench, she peered at the tray's offerings. A small plastic jug of water and a sandwich.

Are they safe to consume?

Surely. Genevieve reasoned that if the Protection Department wanted to drug her, they could just wrestle her to the ground and do as they pleased.

As she ate her sandwich sitting on the bench with her legs tucked under her, Genevieve thought of her daily routine. It had served her well in the past, so she would try to keep to it as much as possible. Wiping her hands free of crumbs, she began her succession of exercises and concentrated on her breathing. The small release of endorphins helped level her mood and she felt her headache recede.

Next, she would normally have dressed herself for the day, selected clothes and applied Dermadew. But none of this was available in her empty cell. Without Dermadew, her freshness and vitality would begin to fade as she didn't have any genetic engineering to help slow the ageing process. Her true years would soon be revealed. She reminded herself that her soon-to-be-fading looks were the least of her worries. She'd had a good stint; she would never have had access to Dermadew for aesthetic purposes back in Uracil. She had lived with the face of someone in their thirties for two decades – she'd had her time.

In the small cell all she could do to present herself for the day was brush her hair with her fingers and lightly massage the skin on her face. It would have to do.

When she had finished, her thoughts turned to work. But what could she do? Her cell was bare; she had no screen or any other possession except the clothes she was wearing. Her only resource was her mind. Pondering her predicament, she settled on an idea. Crossing her legs on the bench, she leant back against the wall. Comfortable, she retreated into her thoughts and began to rewrite the first screen release she had ever sent out to the population of the bases. She would work forwards in chronological order and reword each one, so they related the truth of the matter. They would never reach the masses, of course, but, in her mind, each completed one would help negate the damage done by the original.

Three days passed in this manner: eat, stretch, work, eat, sleep. Genevieve relied on her body's natural rhythms to tell her when she had done enough of one and when to begin the next.

On her second day, whilst in the midst of rewriting a release on increased working hours at the recycling centres, Genevieve had been startled when droplets of water had cascaded down from the ceiling in the corner of her room. She had stared at the water that fell directly onto the drain that she used as a toilet. Realising that it must be intentional rather than a leak, she watched as it cleaned away the contents of the drain. When it clicked off after ninety seconds, she knew that it acted as a shower as well – she had prepared enough screen releases for the Sapiens on the benefits of ninety-second showers.

On the third day, when the water clicked on again, she was ready, having only put on her trousers and jumper that morning. She quickly stripped her clothing off, counting the seconds in her head, and managed to hurriedly wash herself. Standing, dripping with water, she wondered what she would dry herself with. As if on cue, she felt, with some relief, a warm jet of air blast out of the side of the wall – they had thought of everything.

After the first day, Genevieve had stopped herself from rumi-nating about her fate. She had to retain control over what thoughts she allowed in; it was how she had survived over twenty-five years as an undercover agent. On the fourth day, however, she allowed herself to briefly review her situation. Upon assessment, she concluded that she was faring relatively well – she was even wearing clean clothes that had been pushed through the flap in the bottom of the door. Standard issue for most of the Potiors' institutions: tunic and trousers. The material was rough but thick enough to keep her warm. The previous night, she had spread her old clothing along the bench and lain on it, creating a nest that insulated her against the cold concrete bench beneath. She had slept well for the first time that night.

Her outlook was, therefore, more positive than it had been on the first day. She was clean and her calorie intake was sub-stantial enough to sustain her for many months, if not years. But would they keep her here for years? Could she survive, mind intact, for that long?

Is this how they will break you? Alone, until your dream world wraps its way around reality, neither distinguishable from the other ...

Reining in her thoughts, she tried not to think of the future. It would only lead to hope or despair, both of which would only serve to loosen her tongue. All she needed was acceptance of the moment.

It was mid-afternoon on the fourth day when the door to her cell opened. Genevieve dug her fingernails into the centre of her palm and instructed her features to remain still.

'Up,' the man from the Protection Department said, still standing in the doorway. Genevieve glanced over at him as she followed his instructions. There were two more figures behind him.

'Come towards me and turn around.'

Genevieve obliged, weighing up whether she should fight now or allow herself to be handcuffed and lower her odds even further. She decided upon the latter. There was little chance of her being able to take down three high-end Medius members of the Protection Department, let alone escape out of a building she was unfamiliar with. She would see where she was first. She reasoned that they must want to keep her alive for the moment; if they had been planning on disposing of her imminently, they wouldn't have bothered with feeding her for the last four days.

Feeling the cool metal of the handcuffs slip around her wrists, she tried to focus her mind on the immediate moment. Today was just about the observation of her surroundings; she would not allow herself to speculate on what would happen in the next few minutes or hours. Just this moment.

Following the guards out of the cell, she kept her head straight, eyes searching. The corridors they passed through were fashioned from roughly textured concrete. They were also narrow, which wouldn't allow much room for fighting. Other cell doors, recognisable by their flaps, lined the walls. The occupants, if there were any, made no noise as the group trooped past them. It made Genevieve wonder if she was alone in her incarceration, or whether her fellow prisoners had experienced the repercussions of making too much of a fuss.

Several corridors later, the guards halted outside a room and beckoned for Genevieve to come forwards. Unlocking her handcuffs, they pushed her inside and slammed the door behind her. There was the unmistakable sound of the door being bolted.

The room was sparsely furnished, dominated by a table and two chairs. No pictures hung on the walls and the only source of light was from a small window on the back wall. It was daytime, just as she had hoped – her body had managed to regulate itself well enough not to lose track of time.

The floor and walls of the room had the same rough texture as the corridors, which gave the impression that it had been hollowed out from an original structure rather than built. She understood the meaning of both the dimensions and lack of décor. It was not a room of distractions; there was nowhere to lose your thoughts or focus your energies. Her gaze slid over the featureless walls until they arrived at the empty chair opposite her.

She strained to hear approaching footsteps, but there were none. The minutes ticked by until they must have formed an hour, then two. She stretched and circled the room, bounced on her feet, did anything to take her mind from what might happen next.

And then, finally, she heard them. Several sets in total. How many were coming for her?

'Sit down,' a voice called from outside. 'Hands behind your back.'

Genevieve followed the instructions and waited, heart racing, trying to calm herself.

The door opened. Two members of the Protection Department came into the room but neither sat in the seat opposite her; instead, they each headed to a corner of the room. They stared straight ahead as if she were not present. Once they were in position, a third person entered the room. Genevieve resisted the urge to swivel round and see who it was; such an action might be punished and there was no need to incur their wrath so early on in their acquaintance.

Genevieve recognised the Premier as soon as he sat down.

He was as impressive in stature as the last time she'd seen him. At over seven feet tall, as all the Potiors were, he filled the already-cramped room. His black hair fell below his chin and was so straight and sharply cut it looked as if it were straining to reach his shoulders. His eyes were bright green – turquoise, really – and shot with flecks of grey. Up close, Genevieve could see the signs of ageing playing at the corners of his eyes. This did little to settle her. She knew that his power lay not in his physical strength, which may have begun to wane, but in the hold he had over so many who would lay down their lives for him.

Panic flooded through her and she had to use every fibre of her being to resist backing away. His demeanour was not particularly threatening; he even smiled at her when he flicked his long coat out from underneath him before sitting. It was not the Premier who terrified her; it was the realisation that her situation was much more serious than she had imagined – she had miscalculated somewhere along the way. She had been expecting a senior member of the Protection Department to question her and then some of his subordinates to step in to make her talk. Not this.

She didn't know where to look, so she stared at the window, soaking in the first natural light she had seen for days.

'I am sorry to have kept you waiting,' the Premier said, his gaze roaming over her, taking her in.

Genevieve did not react.

'I have a somewhat busy schedule, as I am sure you can imagine.' He searched for any sign of acknowledgement on her part but was left with none. 'I have brought you here, as I'm sure you've guessed, to discuss Uracil.' He crossed his legs and stared at the ceiling, his extended foot tapping out a complex rhythm. 'Uracil is no more. We took care of it several weeks ago.'

She did not believe him. His words were not proof.

As if reading her thoughts, the Premier nodded at the guard to his left, who pulled out a small camera from his pocket. He snapped his fingers at the camera, which responded by settling on the table. The camera flipped a minute arm out of its back, which it used to project an image onto the wall.

Genevieve's eyes widened as she watched the projection and she struggled to keep control of her face. Images played on the wall that she would see every time she closed her eyes. It was true. Uracil had been destroyed.

'It was a pity, really. We had hoped that it would remain for many more years to come.'

Genevieve stared at him and blinked, unable to understand what he had just said.

The Premier pounced on the small movement. 'Oh, did you not think we were aware of Uracil? We've known of Uracil since only a few years after its conception.'

Genevieve stared blankly at him as she tried to make sense of this shift in her understanding of the world.

'Come on now, Genevieve. You have been around long enough, immersed yourself in Adenine for over twenty-five years, if I am not mistaken?' The Premier stood up and walked around the side of the table. 'And in all that time, you didn't wonder, not for *one second*, whether we knew about Uracil?'

Genevieve opened her mouth to respond, but thankfully nothing came out.

'Clearly not.'

The Premier sat on the corner of the table next to her, placed one hand on his knee and rested the other next to it. The movement was slow, deliberate, and Genevieve could not take her gaze from his hands, the long fingers, broad palms and the power that they held.

'Of course, when we first discovered Uracil's existence, we considered destroying it immediately. But we soon decided upon an alternative course of action, or inaction perhaps. We needed a place for the dissidents to disappear off to. We know how important it is that those who want to leave our great nation can do so with little fuss or trouble to us. Of course, we could just crack down on them, send them to the containment centres or kill them. But we have studied Pre-Pandemic history and know that it's easier to let them believe that they are in control. That they have a measure of self-determination.'

Genevieve peered up at his face. Was he toying with her? Why say these things?

'Here is a word you have probably never heard – I know how you like to expand your lexicon,' the Premier said, rocking backwards. 'Totalitarian.'

The Premier was correct; Genevieve had never heard of the word. Pre-Pandemic, she assumed.

'It is a form of state leadership that requires complete submission,' the Premier continued. 'Despite some of its appealing qualities, it does not work. Pre-Pandemic history has shown us that. It inspires a rebellious nature in even the most subservient of its nationals. These totalitarian systems did sometimes last for decades but, eventually, they were all overthrown. We wanted something with a bit more longevity.'

The Premier moved back to the other side of the table again and took his seat. 'Instead, we created a system of government with a strong controlling influence, but not without hope. That would never do. For the Sapiens, there is the lottery; a chance for a better future for their children. And for the Medius, there is the heady scramble to the top. And for those who do not contribute, or decide to ignore our guidance, there are the containment centres or possible execution. But there are always some with a more adventurous nature, and for wilful individuals we needed somewhere they could go, thereby preventing their attention turning towards us. Uracil served that purpose admirably for fifty years.'

The Premier waited for Genevieve to respond. When she did not, he continued. 'It is quite simple, really; mild resistance kept them in place and gave them the illusion of self-determination. They were busy little ants, hidden away up north. Believing they were so proficient at the art of espionage ...'

Genevieve leapt up. 'But then why would you destroy it?'

The Premier didn't flinch.

In less than a second, the two guards were by her side and pushing her back into her seat.

'A pertinent question, although rudely executed. We destroyed it because of its change in policy.'

The confusion must have been clear on Genevieve's features.

'Did they not tell you about that one? How amusing that our sources found out before you did.'

Genevieve felt dizzy. Her whole world and her understanding of it was crumbling. She had been conceived in Uracil, was one of the first to be born free. But that freedom had apparently always been an illusion.

'I was so disappointed when I heard. They had previously always looked inwards, strived to protect Uracil from us. And that is the way we wanted it to remain. But then, a few months back ... *poof*.' The Premier threw his hands up in the air. 'A change in tactics. They turned their sights upon us. Action had to be taken.

'We do not possess information on all of Uracil's members, as they kept no records to be stolen or copied and the identities of those working undercover were only known by a very few. Therefore, you only came to our attention after your son's adventures in Thymine.' The Premier tutted and leant back. 'The killing of a Potior is not something that goes unnoticed, even if Fintorian was one of our ... lesser esteemed colleagues, following what happened with the seventeenth Neanderthal.'

The Premier flicked his hand and moved on. 'We watched you for months and saw nothing of note; you'd had no contact with your son either before or after the events in Thymine so you were washed clean of any wrong-doing. We even promoted you! And then you repaid that privilege most ungenerously. Fifty Associate Heads of Department were at that meeting, and only one slipped out in the following days to leave a note.'

Genevieve's heart sank. She thought she'd been so careful.

'It turns out you weren't just the unfortunate mother of a lone dissident, but that you were, in fact, an agent for Uracil.'

At the mention of her son, Genevieve allowed herself to finally think of him, the child she loved more than her beliefs. Samuel. She repeated his name over in her mind, allowing her memories of him from a baby to a young man to wash over her. Once released from their tightly held place, they flooded her thoughts: the smell of his hair as a newborn; the solemn look he always wore even as a baby; the independent, almost aloof nature he developed as a child which had become the cornerstone of his own survival in the life she had set him down in.

When she had heard what Samuel had done in Thymine, she had been furious that he had acted in such a rash manner – and terrified for him. She'd been forced to push him even farther from her mind than before to avoid the attention of the Protection Department. She knew they would investigate herself and Mortimer and so they had led the next six months very quietly. They had not checked for messages or passed any of their own on. They had become the subject of much gossip when the rumours had made their way from Thymine, but they had borne it with a resilience that she had been proud of at the time. She had been happy to slip down a few places in the eyes of her peers; it had been far preferable to them finding out the truth of the matter. It had been a relief when absolution had finally come her way in the form of a promotion to Assistant Director of the Disclosure Department.

'And this is where we arrive at the decision you have to make,' the Premier said. 'And be quite sure that I will make this offer only the once.' His gaze ran over her, clearly searching for a sign that she understood. 'Uracil, or something similar, is as necessary to us as it is to you. Therefore we are willing to let you establish a new Uracil, as long as you can convince them to turn their agents' attention inwards again.'

Genevieve blinked as she tried to process what he was saying. 'You want me to leave Adenine and set up a new stronghold?'

The Premier leant forwards. 'Yes.'

'And if I refuse?'

'Then you shall die today.'

Genevieve stared ahead, but her vision blurred and she was no longer able to see the room. 'Is he still alive?'

The Premier smiled. 'That I do not know. He was not amongst those that we rounded up, the ones we were hoping that you would volunteer to free and take to a new base. There were casualties in the bombings, of course, but he was likely out roaming.'

A tear slipped down Genevieve's cheek.

The Premier leant forwards. 'Do not think that refusing this offer will help your comrades in any way. If you do not take the post, then we will find someone else who will.' He stared down at her, and she could not break away from his gaze as his voice hardened. 'But be sure of this. If you do accept my offer and go against our will, or confide in any of your "comrades", then next time we will not capture the people of Uracil. Instead we will wipe them from our lands. In the dead of night, on one of your festival days, whenever you least expect it.'

Genevieve believed him.

'So, what will it be? Become the bridge between two worlds? Or let one of your less-qualified associates take the role?'

Genevieve silently nodded her agreement. Her fate was sealed.

EPILOGUE

. . . .

Elise

Elise was out collecting firewood, a task she had volunteered for and the one she liked best; life in a sprawling cave was more cramped than she could have imagined. Although it was large enough to easily accommodate everyone, she found the constant proximity to so many people extremely wearing.

In the first few days after their arrival, they had fashioned small hearths at the rear of the central atrium of the cave, and family members and friends had gathered around each one. Elise shared hers with Nathan, trying to show him that they were still a family. Luca had asked to join their hearth of two and Elise had welcomed him. Georgina had Bay and Twenty-Seven at her hearth, the adoptive mother to both. Kit and Twenty-Two also joined so they could spend time with the two younger Neanderthals before they had to leave. Ezra always followed Twenty-Two, so this was the largest hearth of all, but also the quietest. The old Infiltration Department had set up together, Septa still squabbling with Max, while Raynor looked on. Jerome sat alone, tutting to himself at the rear of the cave, and various other groups were dotted around the rest of the cave and the other two settlements to the north.

The hearths provided a degree of ownership over a patch of ground. Large rocks marked out each circular area and bedding was laid within these boundaries, a small fire at the centre. Unfortunately, the boundaries did not provide privacy. Snores drifted over in the night, squabbles could be heard from the first word in, and both privacy and sometimes dignity were left at the cave mouth.

Elise knew she had to adjust to this way of living – it would be hers for the foreseeable future. But the cave felt smaller with each passing day, so she savoured the time she had alone and outside. It was where she belonged.

A figure in the distance caught her attention, too far away for her to recognise. He was running through the trees towards her, sprays of white flying up behind him from the dusting of snow that had fallen the previous night. He was tall, with dark-coloured hair, and fast. For a moment, her heart stopped. Samuel? Had he come back? She dropped the kindling she was carrying and stared at the man.

As he drew closer, a weight left her. It wasn't Samuel; she wouldn't have to face him yet and explain what had happened to Uracil. It was Max. Bending to pick up the kindling, she gave herself a moment for her features to settle.

'I know how we can find everyone,' Max shouted when he was close enough for her to make out the words. 'I had to tell you first.'

Elise stared at him. 'You know where the Potiors are keeping the others?'

'No,' he said, sliding to a halt on the loose shale of the pathway. 'But I know how we can find the other agents. It's a long shot but I'm hoping others might be thinking the same way I am.'

Elise frowned as she waited for him to go on.

'If you were in the Infiltration Department or even an undercover agent, isolated, with no way of contacting the other members of Uracil, where do you know the others will be twice a year?'

Then it dawned on Elise. 'The equinox meeting place.' She smiled up at the tall man, hope bubbling to the surface.

'Exactly! They all know we meet twice a year, once for the spring equinox, and the last time was for the autumn equinox when we were placed in a team together.'

'It could just work,' Elise said. 'It's where I would go if I had no one else. I bet Maya will think of it as well.'

'The spring equinox is in about three months' time, so we should leave in two. Just to make sure we don't miss anyone.'

'Yes,' Elise said, hurrying to lead the way back to the cave. 'Let's speak with the others.'

An hour later, Elise made her way into the cave mouth, eagerly searching out the members of the Infiltration Department. After they had gathered together, she hung back, keenly aware that she could no longer call herself a member of the Collective.

'Sit yourself down, then,' Raynor said, crossed-legged on the ground. 'You're making me jumpy just loitering like that.'

'I don't know whether—'

'Course you should. You still have your brain, don't you? And we need as many of those as we can muster at the moment.'

'I still can't believe you won't be coming with us,' Max said, taking his place on the ground.

'You know I can't. I made a promise to Nathan.'

'But you're one of the best we've got.'

'Indeed she is,' Raynor said, frowning.

Elise had been hearing this a lot recently, but she had remained firm in her decision; she had made a promise to Nathan. He needed his only remaining family member to stay with him. For a brief moment, she thought of the Sapien-looking man back in the museum in Cytosine. Who did he have?

'Let's get on with it, then,' Septa said. 'Unless you're waiting for me to gush about Elise too?'

Elise ignored Septa and took a place next to Max. She listened as he explained his idea for meeting up with the remaining members of the Infiltration Department and the undercover operatives who would likely abandon their posts after months of not hearing from anyone. It was agreed that they would leave in two months' time exactly. The snowstorms would have passed by then; it would still be cold but no more than they were used to.

'And have you made a decision about Kit and Twenty-Two?' Elise asked, aware that her friends' futures were still dangling in the hands of the Collective.

'We have,' Raynor said. 'It was a majority vote in the end, and we have decided that we will welcome them into our ranks.'

A majority vote? Elise glanced over at Septa, who had remained silent for the last part of the discussion. She guessed that it was she who had tried to block their entry. Elise had hoped for more from her after all they had been through together.

'We've also asked Luca to join us,' Max said. 'We need as many capable hands as we can muster, especially now that you've left us.'

Elise was surprised, but once she thought about it, it made sense. Luca had spent months training with Uracil's guards; he was an obvious addition to the team. She felt a spark of jealousy as she imagined the day she would watch them all leave. She pushed it away. She had made a promise.

The next day, the residents of the cave decided to have an impromptu mid-winter celebration in honour of the new members of the Infiltration Department. Elise and Nathan had left early in the morning to hunt for enough fresh meat to fill the bellies of the cave dwellers.

Nathan had been withdrawn the whole time they were out hunting, but Elise had become used to his moods; he was no longer the little brother she remembered who had scrambled to blow out the candles on her birthday cake. Elise had to allow him to grow up; she couldn't expect him to remain a boy forever.

'What's wrong?' she eventually signed. 'Is it being cooped up in the cave? We can go out tomorrow, practise the blocks that Dad taught us, if the weather is better.'

Nathan ignored her question. 'Is it true that you're one of the best of the Collective?'

Elise stared at him.

'I was in the cave yesterday when you all met,' Nathan continued. 'I read Max and Raynor's lips. I spent the rest of the day with Raynor and she told me it was true.'

Elise gave herself a minute to think before answering. Was she one of the best? All her life she had been taught to downplay her abilities, to be demure and self-effacing. Working for the Infiltration Department for the past two years and being promoted to the Collective had given her confidence in her capabilities, the courage to know her strengths.

'Yes, I suppose it is.'

Nathan reloaded his sling and took aim at a pheasant that was pecking its way around a bush. The stone flew true and he walked over to collect his reward.

When he returned, he dropped it at Elise's feet. 'You should go, then, with the others. I can hunt for the cave, collect the wood.'

Elise tried to shrug off his comment. 'You don't mean that, Nathan. Anyway, I've told you, I'm happy to stay.'

'No, you're not. You'll never be happy unless you're out there.'

'That's not true!'

Nathan's face reddened. 'Yes, it is. And don't lie to me. I'm not a child any more. I can tell when you don't mean something.'

'Come on, Nathan, don't be cross with me. I'm doing my best.'

'You're doing your best to pretend that you're my parent, but you're not. You're my sister. I don't even know if I have any parents any more ... but perhaps you could find Mum and bring her back.'

'The others can find Mum; it's not just me.'

'But the more of you there are, the better the chances.'

'Is that what you want? For me to go and find Mum?'

Nathan nodded. 'I don't know where they've taken her, but I think about her every day. We have to bring her back.'

Elise was torn. Part of her knew she should stay with Nathan, let the others try to locate and rescue her mum, and be there for him when he needed her. The other part knew that she couldn't hide away in a cave and hope for the best. That wouldn't make Nathan safe in the long run. The Potiors would find them eventually.

'What do you want to be when you turn fourteen?' she signed.

'I want to be a fighter ... like Dad.'

Elise swallowed. She wouldn't be able to keep Nathan safe forever and the route she had been taking seemed only to lead to him hating her. She had to face this head on.

'If I leave in the spring, do you want to train with me and the others over the next two months? I'll try to teach you everything that Maya taught me.'

Nathan eyed her suspiciously. 'What will happen when I turn fourteen?'

'I'll help you find a job working with me. If that's what you want.'

Nathan nodded. 'We can start tomorrow.'

The evening celebrations had become a raucous affair. Everyone in the cave had felt a glimmer of hope, and they needed to shake off the weeks of monotony in the caves. Raynor had produced some bottles of liquor she had found in the remains of Uracil and most had tucked in. The children whizzed between the legs of the adults, pleased to be allowed to stay up late.

Elise had informed the Collective of Nathan's decision as soon as she had returned to the cave. In celebration of her news and much to Nathan's delight, Raynor had proposed that they make him an honorary member of the Infiltration Department and the others had agreed. He smiled for what seemed like the first time in weeks and Elise took pleasure in watching him join in with the celebrations.

The evening turned into the early hours of the morning, and one by one, the children fell asleep in the arms of an adult, before being tucked up in bedding at the rear of the cave. Nathan had held out the longest, but eventually he fell asleep on Elise's shoulder and she guided him to his bed.

When she returned to the main cave, she held her breath as she watched an inebriated Luca brazenly flirt with Septa. Much to Elise's surprise, the equally inebriated Septa laid an encouraging hand on Luca's shoulder and pulled him closer. She smiled to herself at the unpredictability of attraction.

Settling down outside the cave, Elise pulled on Samuel's grey jumper and watched as the coral shades of dawn crept into the skyline. One by one, her friends came outside, all winding down from the night of celebrations. They sat cross-legged in a line staring out over the cliff edge, the bottle of liquor passing between the few of them that still remained. Elise passed it straight on to Georgina when it came to her turn, aware that she was close to sleep and not wanting to miss the sunrise.

Twenty-Two, who was sitting next to Elise, had also passed on the liquor, having tried it once earlier in the evening and scrunched her face at the sharp taste.

'When I was imprisoned, I read many Pre-Pandemic works of fiction,' Twenty-Two signed to Elise. 'And there was a saying in one of them that "it is always darkest before dawn".'

Elise nodded her encouragement. It was rare for Twenty-Two to start a conversation with her.

'It is not true, of course,' Twenty-Two continued. 'The darkest hours are the ones after sunset. For my first fourteen years, I had only natural light to guide me.'

'Yes, I've noticed that too, since leaving Thymine,' Elise responded.

'Do you think we have passed through the darkest hours?' Twenty-Two signed, turning towards Elise.

She peered at her in the brightening dawn light.

'I don't know,' Elise eventually responded. 'I hope so.'

She thought back to only a few months ago when she had been fixated on the deaths in the containment centres. Now those defeats were much closer to home and she had still more to lose.

'Back in Cytosine I thought I was going to die,' Twenty-Two continued.

'I thought I was going to die in Cytosine too.'

'But then Ezra found me, and I began a new life.' Twenty-Two glanced over at her friend. 'Perhaps the darkest times do happen before the better ones.'

Elise held on to this thought as she made her way back into the cave and waited for sleep to take her.

Names of Bases and Characters from Previous Books

<u>Adenine: Guidance and Governance</u>

The Premier: Leader of Zone 3.

<u>Cytosine: Ingenuity and Innovation</u>

Ezra Thippen: Former cleaner in Cytosine's Museum of Evolution and Twenty-Two's best friend.

Hadrian: Collection's Assistant at Cytosine's Museum of Evolution.

Marvalian: Director of Cytosine's Museum of Evolution.

Twenty-Seven: The twenty-seventh Neanderthal to be brought back from extinction. A young boy who escaped Cytosine with Twenty-Two and now lives in Uracil.

Twenty-Two: The twenty-second Neanderthal to be brought back from extinction. She escaped Cytosine and now lives in Uracil. She was sentenced to eighteen months' imprisonment as punishment for killing Faye.

Guanine: Education and Enlightenment

Thymine: Purpose and Productivity

Aiden Thanton: Elise's dad.

Bay: The thirty-second Neanderthal to be brought back from extinction. Daughter of Seventeen and adopted daughter of Georgina, who now lives in Uracil.

Elise Thanton: Companion to Kit at Thymine's Museum of Evolution. Helped him to escape and now works for Uracil's Infiltration Department. Was captured and kept in Cytosine's containment centre for several months.

Fintorian: Director of Cytosine's Museum of Evolution before moving to Thymine's museum and taking the same role. Killed by Samuel when he tried to stop them leaving Thymine's museum.

Georgina: Formerly a nurse in Thymine's Museum of Evolution. Escaped the museum to live in Uracil.

Harriet Thimble: Member of the Worker Profiling Department in Thymine's Museum of Evolution.

Holly: Elise's childhood friend.

Kit: The twenty-first Neanderthal to be brought back from extinction. He escaped Thymine's Museum of Evolution and now lives in Uracil.

Lewis Thetter: Holly's partner, who was hired to become Kit's new Companion at Thymine's Museum of Evolution. Georgina's brother.

Luca Addison: Former Companion to Seventeen in Thymine's Museum of Evolution. Now works as a guard for Uracil.

Nathan Thanton: Elise's brother.

Samuel Adair: Former Collection's Assistant at Thymine's Museum of Evolution. Helped Kit escape the museum and took him, Elise, Georgina, Luca and Bay to Uracil. Son of the founding member of Uracil, Vance, and Faye's brother.

Seventeen: The seventeenth Neanderthal to be brought back from extinction. Died while giving birth to Bay.

Sofi Thanton: Elise's mum.

Uracil: The Fifth Base

Faye: Acting member of the Tri-Council when her father, Vance, went missing. Samuel's sister. Killed by Twenty-Two.

Flynn: Founder of Uracil and member of the Tri-Council.

Maya: Member of the Infiltration Department and Elise's trainer. Samuel's mother's best friend.

Michael: One of the Heads of the Agricultural Department.

Raul: Founder of Uracil and member of the Tri-Council.

Septa: Member of the Infiltration Department who posed as Nurse Roseanna to help Elise escape Cytosine's containment centre. Was ordered to kill Elise by Faye.

Tilla: Born in Uracil and Georgina's partner.

Vance: Founder of Uracil and Samuel and Faye's father.

ACKNOWLEDGEMENTS

I would firstly like to thank my friends and family who reviewed this in its earlier stages, including Jo, Lee, Darryl, Julie, Lorraine, Mike, Lindsay and Kat. Yet again I owe you hours of my time and want to thank you for yours.

I'd also like to thank Bev James, my agent extraordinaire, for making all of this possible, and the whole team at Del Rey UK, particularly Sam Bradbury, whose direction and insight has been invaluable. Thanks also to Kasim Mohammed, Ben Brusey, Rachel Kennedy and Róisín O'Shea for all your expertise.

Finally, I'd like to thank everyone who has bought, reviewed or contacted me about my books. Writing is a lovely, but sometimes lonely, job and these messages often make my day. Thanks also to my original readers from when I was self-published, for waiting three years between the second and third instalments – I owe you an apology in the form of cake and a handmade card.

ABOUT THE AUTHOR

After spending eight years working as a lawyer, A. E. Warren began to write in the evenings and early mornings as a form of escapism from life in a very small cubicle with lots of files. She self-published her first novels in her spare time, which were picked up by Del Rey UK which is the science fiction and fantasy imprint of Penguin Random House. She is an avid reader, an occasional gamer and a fair-weather runner. *The Fourth Species* is the third book in the Tomorrow's Ancestors series. She lives in the UK with her husband, daughter and, hopefully one day, a wise border terrier named Austen.

You can find her at aewarren.com or one of the following:
Instagram: @amauthoring
Facebook: @amauthoring
Twitter: @amauthoring
Pinterest: @amauthoring